# Cat's People

# Cat's People

## A NOVEL

### Tanya Guerrero

DELACORTE PRESS
NEW YORK

Published in the United States by Delacorte Press, an imprint of Random House, a division of Penguin Random House LLC, 1745 Broadway, New York, NY 10019

DELACORTE PRESS is a registered trademark and the DP colophon is a trademark of Penguin Random House LLC.

LIBRARY OF CONGRESS CATALOGING-IN-PUBLICATION DATA
Names: Guerrero, Tanya, author.
Title: Cat's people : a novel / Tanya Guerrero.
Description: First edition. | New York : Delacorte Press, 2025.
Identifiers: LCCN 2024055082 (print) | LCCN 2024055083 (ebook) |
ISBN 9780593873847 (hardcover ; acid-free paper) | ISBN 9780593873854 (ebook)
Subjects: LCGFT: Novels.
Classification: LCC PR9550.9.G78 C38 2025 (print) | LCC PR9550.9.G78 (ebook) |
DDC 823/.92—dc23/eng/20250101
LC record available at https://lccn.loc.gov/2024055082
LC ebook record available at https://lccn.loc.gov/2024055083

Printed in the United States of America on acid-free paper

randomhousebooks.com

First Edition

Book design by Jo Anne Metsch

The authorized representative in the EU for product safety and compliance is Penguin Random House Ireland, Morrison Chambers, 32 Nassau Street, Dublin D02 YH68, Ireland, https://eu-contact.penguin.ie.

For all the cat people in the world,
especially
the suckers who always fall victim to
the cat distribution system;
the kind souls who adopt the oldest, sickest,
and "ugliest" cats in the shelter;
the hardworking, selfless, and brave cat rescuers;
and the TNR volunteers
You are my people, my favorite people

# Cat's People

# The World According to Cat

Cat knew to stay in the shadows. At night it was a piece of cake. But in the daytime, when shadows were few and far between, he had to search for objects that would hide him from strangers—shiny black dumpsters, alleyways with fresh asphalt, planter boxes with overgrown hedges.

Because Cat was wise. In the many years he'd spent living on the streets, he'd figured out two things:

1) Most people didn't like strays.
and
2) Black cats were considered bad luck.

He knew that was nonsense, of course. What did the color of his fur have to do with anything? Tons of people milled around Brooklyn clad in all black, and nobody ever stared at them suspiciously, or shooed them away, or did that silly thing where they touched their foreheads and crossed their hands from one side of their chest to the other. To add insult to injury, on one day *every* year, he would see plastic statues and cardboard cutouts of himself on windows while kids marched around in costumes carrying pumpkin-shaped purses. It was the only day he ever felt safe. Well, sort of safe. At least, he could skulk out of the shadows and still blend in.

But Cat did have a few friends. Maybe not quite *friends*, but people he trusted enough not to hide from. People with kind eyes, soft voices, and hearts that weren't completely made of stone. Those people were his people. In fact, they were the only people in his universe. Everyone else was a blur, a movement, a shape. They were just there. And he didn't care one bit about them. Because he wasn't one of those silly dogs who'd wag their tails at every single stranger who passed by. Cat was too proud to stoop so low. His people would come to *him*, not the other way around.

People were there to serve cats.

And maybe, once in a blue moon, if they were so inclined, cats would do something in return.

# ONE

## Núria

Núria didn't need an alarm clock. Every morning at six on the dot, three sets of paw daggers would stab her legs, her stomach, her chest, her face. Sandpapery tongues groomed her hair until finally, she shifted and groaned. At which point the owners of the daggers would meow in chorus until she staggered out of bed, bleary-eyed.

"Okay, I'm up!" she said, finding her way into her tiny kitchen. The three ingrates followed her, circling her legs, meowing as if it were the end of the world. She tripped over a ginger-colored cat before reaching her destination—the cupboard that held stacks and stacks of salmon-flavored Gour-Meow, the ingrates' favorite canned food.

*Meeeooowww!*

The howls became even more desperate as she popped a can open, scooping the foul-smelling pâté into the clean bowls she'd left on the counter the night before. It was only when she'd carefully placed the bowls on the floor, spaced one foot apart, that silence finally reigned. Well, not total silence, since she lived in a second-floor walk-up on one of the busiest streets in Brooklyn. Still, it was quiet enough for her to relax and get on with her day.

First, coffee. Núria scrounged around, searching for some beans. But there were none. "Crap," she mumbled.

Somehow, she always remembered to restock the ingrates' food, but when it came to her own needs her brain turned to mush. No coffee. No toilet paper. No food. She opened the fridge and glared at the one Granny Smith apple. The only other items were a stick of vegan butter, a carton of expired oat milk, a jar full of ketchup packets, and a lone bottle of something that had rolled to the back of one of the shelves. She reached for it and pulled it out, grinning when she realized it was the rest of the cold brew from the other day that she'd forgotten about.

Maybe the day wouldn't be so bad after all.

She plopped down on one of two chairs, part of a Formica dining set she'd picked up at the Salvation Army, the table only as big as two pizza boxes. By then, the ingrates had finished their breakfasts and scurried off to call dibs on their favorite spots in her cluttered studio apartment. Miel, the ginger tabby, hopped onto the windowsill next to her half-dead cactus. Gazpacho, the chubby calico, curled up on her pillow. Last but not least, Churro, the chocolate-colored cat, crawled under the bed where nobody would bother him.

While drinking her cold brew, Núria scrolled through her emails, reading but not really, as if her mind was somewhere else. It had been a while since she'd really cared about anything. Even the things she'd loved, like volunteering with the Meow-Yorkers, a rescue and trap-neuter-return organization, and her job as a barista at a nearby café had lost their luster. She didn't know why, but for the last year, she felt like she'd been walking through life half-asleep. A zombie. A robot. A shell of the human she'd once been.

*Beep!* A text from her mother popped onto the screen.

Oye! Look! Even the Pope says that pets aren't children.

Attached to the text was a link to an article titled, "Pope Scolds Couples Who Choose Pets over Kids." Núria sighed. She didn't even bother reading it. What was the point? Ignore and delete. That had been her coping mechanism for the last few years, since her mom had started harassing her about grandchildren on her thirty-fifth birth-day. Núria hadn't had the courage to tell her that she had no plans on birthing a bunch of mini-Núrias. Not because she thought she'd ever change her mind, but because she wasn't mentally prepared to deal with the fallout. Spanish women of a certain age dreamed of having grandchildren, and the thought of taking that dream away from her mother made her break out in hives.

Núria went over to the windowsill, where Miel was busy chirping at some birds. She scratched his furry chin, the gesture soothing to them both. An instant Xanax of sorts. She needed as much calm as she could get. Because it was Núria's day off. Instead of languishing in bed bingeing on Netflix, she had to venture outside to do her regular feeding. Since she would have more time on her hands to do her rounds properly, she would also have more time to work herself into a nervous ball of energy. Part of her volunteering duties involved making sure that none of the strays had any medical issues requiring emergency care. For her, that was the most stressful part of her vol-unteering duties. Finding a sick and injured stray cat was something she dreaded.

It was exhausting work, physically and mentally. There had been times she'd come close to quitting. Wouldn't it be easier *not* to care? But those moments of self-doubt were fleeting. Truth be told, there was just one thing that Núria took pride in—her steadfast commit-ment. It was probably her only redeeming quality. She sucked at re-lationships. She sucked at cooking and cleaning. And she especially sucked at taking care of herself. Self-care? What the hell was that?

Miel suddenly swiped at Núria's hand, which meant he'd had enough attention. She plucked some relatively clean clothes from a nearby armchair and got dressed. There wasn't any point in wearing truly clean clothes when she was going to go out and sweat. Not to mention the stink of canned food, cat piss, and the occasional coppery odor of a bloody cat scratch that always clung to her after her rounds. The life of a community stray cat caretaker was all so very glamorous.

When she was somewhat presentable, she grabbed her backpack and stuffed several cans of cat food, a Ziploc full of kibble, and some disposable plastic containers that she used as water bowls inside.

Then she filled her insulated bottle with tap water and headed for the door.

*Twinkle-twinkle . . . Twinkle . . . Twinkle-twinkle . . .* It was the sound of her supposedly Zen ringtone. Núria pulled her phone out of her back pocket and glanced at the screen. Her shoulders instantly slumped. It was her mother. Again. As much as she wanted to ignore the call, she knew that she had to give her mother a modicum of attention. It was kind of like the ten minutes a day that she had to play aluminum-foil-ball or catch-the-string with the ingrates. If she didn't, they'd spend all night doing the zoomies from one side of the room to the other.

Núria answered, "Hola, Mamá."

There was some fumbling on the other end. "Núria! Por fin!" There was a pause. "Mira, I have some exciting news for you."

"Exciting news?" Núria rolled her eyes.

"Yes, are you sitting?"

Núria went over to the bed and sat. "Yes."

Another pause. "Enrique . . . He's single again!"

Enrique was the handsome son of her mother's best friend down in Florida. He lived in New Jersey, but commuted to the city for his job at a law firm. He gelled his hair and wore designer suits and drank single malt whiskey at fancy bars with fancy blondes.

"*And* you're telling me this because?"

"Because I think you should go out on a date with him, mija. . . . It really is time for you to quit acting like a teenager and settle down," she said.

"Ma!"

"What? I'm your mother! It's my job to point these things out to you."

Núria could feel the sweat trickling down her temples. Her palms were clammy and she could sense the beginnings of an anxiety attack. She had to think quickly.

"I'm already seeing someone!" she blurted out.

"Qué?" Her mother sounded like she'd just run face first into Julio Iglesias, her idol. "Who? Who are you seeing? Por díos! Dígame!"

For a second, Núria panicked. *Shit.* What the hell was she thinking? If she didn't say something soon, her mother would hop on the first plane to New York City and demand answers.

"Uh. Um. Well . . ." Núria fumbled with her words. But then, she felt something on her leg and looked down. Churro was peeking at her from underneath the bed, swatting at her untied shoelace. "Ch-Chu . . . his name is Charles."

# Bong

Bong was lonely. It had been almost a year since his wife, his beloved Conchita, had died suddenly of a stroke. There hadn't been a day since they'd been married that they'd been apart. Not one day. Now that she was gone, he felt lonely and lost, as if *he* were the one who had died—as if he were merely a ghost floating through a life he no longer wanted. He often fantasized about dying and being reunited with her in Heaven, his corporeal form lying next to hers in their side-by-side cemetery plots. But he knew that Conchita would have wanted him to carry on.

So carry on he did. In fact, he probably carried on *too* well, working at his bodega day in and day out. It was exhausting. At least he was surrounded by people. It made him feel less lonely, even though they were mostly strangers. He did have his regulars, of course. Although regulars in Brooklyn meant only that he recognized them and they recognized him. The most he ever got was a nod or a half-hearted *good morning*. New Yorkers were way too busy to make friends outside their circles. In fact, avoiding eye contact was preferable. There were just too many weirdos out there. But none of that mattered to Bong. In a way, it was better. The last thing he wanted was to get close to anyone new and, God forbid, have them yanked out of his life like Conchita had been.

*Ding. Ding. Ding.*

Bong glanced at the door. It was Freckles. That's what he called this woman in his head. She was one of his regulars who stopped by two or three times a day. Their exchanges were limited to small talk, but he felt like he kind of knew her. He would often pass the time behind the cash register imagining what her life and the lives of his other regulars were like. Did they have someone like Conchita by their sides? Or were they as lonely as he was?

Freckles wandered the aisles, perusing. He was pretty sure that she would end up buying her usual: a peanut-butter-chocolate protein bar, a bag of Lays potato chips, and a banana. After about five minutes, she approached the cash register and presented him with exactly those items, plus an additional one—a bar of dark chocolate. She must have been having a lousy day.

"Good morning." Her olive-green eyes found his before glancing down at the items on the counter.

Bong smiled. "Good morning to you too." He rang up her items. "That will be five dollars and seventy-five cents, please," he said, not bothering to reach for a brown paper bag since he knew she would refuse and stuff everything into her backpack.

She handed him six crumpled dollars and proceeded to toss the stuff into her bag. While she did that, Bong carefully flattened each bill before placing them into the cash register. He handed her a quarter. For a moment, Freckles idled like a car waiting for a parking spot. Bong furrowed his brows, but after a brief awkward pause, he grinned. "Hold on," he said, bending down to retrieve something.

"Thanks," she said.

He straightened back up and handed her a stack of small paper plates. It was an exchange that had been going on for well over a year. One day she'd inquired if he could spare some. Without asking for an explanation, he'd handed her a dozen or so. Since then, he'd been regularly supplying her with them. Of course, it cost him to give them away for free. But Bong was certain that she had a good reason for needing them. It was a feeling he had in his gut. And his gut was pretty much the only thing he had to rely on these days.

Freckles took the paper plates and waved. There was a slight smile on her face, one that reminded Bong of spring's first crocus buds un-furling, a tiny sliver of hope in a cold world.

He watched her disappear through the entrance, bathed in the mellow morning sunlight. Maybe one day, he would ask her what she did with all those paper plates. In the meantime, he was content to leave it a mystery.

# THREE

## Collin

Collin sat at his desk. In front of him was his laptop, and beside it, a ceramic mug of piping-hot coffee—his third cup of the day. He'd been sitting there since five A.M., convinced that waking up at an ungodly hour would inspire the words to magically appear on the screen. Words that his editor had been expecting eighteen months ago. Yet the page remained blank. Collin glared at the hardcover of his first book, which he kept nearby to remind himself that he wasn't a total impostor. He reached out to touch it, his fingers tracing the NEW YORK TIMES BESTSELLER banner at the top. It was proof. He *did* have talent. Readers loved his writing. The awards had been abundant. But then his second book had flopped. The pressure for his third was on. From his agent. From his publisher. From his readers. And most of all, from himself. He had to make a comeback.

There was a huge problem, though. Since achieving what most aspiring authors could only dream of, Collin had become a bit of a hermit. Well, maybe not quite a hermit. He was definitely antisocial, preferring to be by himself in his three-story Brooklyn brownstone. That's why writing was the perfect career choice for him. Authors spent most of their days holed up in their writing caves, only emerging when it was time to come out of hibernation—meetings, book tours, signings. When forced to do those things, he would don his armor: his tortoiseshell glasses, his tweed coat, and his fake smile that he'd practiced in front of the mirror. After all, isn't that what adoring fans expected from a successful male author? It was a chore. But it was part of his job. So he did what he had to do.

He glanced out of the second-floor window, something he did way too often. It was easier to look at the outside world than at the blank screen in front of him. But he told himself that it was for inspiration. Maybe a Greek muse would appear in the form of something or someone on the street. Then, *bam!* An idea would form in his head. Another bestseller. Another award winner. Another brilliant fucking book.

But so far, all he saw outside was a view of the alley where he kept his trash cans and composting bins. Farther down was a slice of sidewalk where occasionally a passerby would appear. Most of them were completely forgettable. Except for one.

Collin glanced at his watch. In a couple of minutes, she would appear. He'd spotted her several months ago, walking slowly, her face turning from side to side, stopping to crouch or stand up on her tippy-toes as if searching for something. That's what had caught his attention. For the most part, people strolled by so fast that he could barely get a good look at them. But not her. She had stayed in his eyeline for a long while, looking like she was putting on some sort of weird avant-garde performance, like a mime on the streets of Paris. At first, he couldn't quite tell what she was up to. One day, though, a scruffy black cat peeked out of his neighbor's hedges. He could tell the woman was excited to see the cat.

She'd placed a small paper plate with food on the sidewalk, about three or four feet from where the cat was. Beside it, she'd situated one of those flimsy takeout containers and poured some water about halfway up. When she was done, she'd said something to the cat. And then she'd walked off, turning once or twice before disappearing from his view. The cat had waited a couple of minutes before darting out of the hedges to devour the food she'd left.

Collin had never been much of a cat person. Not even as a little kid. But seeing this act of kindness gave him hope. Maybe it was worth venturing outside of his cocoon. Maybe there were still people out there that could inspire him.

*Pssspsssspssspss!* The sound drifted through the open window even before he could see her. A second later, the woman appeared in one of her usual outfits, which reminded him of what some of the girls he'd gone to college with had worn. It was that woke-up-too-late-so-I-put-on-whatever-was-on-the-floor look. Today's ensemble featured neon-orange yoga pants, a black T-shirt with Salvador Dali's face on it, shiny gold Birkenstocks, and a purple backpack that could have belonged to Dora the Explorer. As usual, her auburn hair was tied in a messy top-bun that leaned to the side.

He stood so he could get a better look, hoping she wouldn't catch him spying on her. Just the thought of it made his cheeks warm.

*Pssspsssspssspss!*

It didn't take long for the black cat to appear. He jumped out of the hedges without hesitation. Clearly, she'd earned his trust. Still, the cat wouldn't let the woman touch him. She had to stay a few feet away, otherwise he would dart back into the hedges. Collin could relate. He too kept people at a distance. He too was skittish. Perhaps he had something in common with cats after all.

Before leaving the cat to his meal, she crouched down on the sidewalk and spoke to him. Just a couple of words. And then she stood and adjusted her bra before walking out of his view again. Collin ran to the front of his brownstone, hoping to catch another glimpse through the street-facing windows. But by the time he got there, she was gone, probably off to find some other stray cat in the neighborhood.

Collin's shoulders slumped. He glanced down the hallway that led back to his study. The laptop with its blank page was still there waiting for him.

"Crap," he mumbled to himself.

What was the point? Still, he lumbered down the hallway back to his study. Collin was tall, the kind of tall that made people notice whenever he walked into a room. He was solid too, with wide shoulders, thick forearms, and big hands and feet. It was a man's body, but the way he carried himself was like a little boy traipsing through life in his daddy's work clothes and shoes.

When he reached the mid-century walnut desk that his parents had gifted him after his first book deal, he hovered beside it. The thought of sitting back down repelled him. His eyes landed on the pad of neon-orange Post-it notes that he kept around to jot down ideas. It was the same exact shade of orange as the woman's yoga pants.

Collin twitched. He reached for a pen and scribbled something on a Post-it. Before he could change his mind, he peeled it off the pad and jogged down the stairs toward the front door. For a second, he hesitated with his hand on the doorknob. After a deep breath, he turned it and stepped outside in plaid pajama bottoms, a white T-shirt, and slippers. Without even caring if anyone noticed him, he grabbed one of the decorative stones from his planter of geraniums and hurried to the spot where the woman had placed the paper plate and plastic container. By then the food had been gobbled up and the black cat was nowhere in sight. But he knew she'd be back. He'd observed that the cat's place setting was always gone within an hour or two.

His hand tightened around the stone, knuckles white. There was a warmth in his gut, like the oozing center of a chocolate lava cake, compelling him forward. What was the purpose of this exercise? Did he really want to entangle himself in a potentially complicated situation?

Despite his hesitation, he bent down and stuck the Post-it to the empty paper plate, weighing them both down with the stone. There. He'd done it.

Collin was about to escape back to the confines of his brownstone when, suddenly, a furry black head poked through the hedges. It was the cat, staring at him with green eyes that reminded him of sea glass. He stared back. Collin assumed that the cat would run away at the sight of him, but it stayed put, sizing him up as if he were the new kid walking into the classroom on the first day of school.

"Um. Hey, how are you doing?" he said, immediately feeling ridiculous for trying to speak to the cat.

*Meow.*

It was a soft, shy meow. Barely a meow, actually. But hearing the cat's whisper brought a grin to Collin's face. He couldn't recall the last time the corners of his mouth had curled up like that. For the briefest of moments, he understood why the woman did what she did.

Collin waved at the cat. "Have a nice day," he said, before walking back to where he'd come from.

# FOUR

❦

# *Cat*

C at waited. It was still cool under the shade of the hedges.
He'd spent the night patrolling the neighborhood, so he was
due for a catnap pretty soon. But he was also really hungry, so
first, he'd wait for Rainbow Lady to show up.

Early on, he'd given her that nickname—Rainbow Lady—because
she walked around looking like the human equivalent of the rainbow-
colored flags that were proudly displayed in front of many Brooklyn
establishments. Over the past few months, though, he'd observed
that her insides didn't seem to match her outsides. Whenever he'd
see her walking down the street, her expression was blank, even sad
at times. Her eyes were lifeless. She was always alone too, not like
some of the other cat feeders in the area who made their rounds in
groups of two or three.

Whenever she saw him, though, her sparkle would return. She
would smile, making the freckles on her face dance. Cat showed up
at that same spot every day, at the exact same time, not only because
he craved a good meal, but because he knew that Rainbow Lady
needed him as much as he needed her.

*Pssspssspssspsssss . . .*

Cat's ears perked up. Through the hedges, he spotted a pair of familiar-looking legs coming toward him. Immediately, he sprung out, meowing a greeting when he landed on his paws.

"There you are," she said, unzipping her backpack so she could retrieve her supplies. While she arranged the paper plate and plastic container on the sidewalk, Cat circled, round and round. He never got too close, but Rainbow Lady knew that it was his way of telling her he was happy to see her. "You hungry?" she asked.

*Meeeooow!* Cat answered, circling closer. There was a tiny part of him that was desperate to rub up against her legs. But the rest of him was too afraid. When he was a kitten, he'd been more trusting, more naïve. Unfortunately, that ignorance had gotten him in trouble. The assumption that most people were good only got empty beer cans and boiling water thrown his way and pellet guns shot at him—one pellet was permanently lodged in his flank muscle. A couple of times, strangers had even tried to kill him with rat poison. In order to survive, he'd had to learn to be much less trusting.

Finally, Rainbow Lady popped a can open, scooping half of it onto the paper plate and pouring some fresh water into the container.

By then, Cat's tail was flitting at warp speed, but Rainbow Lady knew that he wouldn't touch the food unless she stepped back a good three or four feet. One step, two steps, three. Cat glanced at her to make sure she was far enough.

"I'm not going to hurt you. Go on, eat up, buddy," she said with a smile and a nod.

Cat pounced on the paper plate. Rainbow Lady watched him eat for a couple of seconds before turning around and going off on her merry way.

It only took a couple of minutes for Cat to finish his meal. It was too dangerous to take his time; there were people who might kick him, dogs who might chase after him, strollers that might run over his tail. So he lapped up some water, licking the droplets off his chin, before darting back into the safety of the hedges.

Cat curled up into a ball on the cool morning dirt. His eyes drifted closed, slits of white still visible as he dozed off. *Clomp. Clomp.* Cat startled awake. Was Rainbow Lady back already? No, the sound of the footsteps was different. Cautiously, he peeked through the bushes.

A tall man in pajamas stood there, staring down at his plate. His hair was overgrown and black, the same color as Cat's fur. Instead of shoes, he had on house slippers. In one hand he held a piece of paper and in the other, a stone.

For a moment, Cat considered running off. This man could be dangerous. But despite the potential threat, he was intrigued. So he stayed put. The man bent down and placed the paper on top of his plate, and then he situated the stone on top of it before standing back up.

Even though the man was tall and big like those supermarket delivery guys that flicked their cigarette butts at Cat, there was something different about him. The way he moved his limbs was slow and awkward, as if he hadn't yet read the user's manual to his own body. And though his eyes were brown, not green, he had the same vacant gaze as Rainbow Lady.

It was obvious to Cat that this man needed something. What exactly, he wasn't quite sure. For some strange reason, Cat wanted to find out. He popped his head through the bushes and meowed.

# FIVE

# Omar

Omar was every neighborhood's dream mailman. He took his job seriously. He not only delivered the mail with care and precision, but he also always had a smile that made even the grumpiest of people smile back. It wasn't uncommon for him to be invited in for a cup of coffee or an ice-cold lemonade. Pretty much everyone adored him, especially the older folks and kids. Even the various cats and dogs on his route would sit by their windows and wait for him because he always kept treats in the little bag he wore around his waist. On some days, he'd take selfies with his various furry friends, posting them on his Instagram with amusing anecdotes for the world to see.

He opened the creaky gate leading to Mrs. Lewis's home—the first in a row of brownstones on what was probably the prettiest block in Crown Heights. Before proceeding up the stairs to her door, he halted and unzipped the bag at his waist. Inside was a pocket-sized bottle of WD-40 that he always had on him for emergencies. He spritzed a generous amount on the gate's hinges, testing it a few times to make sure the creak was gone. Mrs. Lewis was a widow, so he made sure to help her out, even offering to dog-sit Sinatra, her blue-eyed Chihuahua, whenever she went to Boston to visit her grandkids.

*Yap! Yap! Yap!*

Sinatra was already making a racket even before Omar reached the landing. That dog had hated *everyone*, including Omar, when he'd first started his mail route. During the first few months, Sinatra had bitten his finger, peed on his shoe, and shredded the mail because it had Omar's scent on it. What Sinatra hadn't realized, though, was that Omar was just as hard-headed as he was. For every growl, Omar would speak to him with gentle, sweet words. For every bark, he'd give him a dehydrated liver treat. It had taken a lot of patience and persistence, but eventually Omar had won Sinatra over.

"Good morning, Omar!" said Mrs. Lewis as she opened the front door. Sinatra darted through her legs so he could hop on Omar like a furry jack-in-the-box.

"Good day to you, Mrs. Lewis," Omar replied, scooping up Sinatra and carrying him like a baby. "Smells like you just had a bath, my man!" He rubbed Sinatra's belly until his leg twitched.

Mrs. Lewis chuckled. "Well, enjoy that freshly cleaned doggie scent while you can. I'm afraid it might be a while until he gets another grooming. Donna, the only groomer he tolerated, quit, and the rest of the staff are too scared to deal with him."

Omar cuddled Sinatra, kissing him on the head. "He's just misunderstood."

"Aren't we all?" Mrs. Lewis shrugged and opened the front door wider. As usual, her silver hair was braided from one side of her head to the other, which somehow went perfectly with her collection of multicolored caftans. "You want to join me for some chai and cookies? I made some extra-buttery shortbreads with a hint of orange zest."

Omar put Sinatra back down so he could hand Mrs. Lewis her mail. "I'm a bit behind today, but I'd love a cookie to go if that's okay? You know I love me some butter."

"Of course! Hold on." She disappeared back into the house, leaving Omar petting a wiggly Sinatra.

"Hold your horses, my man." Omar unzipped his bag and pulled out his Ziploc of liver treats. "Okay, let's take one for the 'gram, shall we?" He knelt on the landing and held up one of the liver treats so that Sinatra would stand on his hind legs. At the exact right moment, he took a selfie. "Your fans are gonna love it," he said, giving Sinatra the treat before standing back up.

"Here you go." Mrs. Lewis returned with a tiny brown pastry box with a perfect pink bow tied around it. "I know it's a bit much, but I have a lot of time on my hands."

Omar grinned. "You *know* I'm a fan of extra. Thanks, Mrs. Lewis. See you tomorrow." He tucked the box into his bag and gave Sinatra one more pat before setting off to the next brownstone.

By the time he reached the second-to-last apartment on the block, he was out of breath, but in a good way. Heat, sweat, and exhaustion were all blessings, because those were things that made you feel alive. Omar's abuela had told him over and over again that hard work was the key to a long life. Even after she'd retired from teaching, she'd still volunteered with her church group, made meals at the local soup kitchen, and tended her small vegetable garden. That kind of productivity had kept her alive until the ripe old age of one hundred and three.

Omar trudged up to the home of Collin Thackeray, the pseudo-celebrity of the block. Considering the man worked from home, Omar hardly ever saw him. Once in a blue moon, though, the best-selling author himself would open the front door and take the mail, usually still wearing his wrinkly plaid pajamas. On one of those occasions, he'd even gifted Omar a signed hardcover of his book, which Omar had read in one sitting. Truth be told, he hadn't cared for it much. It was obvious that Collin was a great writer, but Omar thought the story had too much white cis male angst for his liking.

On that day, Collin decided not to make an appearance. Omar pushed the solitary envelope through the mail slot. Oddly, after the envelope fell through, he caught a glimpse of a pair of navy-blue slippers and plaid-clad legs, as if Collin had been standing on the other side of the door waiting for him. So why hadn't he opened the door or said anything? Maybe the dude just wasn't in the mood to chat. He did seem like the type of guy who kept to himself. After all, he lived in a brownstone all by himself—no girlfriend or wife, no kids, no pets that Omar could see. Unless he counted that scruffy black cat who slept in the hedges. Speaking of the devil . . .

Omar hurried down the steps, making sure his shoes *clomp-clomped* on the way down, because he knew that sound was his little buddy's cue. As soon as the sole of his shoe hit the sidewalk, the cat peeked out of the shrubbery and meowed.

"Well, hey there, Gatito. You ready to make the rounds?"

Gatito meowed again before emerging from the hedges. While he did a couple of stretches, Omar straightened out his mail cart. "C'mon, when we're done, I'll get you some refreshments at the bodega."

So off went Omar to deliver the mail with Gatito galloping beside him.

~⁓

# SIX

# Núria

By the time Núria had finished with her cat feedings it was almost lunchtime. Every inch of her was covered in sweat. Thankfully, all the strays on her route seemed okay. All she had left to do was go back the way she'd come to retrieve the paper plates and plastic containers. The last thing she needed was for some homeowner to accuse her of littering. But she needed to hurry because of her lunch date with Raquel, aka Rocky, the only close friend she had. Rocky had been bugging her for a catch-up sesh, and even though she hadn't been in the mood, she'd agreed to meet up for a quick bite. In a way, Rocky was kind of like her mom; if Núria didn't give her a bit of time once in a while, she would come for her and demand an explanation.

*Psspssspssspssspsss . . .*

She approached the hedges, looking for Cat. For whatever reason, he was never there whenever she went back to clean, which always made her wonder. Did he have other cat friends? Human friends? What kinds of trouble did he get into and out of? She'd been feeding this particular stray for a while, but she still didn't know much about him. She hadn't even been able to come up with a proper name other than Cat.

Núria reached into her backpack to pull out a small trash bag.

Something caught her eye, making her stop what she was doing. On the paper plate she'd left on the sidewalk was a bright-orange Post-it note with a rock on it.

*Hmmm. Strange . . .*

She gazed right and left and over her shoulder to see if anyone was watching. There wasn't anyone around. With the tips of her fingers, she picked up the smooth rock, tossing it in the side pocket of her backpack so she could get to the orange piece of paper below it. Once it was right smack in front of her, she stared at it, her brow furrowing with confusion.

*Do you think the cat understands you?*

That was it. That's all it said. It was obvious someone had been watching her. A weirdo? A pervert? An admirer? No. She couldn't possibly have an admirer. Oh, well, at the very least, now she'd have something to talk about with Rocky over lunch.

Núria tucked the note into her pocket and went off to shower and change before twenty questions, otherwise known as lunch with Rocky.

As usual, Núria was late. When she arrived at El Rincóncito, the hole-in-the-wall Cuban restaurant that was one of their favorite meeting spots, Rocky was already situated at their booth with a café con leche.

"*Finally,*" she said, rolling her eyes. "I was beginning to think your cats had finally murdered you."

Núria sat across from her. "Ha! Not yet. But they're probably plotting it as we speak."

Carmen, the one and only server, appeared with a tray of food. Her usually brassy-blond hair was now a vibrant shade of burgundy, which clashed with the fuchsia uniform. "Un Cubano, arroz con habichuelas, tostones, yuca con mojo, y dos batidos de guanábana," she said, arranging the plates on the table. "Algo más?"

Núria and Rocky shook their heads. "No, muchísimas gracias."

Carmen smiled and said, "Buen provecho," before leaving them to their meal.

They'd been going to El Rincóncito for years, even though there were tons of trendy new restaurants in the neighborhood. It was easier and more comforting to not have to think about what to order, and the staff never seemed to mind that they sometimes stayed for hours. Not to mention that the food was delicious and cheap.

Rocky bit into her Cubano, making her usual orgasmic facial expression after swallowing. "God, it's a good thing you got here when you did, because this *hangry* girl would have bitten your head off if you'd been any later."

"Sorry," said Núria. "I was busy . . . you know—"

"I *know. I know.*" Rocky shook her head, making the sun-kissed curls on her head bounce. "*Girl,* why did I buy you all those lint rollers for Christmas if you aren't going to use them?" she said, eyes zeroing in on the copious amounts of cat hair on Núria's T-shirt.

"I do use them! For work. I mean, it's not like you care what I look like," said Núria defensively.

"*Hello!* I care! That's why I gave them to you!"

Núria slouched. "All right. Can we move on now?"

"Fine," said Rocky, gritting her teeth.

Núria scooped a forkful of beans and rice into her mouth and groaned.

Rocky glared at her with her honey-brown eyes. "Let me guess. This is your first meal of the day, isn't it?"

"*And?* It's not like I'm going to die of starvation. I mean, isn't intermittent fasting a thing now?" said Núria.

Rocky pointed her fork at her. "There's a difference between intermittent fasting and not eating because you care more about those damned cats than yourself."

"Okay, *Mom.*"

Rocky took a deep breath, something she usually did to not blow a fuse. "Listen, Núria. I just want you to take better care of yourself. If you get sick, if you lose your damned mind, then who's going to take care of those cats? Can you at least look at it from that perspective?"

"Fine. I guess you have a point," Núria conceded. "I promise, I'll go to the supermarket after lunch and buy some real food. Okay?"

Rocky smiled. "Good. That's a start."

Núria reached for her shake and took a long sip, letting the cold, creamy goodness soothe her. "So, something kind of weird happened today."

"Good weird or bad weird?" Rocky leaned forward.

Núria shrugged. "I don't know." She reached into her backpack and pulled out the orange Post-it note, placing it on the table for Rocky to see. "Someone left this for me."

Rocky squinted at the note. "Oh my, that *is* weird. But also intriguing . . ." She sat back and grinned. "Hmmm. Methinks *someone* wants to get into those pants of yours, cat hair and all."

"What! No! Of course not," said Núria, her face suddenly flushed.

Rocky poked her finger at the note. "*Girl*. It may not seem like it to you, but that there is a pickup line."

"You think?" said Núria.

"I sure do."

Núria stared at the note so hard her eyes watered. "Huh. Should I, like, write them back?"

Rocky grinned. "Only if you want to."

Núria wasn't so sure she did. Did she want to invite that kind of complication into her life?

# SEVEN

# Cat

What was taking him so long?

Cat was on the bench outside the bodega, waiting for the mailman to return. He'd gone inside for refreshments. It wasn't as if Cat was starving or anything. But he wasn't one to refuse a meal, especially those irresistibly creamy treats that came from inside the bodega.

Truth be told, he didn't love this part of the neighborhood. There were way too many people milling around for his liking. The kids always wanted to touch him, but their moms or dads would pull them away, mumbling something about strays and rabies. Then there were the weirdos, who were prone to unpredictable behavior. One guy with a really red face and ripped-up clothes had tried to grab him once, for what, Cat had no clue. Another time, a man wearing a tin-foil hat had shouted at anyone walking by, pointing to Cat and pro-claiming him to be the king of an alien race that would soon take over the world. And then there were the clingy old ladies who were desperate to bring him home and convert him to a housecat. Cat preferred the quieter streets where he could lay low and be left alone.

However, for Cheery Mailman he made an exception. He was one of the few humans who treated him like an equal. He never baby-talked to him, instead telling him stories as if he were an old friend.

Cat had learned all about his abuela, and his boyfriend-slash-roommate Carl, and how sometimes he daydreamed about doing something new with his life.

One cold winter day, Cheery Mailman had confided in him that even though he loved being a mailman, sometimes he wished for a higher calling, something that would give his life a greater purpose. In his own way, Cat had understood where he was coming from. There had been a time when he'd thought about what it would be like to live with a human.

Cat had been born on the streets. His mother had eventually run off. His siblings had died, one by one. He'd never known a life other than being a stray. Sometimes, he passed by windows with chubby cats staring at him from inside a home, and he would wonder what it was like on the other side. But those notions usually left as quickly as they'd appeared. Cat loved his freedom. There was a wildness inside of him that couldn't be tamed. He'd come to peace with that.

Where the heck was Cheery Mailman, anyways?

Cat stood on his hind legs with his front paws on the bench's backrest. Once he had a good vantage point, he peered through the storefront window. It was a bit dark and there was a glare on the glass that made it hard for him to see the store's interior. He jumped off the bench and sauntered over to the door, hoping for a better view. After a couple of seconds, he spotted Cheery Mailman standing several feet away from Sad Bodega Man, the one whom Smiley Lady had called "mahal," whatever that meant. Cat understood that Smiley Lady had died. She'd been there one day, gone the next. Of all his feeders, she had been the most dependable, the one who showed up every day at the exact same time, rain or shine. That's why he knew something had happened to her. It had made him sad. *Really* sad. His little heart ached at the thought of never again seeing the way her entire face would light up every time she spotted Cat through the back door. For weeks, he'd stayed away from the bodega. One day, though, Cheery Mailman managed to convince him to join him for a walk, a chat, and some creamy treats. Since then, he'd been visiting the bodega with him almost daily.

Most of the time, he avoided looking inside at Sad Bodega Man.

Seeing him reminded Cat of Smiley Lady's absence. But today, he felt braver than usual. Through the glass, he stared right at him. The old man looked different. Much older. He'd lost some weight too. It was as if the life had been zapped out of him. Seeing him like that brought the feelings of sadness out of Cat once again.

He went even closer to the glass door, craning his neck to figure out what was going on. After a moment, he realized that Sad Bodega Man was seated on a box, crying. His face was moist, covered in tears and mucus. His body sagged, making it seem as if his bones had suddenly melted. It was as if he was broken, like those discarded toys Cat would see out on the sidewalk on trash day.

Part of him wanted to hightail it out of there. But the other part of him, the one that had loved Smiley Lady so dearly, knew he had to do something. He owed her that much. So when he saw Cheery Mailman trying to leave the store with embarrassment stamped all over his face, Cat stood his ground at the door, as if his butt and paws were cemented to the sidewalk. If he didn't move, there was no way for Cheery Mailman to escape. He would have to stay inside and help Sad Bodega Man. If anyone could help that pile of depressed flesh and bone, it was Cheery Mailman. There was a reason that Cat had nicknamed him "Cheery," after all.

And it worked!

Cheery Mailman turned back around and said something to Sad Bodega Man. After a second or two, he went over and sat next to him, not saying anything, while the old man's tears streamed down his face, his body hunched over as he rocked back and forth.

Even though Cat was incapable of crying, he *had* experienced sadness in his life. When his mother left, he'd felt abandoned and heartbroken. When his siblings died, leaving him all alone, he too had hunched over, curling into a ball of misery for days on end. It wasn't until he'd found the kindness of strangers—strangers like Smiley Lady—that his grief had begun to subside. Until, finally, life had become bearable again.

Now it was his turn to pay it forward.

## EIGHT

~

# *Bong*

There were boxes of beverages waiting to be unloaded into the refrigerated cases. Bong stood in the midst of them, not knowing where to start. His arms hung limply at his sides. He'd been feeling this way more and more lately. Lost. Hopeless. Sad. Teresa, his eldest daughter, had encouraged him to get grief counseling. But how could a total stranger help him move past the grief he was feeling? It seemed improbable. Not to mention the cost, which wasn't covered by his health insurance.

Bong sighed, reaching for the nearest box and slicing it open with a box cutter. Inside were four cases of LaCroix flavored seltzers. As soon as he read the label of the first can he extracted—*pamplemousse*—his chest tightened. It had been Conchita's favorite drink. Bong used to make jokes about it, saying that the word "pamplemousse" sounded like a diaper-flavored dessert. She still loved it, though. And he loved teasing her about it even more. When she was alive, he'd always made sure to stock extra cases of it for his beloved.

Now she was gone. He stood there holding the can with tears streaming down his cheeks. He didn't even realize he was crying until he saw the wet marks by his shoes. That's when he completely lost it, the tears gushing so hard and fast it made him think of Niagara Falls, which in turn made his bawling even worse, since that's where he and Conchita had spent their twenty-fifth wedding anniversary. He sat down on a pile of boxes, covering his face with his hands. His chest heaved, and then he wailed, rocking back and forth to the rhythm of his crying. Bong was so wrapped up in his sadness that he didn't notice a customer had walked in.

"I'm sorry. I'll come back later," said the mailman, turning back around toward the door. But something stopped him. In front of the door, on the other side, a cat was blocking the way.

Bong blinked as if he were seeing an apparition. The cat was black and looked an awful lot like Itim, the stray Conchita used to feed. He hadn't seen it for months, as if the cat had sensed she was gone. Truth be told, he'd forgotten all about the poor creature that had meowed for food every day outside the bodega's back door.

But it really *was* Itim, alive and well, preventing the mailman from making an exit. His green eyes stared up at the uniformed man, almost as if to scold him for trying to leave Bong in such a state.

Slowly, the mailman turned back around and approached Bong. "Are-are you okay? Should I call someone for you?"

Bong wiped his face and looked up at the mailman with red-rimmed eyes. "No. I-I'm not okay." Bong flinched, surprised by his own frankness. Up until that moment, he hadn't admitted that to anyone. Not even his children. But there he was, saying exactly what he'd been feeling to the mailman he barely knew.

"You need someone to talk to?" said the mailman, taking a few more steps toward him. "I'm a good listener."

The mailman's offer was too much, too soon. Today was the first time Bong had really, truly cried. Adding in a heart-to-heart might just throw him over the edge. Bong shook his head. "I think I just need someone to sit with me for a while."

Without speaking, the mailman sat down on a stack of boxes beside him. They listened to the cars speeding outside, to the hum of the refrigerators, to the sounds of their breathing. Bong was still crying. It was a gentler sobbing, though, like the tail end of a storm before it passes. Eventually, Bong's tears ran out.

"Your name . . . It's Omar, right?" said Bong in between sniffles. Omar nodded. "It is."

Bong pulled out a handkerchief from his pocket and wiped his eyes and face with it. "My wife, Conchita, died almost a year ago," he explained, feeling the tightness in his throat return.

"I'm sorry. I didn't know." Omar paused. "I lost my abuela a couple of years ago. She was like a mom to me."

Bong nodded. "I'm sorry." And then he stood abruptly, suddenly remembering all the work he had left to do. He cleared his throat, fumbling with the cans in the box. "Thank you, Omar," he said softly.

"Anytime." Omar headed toward the door.

"Wait."

Omar turned back around.

"Did you need something?" said Bong, gesturing to the aisles of his store.

"Oh yeah. I need some of those cat treats. You know the ones in the sachets?"

Bong glanced at Itim, who was still watching them from the other side of the door. "For the cat? Outside?"

Omar smiled. "Yeah. He's sort of my sidekick. . . . He lives down the block, not too far from here."

"Yes. I-I know—" Bong stopped himself from speaking. For a moment, he thought about telling him all about Conchita and Itim. But he changed his mind. The story would have opened up a whole other can of worms that Bong wasn't quite ready to discuss. "Yes, I know those treats." Bong went to the pet food aisle and grabbed a handful of Sheba creamy tuna cat treats. He handed them to Omar. "On the house," he said.

"Oh, no. I couldn't possibly," said Omar.

"It's okay. Thank you, my friend," said Bong. And he meant it. For the first time in a long time, he was grateful for the presence of another person.

He watched Omar leave. Itim moved away from the door, almost as if he knew Omar's business inside the store was done.

# NINE

# Lily

Lily had been working as a checkout girl at the Foodtown for a month. She'd waited patiently for a job opening there. Not because she had dreams of manning a cash register in Crown Heights, but because it was the right location for what she needed. For the interview, she'd printed out two copies of her resume, which she'd embellished since the only real experience she had was one summer of playing hostess at Denny's. And she'd also taken the time to style her dark, wavy hair in a way that made her blue eyes stand out. Her favorite coral sundress was the finishing touch. Thank God the store manager had been a middle-aged man, because they always seemed in awe of Lily's Southern charm and good looks.

Truth be told, the job was a real bore. However, it served its purpose, not only for the salary, but for the opportunity it gave her to see the person she'd come all the way from Georgia to see. Since day one, she'd managed to stalk this unsuspecting person six times. In each instance, she'd observed something new—what kinds of items they liked to buy and unusual gestures, expressions, and habits. It was like watching one of those nature shows on *Nat Geo*—Lily was the unseen nature documentarist taking note of her subject.

"*Excuse* me."

Lily blinked and looked up at an irate customer. There was a conveyor belt full of items in front of her and she hadn't even noticed.

"Oh, sorry," said Lily, avoiding eye contact with the muscular, tattooed woman who looked as if she could have been a member of a biker gang. Lily had seen a lot of strange people since leaving her small town in Georgia for New York City. Some were downright scary.

*Beep . . . Beep . . . Beep . . .*

She scanned the items one by one as the biker lady bagged her haul in her reusable totes. "That'll be one hundred and five dollars and twenty cents, please," she said when everything had been tallied.

The biker lady wordlessly handed over a credit card, which was fine by Lily. The last thing she wanted was to chitchat with this woman. She might try to enlist her into a cult or something. Her mother had warned her about big city folks. She'd even gone as far as to try and dissuade Lily from going to New York City to pursue acting. That was all a crock, of course—an excuse Lily had made up so she could move far away. Much to her mother's disappointment, Lily *had* no real aspirations. She'd always been crap in school, but she'd scraped by because of cheerleading. Eventually, though, everyone in her squad had moved on to college, leaving her back home with nothing to do.

The biker chick finally left and Lily was free to stand around and zone out. Midafternoons were always kind of slow at the store, so it was her preferred shift. It allowed her to daydream, to make up stories in her head about her coworkers, who in real life were either boring or weird or basic. But in her head, Lily had convinced herself that Hank, one of the stock clerks, was either a serial killer or a rapist. She'd watched enough episodes of *Unsolved Mysteries* to know the look—darting eyes, sweaty forehead, always skulking around suspiciously. One day his mug shot would appear on the evening news and Lily would tell everyone that she'd suspected it all along. Unless, of course, *she* was the one who ended up getting murdered.

"Good afternoon, Lily." Bill, the store manager, passed by and smiled.

"Oh, good afternoon, Bill," she said, pretending to wipe the conveyor belt down with a rag.

"It's a lovely day, isn't it?" he said with a grin.

She grinned back. "It *sure* is."

He waved and left. *Thank God.* Bill had a knack for starting endless conversations about subjects she had zero interest in. She'd gotten pretty good at nodding and ignoring him. The skill had come in handy with her two roommates, whom she'd found on Craigslist; one was an intern at a media company in Manhattan, and the other worked at a glassblowing place, which, at first, Lily had thought was some sort of lab where they blew up glass to, like, test how different glass items would shatter. He'd laughed at her after she said it out loud when she first met him, and she still hadn't forgiven him for making her feel so stupid.

When Lily was done pretending to look busy, she scanned the store, hoping to find some entertainment. She spotted the person she'd gotten this job for in the first place. Lily glanced at her watch. It was almost three, an unusually early appearance. *Huh.* Maybe it was her day off.

Lily's gaze followed her subject as she grabbed a shopping cart, quickly going from aisle to aisle, tossing seemingly random items into the cart with a frown. Clearly she didn't want to be in there. The previous times Lily had observed her, she'd bought only the bare minimum, stuff like bananas, apples, prepackaged salads, and granola bars—items that always seemed like an afterthought compared to the shit-ton of cat food and cat litter she usually bought.

For a second, Lily lost sight of her. She craned her neck to get a better look, spotting her again when she emerged from the toilet paper aisle. She was headed for the registers. Suddenly Lily's palms got clammy. Thus far, she hadn't ended up at Lily's register, but that day, it was only her and Sandra on checkout duty. Lily watched her subject veer toward Sandra. Her heart sank. But at the last minute an old lady with a granny cart cut ahead, forcing her to go to Lily's register instead. The cart slid into place and she began to unload her stuff.

"Uh, good morning. I mean, good afternoon," said Lily.

Without even glancing up, her subject replied, "Afternoon."

In a way, it was a blessing in disguise, because Lily's hands were shaking. Despite the air-conditioning, she could feel sweat trickling down her forehead and neck.

When all the stuff had been unloaded, the customer stared off into the space above Lily's head, as if she were invisible.

*Beep . . .*

Frozen vegan orange chicken.

*Beep . . .*

Frozen bean burritos.

*Beep . . .*

Tofurky deli slices.

*Beep . . .*

Vegan cheese slices.

*Beep . . .*

Sliced multigrain bread.

*Beep . . .*

Coconut yogurt.

*Beep . . .*

JUST Egg.

*Beep . . .*

Hummus.

*Beep . . .*

Pita chips.

*Beep . . .*

Almond butter.

*Beep . . .*

Tomatoes.

*Beep . . .*

Lettuce.

*Beep . . .*

Avocados.

*Beep . . .*

Toilet paper.

*Beep . . .*

A six-pack of Estrella Galicia beer.

*Beep . . .*

Eighteen cans of Gour-Meow cat food.

Lily opened her mouth to speak. But she couldn't. The woman's eyes and freckles were so familiar. For a moment it was as if she were staring at her dad, except her dad had died well over a year ago.

"Um. That'll be eighty-five dollars and seventy-five cents, please," she mumbled.

The customer handed her a debit card. Lily took it. She turned her back on her, as if to swipe the card, but really what she was doing was staring down at the raised letters that spelled out *Núria Rey Andreu.*

Her long-lost half sister.

# TEN

## *Núria*

Núria didn't sleep well most nights. She had a hard time turning off her thoughts, so she'd toss and turn until eventually she'd give up and stare at the ceiling. At that point, instead of trying to shove her thoughts aside, she would allow herself to drown in them. Often, she would imagine horrific scenarios that would make her insomnia even worse.

What if some sicko hurt one of her strays in the middle of the night?

What if a car sped down the street and ran one of them down?

What if she died in the middle of the night of a heart attack, and all the cats starved to death?

That night, though, what occupied her mind was the neon-orange Post-it note and the person who'd left it for her. Who were they? What did they want? What were they like? Rocky was convinced that the person was a man, one with amorous intentions. But Núria wasn't so sure. She wasn't exactly beautiful, especially since she made zero effort with her appearance. One of these days, she fully expected the *Queer Eye* folks to come barging into her apartment to make her *and* her apartment over.

Would that be so bad, really?

Rocky was always nagging her that if she didn't make a change soon, she would end up like one of those ladies on *Hoarders,* with too many cats and too much stuff. But she brushed it off. Frankly, the "crazy cat lady" stereotype was annoying. There were people out there obsessed with all sorts of things—plants, sports, cars, fitness. Nobody called *them* "crazy."

Even her own mother had accused her of "crazy" behavior since she was a little kid. Six-year-old Núria would save her allowance to buy cat food for the neighborhood strays. In Florida, there were tons of them, some friendly, but most feral. One day, she'd come home with a tiny kitten she'd found in a plastic bag. Of course, her mother had freaked out, saying that cats were filthy. While driving her to the nearest shelter to surrender it, she'd scolded Núria, saying that she should care more about homeless people instead of those disgusting strays. To make up for it, her father, who'd still been around at the time, had driven her to Key West once a month to visit with the six-toed cats at The Hemingway Home and Museum.

As Núria stared at her ceiling, she thought about those trips with her dad—the five amazing visits where they'd wandered around the property, petting as many cats as they could, learning all their names and personalities and fantasizing that one day they would live in a place just like it. Those memories were bittersweet, though. They were the best memories she had of her dad, but they were also among the last. A few weeks after their fifth visit, her father left and never came back. No explanation. No letter. Nothing to indicate why he'd packed up all his stuff and disappeared.

Núria's chest hurt. Her stomach fluttered. Her throat tightened. At that moment, lying in bed, she still felt like that little girl bawling her eyes out as her mother screamed about some other woman— some bitch who'd stolen her husband. It was why Núria had vowed to never have children. She didn't want to ever fuck up some innocent kid's life. Her own life was fucked up enough.

Besides, even if she *did* want kids, she was in no position to care for them. She lived practically the same way as she had since she dropped out of college after freshman year. It wasn't that she couldn't hack the work or anything. Núria was smart. When it came down to it, though, she just didn't see the point. All her mother seemed to care about was that she would one day find a good husband, settle down, and pop out some kids. Her dad was God-knows-where doing God-knows-what. And unlike her classmates, she didn't have big career aspirations. The only two things that she was *really* passionate about were cats and coffee. When she decided to leave school for good, she packed up everything she owned in a backpack and moved to New York City, where she'd been living ever since.

*Meow.*

Gazpacho burrowed into her armpit, purring as if he knew she needed a cuddle. She wrapped her arm around his furry belly and nuzzled his head, sniffing that dusty cat smell. Once again, she tried to push the flurry of thoughts aside, focusing only on the purring in her armpit. She closed her eyes, longing for the fuzzy darkness to lull her to sleep. But all she saw were flashes of neon orange. Her heartbeat quickened. Her eyes fluttered open.

The damned Post-it note. It taunted her. Still, at least it was a distraction from the painful memories. Something new and a little bit exciting. Maybe even something to get her out of the rut she was in.

Núria nuzzled her pillow and hugged Gazpacho tighter.

# ELEVEN

# Cat

Cat was back at his hedge. But he was restless. He would have loved to go on a walk, but he wasn't in the mood to deal with the potential risks. Sure, it was dark, even with the streetlamps on. For the most part, he was safe in the shadows. Sometimes, though, cars drove recklessly, speeding down the roads, occasionally driving onto the sidewalks. Not to mention the drunk people, some of whom were downright mean, as if drinking gave them a free pass to harm innocent creatures.

Instead of venturing out, he decided to explore the alleyway where the tall man with the slippers lived. They were neighbors, after all, and Cat knew nothing about him.

He stuck his furry black head out of the shrubbery to check if the coast was clear. Once he was sure it was safe, he crept out, staying low to the ground. He hurried to the wrought-iron gate securing the alleyway. Thankfully, the bars were wide enough that he could slip through. *Phew.* The alleyway was wider than he'd expected. It was more like a narrow side yard with numerous potted plants and a garbage area that was neat and clean.

Why on earth had Cat been sleeping in the hedges when this amazing place had been here all along?

Cats were curious, so naturally he was itching to get a look at the inside of the house. The man was probably upstairs asleep. Surely it was safe, right? Cat leaped onto one of the trash cans, and then onto the large wooden box that held the recyclables. If he stood on his hind legs and stretched his neck as far as possible, he could peek through the bottom of the ground-floor window, where the interior was visible through the slats in the wooden blinds.

The room he was looking at was even more pristine than the alleyway. It was the kitchen, painted a dark navy blue with light-gray cabinets and white countertops. Everything was clean, in its place. There were a couple of plates and bowls on a dishrack and on a small table in the corner that sat four.

Cat tried to imagine the tall man eating his breakfast there. It seemed pretty sad for him to have such a beautiful kitchen and no one to share it with.

Perhaps he was trying to rectify the situation. Was that why he'd placed that note on Cat's plate? Did he want to meet Rainbow Lady? *Hmmm . . .*

It was kind of hard to imagine her in such a place. Everything about her screamed chaos. Maybe that was it, though. Cat hadn't fully figured out humans, but it seemed to him like sometimes opposites were attracted to each other. Sometimes the couples he saw on the street walking hand in hand matched, and sometimes they clashed, like the streaks of rainbow oil he saw floating in puddles of street water. Maybe Rainbow Lady was the oil and this guy was the water.

Cat's hind legs were getting tired, so he went back down on his four paws before hopping down onto the trash can. Except the trash can lid wasn't on straight, and when his weight leaned to one side, it slipped and fell off. Thankfully, Cat was able to twist his body around, landing on the pavement unscathed. But the metal trash can lid hit the ground with a loud bang.

Cat crouched, whipping his head right and left before darting back to the hedges he'd come from.

# TWELVE

## *Collin*

*Bang!*

Collin startled awake, untangling himself from the bed-sheets. The loud noise had come from somewhere outside. His breathing was rapid, shallow.

What if someone was trying to break in?

As quietly as he could, he tiptoed to the closet to retrieve his childhood baseball bat. He wasn't certain he'd actually be able to use the bat if push came to shove, but holding it made him feel safer. When he reached his bedroom door, he turned the knob and opened it, pausing for a couple of seconds as he stuck his head out. All seemed quiet. At the top of the steps, he halted again.

Maybe he was being overly paranoid.

Still, he proceeded down with caution. Collin wouldn't be able to go back to sleep unless he was 100 percent sure that the coast was clear. He gripped the baseball bat tighter, knuckles turning white as he reached the ground floor.

One by one, he checked each room. Everything seemed to be in order. Collin was relieved, but rattled. Maybe some chamomile tea would help him relax. He made his way to the kitchen and grabbed the electric kettle so he could refill it at the sink. While he was doing that, his gaze drifted through the open blinds, spotting the trash can lid on the pavement. He frowned and put the kettle down. Trash can lids didn't fall off on their own. What if the intruder was out there?

Once again, he took hold of the baseball bat and headed for the back door. Collin opened it and peeked outside. Nobody was there. What a relief! He left the baseball bat leaning by the doorframe so he could retrieve the trash can lid. It was New York City, after all, and rats were everywhere. The last thing he needed was a huge mess to clean up in the morning when he had an early meeting with Quentin, his agent. He'd been avoiding having to meet with him, preferring to make his excuses via email. But Quentin was done with excuses and had insisted on a coffee date.

Collin hurried outside and placed the trash can lid back where it belonged, wiggling it a bit to make sure it was on securely. When he was done, though, he noticed something else amiss. There was a trail of dusty paw prints on top of the recyclables bin leading to the kitchen window. *Huh.* It must have been the black cat. He went closer to get a better look. At the bottom of the window frame, there were two more paw prints, as if the cat had leaned on it while peeping inside.

Collin chuckled, trying to picture the cat snooping around like a burglar. He looked over his shoulder at the hedges, wondering if there was something he could do to make its life better. Because for some strange reason he felt a sort of kinship with it. They were both skittish around strangers, were creatures of habit, and were fearful of unfamiliar places. Never in a billion years had he ever visualized himself empathizing with a stray animal.

Collin was no saint, definitely nowhere near as kind as the woman who fed the cat. Still, maybe there was something he could do. A gesture. A small act of kindness. But what, he wasn't quite sure.

# THIRTEEN

# Bong

Bong's living room was dark, except for the candlelight from the altar he'd made for Conchita. On the console table underneath a framed photograph of her was a silver cross, a vase filled with tulips, a small ceramic bowl with her engagement and wedding rings, a Virgin Mary candle, and her collection of Swarovski figurines—the lovebirds were front and center, next to a smaller framed photo from Bong and Conchita's younger days.

He picked up the lovebird figurine and dusted it with a microfiber cloth before putting it back in its place. When he was done, he tucked the cloth away in one of the drawers and knelt down, hands clasped on his chest, with his eyes closed. It was his nightly ritual. For a few minutes, he would speak to her, visualize his favorite memories in his head, and pray that one day soon they would be reunited.

"I really missed you today, mahal," Bong whispered, opening his eyes and looking up at her portrait.

He imagined her photo coming to life, her smile deepening as she reached out to cup his face with her hand like she used to. For a brief instant he could almost feel her skin next to his. The tingling on his cheek traveled down his neck to his torso until his chest warmed. It was the same kind of warmth he'd felt earlier in the day when he'd broken down in front of Omar. Then, he'd been embarrassed. When he was alone, it didn't matter.

All that mattered was Conchita.

He closed his eyes again, remembering their last few minutes together. They had been in their bedroom, Conchita in the bathroom doing her nightly moisturizing routine, Bong lying in bed in his raggedy white sleeveless shirt, boxer shorts, and socks. The TV had been on, but the volume was low so they could chitchat through the walls.

"Just so you know, I'm going to be busy all day tomorrow making leche flan for the church fundraiser," said Conchita, her voice raised so he'd be able to hear her.

Bong grinned. "Why don't we just buy a couple of trays from Amazing Grace? That way you can spend the day with me . . . It's been a while since we've gone on a date, mahal."

The bathroom door opened a crack and Conchita stuck her cold-cream-covered face through. "I'm supposed to cook something for the fundraiser. Not buy something."

"Does that mean you don't want to go on a date with me?" said Bong, crossing his arms across his chest as if he was offended.

Conchita sighed and rolled her eyes. "Alam mo, you're just too much sometimes!"

"Are you trying to tell me I'm fat?" said Bong, uncrossing his arms and grabbing a handful of his belly roll.

"Ay naku!" Conchita slammed the bathroom door.

Bong knew, of course, that she wasn't at all mad or annoyed. She just had a penchant for the dramatic.

A couple of minutes of silence passed. And then he heard a thud.

"Mahal?" He sat up. "Are you okay?"

Silence.

Bong pushed himself off the bed and hurried to the bathroom. He knocked. No reply.

There was nothing left to do but open the door. So he did. Conchita was crumpled on the pink tile floor next to the toilet. For a split second, Bong was frozen with confusion, panic, fear. But the second passed and he went to her, kneeling on the floor so he could hold her body. "*Conchita*," he managed to whisper. She didn't say anything back. When he bent down to embrace her, though, he felt a shallow breath. His beloved was still alive.

He ran to his phone and dialed 911. By the time the ambulance arrived, though, she was gone.

She wouldn't be making the leche flan for the church fundraiser.

They wouldn't ever have another date night.

He would never hear her utter "Ay naku" ever again.

Bong stood and touched the portrait of Conchita, fingertips tracing her beautiful pink lips. All he could feel was the cold glass. He sighed, blew the candle out, and went off to bed.

# FOURTEEN

## Núria

She had to hurry. Her morning shift started at eight. That meant she had a little over an hour to make her rounds.

*Beep! Beep!* A black sedan barely missed her as she ran across the street.

"Fuck," Núria mumbled, catching her breath in front of the bodega.

Once she was sure that all her limbs were intact and that she was indeed still alive, she pushed the bodega door. It wouldn't budge. She frowned. Then she noticed that the CLOSED sign was still hanging there. *Weird.* The bodega should have already been open. She tried to push the door again. She tried to knock. She tried to peek inside by leaning close to the door with the tip of her nose smooshed on the glass. It was dark. Not a soul in sight.

"Great. Just great," she said to herself. If she'd known this was going to happen, she would have packed her collection of random Tupperware in her backpack. But it was too late to go back home. She would have to improvise.

Núria spun around. Her gaze landed on the bright-yellow box on the corner with free newspapers inside. She went over and grabbed a couple, stuffing them into her backpack before hoofing it down the street. If she hurried, she could still make it to work on time.

Cat jumped out of the hedges at the sight of her. Núria was still rattled by her near-death experience and the strangeness of the bodega being closed. Nonetheless, she greeted Cat with the high-pitched voice she used to talk to her feline friends.

"Hey there, buddy. I'm sorry I'm late."

*Meoooowww!*

Cat circled her legs as she took a newspaper page out of her backpack. First she filled up a plastic container with water, using its weight to hold the newspaper in place. Once that was done, she scooped the cat food onto the paper.

"There. Eat up, buddy," she said, taking a few steps back.

For a good minute, he glared at the newspaper plate with the glob of food on it. It seemed he wasn't so sure about this new place setting.

*Meow!*

Núria frowned. "I'm sorry. That's all I've got today," she said. Cat continued to stare at her, eyeball lasers boring holes through her forehead. "It still tastes good. I promise. Tomorrow, I'll make sure to bring some paper plates. Okay?"

Cat leaned his head down in what looked like a sulk. Still, he marched over to the food and ate, begrudgingly. Núria relaxed her shoulders. *Thank God.* The last thing she needed was more drama.

Núria was about to hurry off to her next feeding spot when suddenly, she remembered the Post-it note. She'd meant to write a response at home and bring it with her, but in the morning rush, she'd completely forgotten.

"Crap," she mumbled to herself. She was a few years shy of forty, but she hadn't yet hit that adulting stage of keeping pens, paper, and other normal sorts of necessities with her at all times. It was hard enough to remember to pay her bills and buy toilet paper, never mind fancy pens and colorful Post-it notes, which, frankly, seemed like luxuries to her. Growing up, she'd never had much money; her mother had been a stay-at-home mom, and her father's police officer salary had barely been enough to cover their basic expenses. After her father had left, her mother had found a job as a legal interpreter. They had had even less money than before, even after they moved into a small apartment in a crappier neighborhood. Now, every time Núria thought about buying something, she would hear her mom's voice in the back of her mind, telling her not to fall prey to the frivolities of consumerism. And colorful Post-its were *definitely* a frivolity.

*Oh well* . . . There was always tomorrow. Whoever had sent her the note would just have to wait. When she turned around to get on with the rest of her route, she found a mailman staring at her.

"So, I finally get to meet Gatito's feeder," he said with a toothy smile.

"Oh." Núria was momentarily flummoxed. It wasn't often that complete strangers engaged with her during her feedings—or even seemed to notice her at all.

The mailman gestured at the black cat. "He's been following me for months now. From here all the way to the bodega. I give him treats when we get there. He responds well to bribery," he said with a chuckle.

For the first time in a long time, Núria smiled—a real smile, with her entire face. Her body almost quivered with happiness. "I-I didn't know. . . . Thank you."

Finally, Cat finished his meal. Instead of jumping back into the hedges, though, he turned around and stared at Núria and the mailman.

"Don't worry, man. You'll have your second breakfast soon enough. Just give me a minute," said the mailman to Cat.

Núria watched him talk to the cat. It had been a long while since she'd met someone else who spoke with animals the way she did. She was opening her mouth to comment on it when suddenly something occurred to her. Was the mailman the Post-it note writer? She furrowed her brows.

"I'm Omar, by the way," said the mailman.

"Núria." She stuck out her hand, except at that very moment her cellphone vibrated. "Hold on a sec," she said, fishing it out of her pocket.

Oye! Are you going to keep me in suspense or what? Who
is this Charles and what does he look like? If you don't
reply I'm going to get on the next plane to New York City.
No estoy bromeando . . .

Her mother. Of course. Just as Núria had suspected, she was already threatening to come see her. Great. Núria shoved the phone
back into her pocket. And then she looked back at the man standing
in front of her.

Núria had an idea. A very bad idea.

"Uh . . . so, like, um, I know we just met and all. But do you
mind doing a selfie with me?" she stammered.

Omar laughed so hard she could see the roof of his mouth. "Lemme
guess. That was either your jealous ex-boyfriend or your mom."

Núria grinned. "Mom. She won't get off my case about settling
down."

"All right, all right. I love me a good selfie," said Omar, shimmy-
ing next to her.

She pulled her phone out and stretched her arm out as far as it
would go. Once both their heads were in the frame, they smiled. And
then she took the shot.

Núria exhaled, relieved. "Thank you, Omar. You have literally
saved my ass."

"I'm happy to be of service. Anything for a friend of a friend," he
said, gesturing at Cat, who was still staring at them. "Anyway, I better get going," he said, grabbing hold of his mail cart.

"Me too. Thanks again. I'll see you around," said Núria.

Omar went off toward the bodega and Núria went the opposite
direction. After a couple of steps, she halted. "Hey, you wouldn't
happen to have a pen I can borrow?"

He turned around and stuck his chest out, proudly displaying the
pen that was sticking out of his shirt pocket. "A pen, you say?"

Núria jogged back toward him. He pulled out the blue USPS pen
and handed it to her ceremoniously, as if he were a knight handing
her his sword. "It's yours. I've got plenty," he said.

"Thank you. Come by Brooklyn Brew anytime. You know, the café by the park? There's a coffee there with your name on it," she said with a smile.

"Cool. I'm gonna take you up on that," he said with a wave.

Núria watched him walk down the street with Cat galloping at his heels. She didn't even care anymore that she was going to be late for her shift. It wasn't often that she had serendipitous moments like that.

Once Omar and the cat were out of sight, she pulled out a fresh piece of newspaper from her bag and scribbled something on it. When she was done, she flattened the page on the pavement and weighed it down with the same stone from yesterday. There. She'd done it. It wasn't as bright, crisp, and clean as a neon-colored Post-it, but it would get the job done.

And her mom would be proud.

≈

# FIFTEEN

# *Collin*

There was a wooden door separating Collin from the outside world. He was in no mood to open it, much less have a casual coffee with his agent in some trendy Brooklyn café. Quentin had emphasized the word "casual" so as to not scare Collin into bailing. But Collin knew that he was in for one of Quentin's tough love talks, which belonged on the list of Collin's most despised things, along with Christmas, Valentine's Day, pickles, unicorns, and anything labeled "artisanal."

He went ahead and opened the door a few inches, allowing himself to acclimate to the humid air. His dark hair was probably already beginning to curl, which unfortunately would make him look like an oafish Cupid in a button-down short-sleeved shirt. He would have preferred his armor of tweed, but it was way too hot for that.

Finally, he was ready to face the world. Except, wait. There were voices coming from the street in front of his brownstone. Collin opened the door a bit wider, but almost immediately closed it again. The woman who fed the black cat was on the sidewalk, talking to the mailman. After what seemed like ages, the mailman went away, but not before he handed her what looked like a pen. She pulled out a sheet of newspaper from her bag, wrote something on it, and placed it down on the pavement with the rock from his planter of geraniums.

She wrote him back!

Collin could hardly contain himself, counting each of the woman's steps as she disappeared from view. After twenty more steps, he opened the door, sneaking down the front stairway to make a dash for it. He picked up the rock and then the piece of newspaper. On the edge, where there was no text or photos, she'd written:

*Duh. Of course.*

Collin laughed. It was a curt response. To the point, yet charming, and somehow adorable. He grinned from ear to ear and then tucked the newspaper into his pocket.

Quentin was already at the café, seated on a rather large leather wing-back armchair. Of course he'd left the tiny slipper chair for Collin. The seating arrangement made Collin feel like a little boy about to be scolded by his father. Rather appropriate, given the situation.

"Ah. Collin. There you are," said Quentin, looking up from the *New Yorker* he was reading.

Collin sat down on the slipper chair, his knees jutting out awkwardly. "Quentin. It's nice to see you."

Quentin raised one perfectly groomed eyebrow. "That's good to hear. I was under the impression you were avoiding me."

"No, of course not," said Collin.

For a moment, Quentin didn't reply. Instead, he adjusted his wiry frame, which was dressed in his usual casual Friday style—pastel-pink shorts, a button-down in a watermelon print, and espadrilles. He placed the magazine on the small table between them before leaning toward Collin with a look of utmost seriousness.

"Collin. Can you be straight with me? Is there something wrong? Are you going through some sort of midlife crisis?" he asked.

Collin exhaled. "Nothing is wrong, Quentin. I'm just feeling uninspired. What can I say? It happens."

"Of course it happens. You don't think I know that? I've been in this business for almost twenty years."

"Okay. Well, there you go," said Collin, slumping back in his seat.

Quentin rolled his eyes. "It's not as if I'm expecting you to send me a polished manuscript tomorrow. But how about sending me a list of story ideas? We can bounce them off each other. I'd even be open to seeing some scribbles from your notebook. I just want to see something."

More than anything, Collin wanted to sit forward confidently, clear his throat, and give Quentin what he was asking for—some brilliant fucking story idea. But he didn't have it. Everything that he'd brainstormed had ended up deflating like a failed soufflé. He just didn't want to admit it to Quentin, because saying it out loud made it all the more real. Collin was failing at the one thing he was supposed to be good at.

"I need a coffee," he said, struggling to get up off the slipper chair before Quentin could say anything.

Collin took a couple of steps toward the middle of the room, where a crowd of people waited in line. After a minute, a large group stepped aside, leaving him with a clear view of the long wooden counter, the shiny espresso machines billowing with steam, and the colorful mural of coffee cups and pastries next to a blackboard menu. And there, right smack in the thick of the coffee-making action, was *the* woman. The black cat was nowhere in sight.

# SIXTEEN

# Núria

Unfortunately, Núria had run out of time. She was already too late for work, so she would have to go back after her shift to clean up all her cat-feeding paraphernalia. Hopefully nobody would rat her out. It *was* Brooklyn, but still, there were all sorts of Karens and Chads lurking in the shadows of their multi-million-dollar brownstones.

When she got to work, she hurried past the crowd to the back room, where she replaced her mismatched sweaty clothes with a clean black T-shirt emblazoned with the Brooklyn Brew logo and black hakama-style cropped pants—her work uniform.

Thankfully, she'd been able to sneak behind the counter without anyone noticing that she was fifteen minutes late. Almost immediately she was slammed with an onslaught of cappuccino, latte, and macchiato orders. Most baristas would have been frazzled by the rush. Not Núria. She almost preferred it that way because time seemed to go by faster when she was busy, and she didn't have to make small talk with her customers. Small talk was probably the only aspect of this job she wasn't all that fond of. In the eighteen years since she'd begun working as a barista—first as a trainee, then a junior barista, a barista, and then eventually a master barista, otherwise known as a coffee master—she'd been hit on, verbally abused, threatened, and even physically attacked by a woman who'd snapped after Núria mistakenly gave her oat milk instead of cow's milk. Despite all that, she did truly enjoy her job, and she was thankful to have flexible hours so she could dedicate herself to her volunteering duties. She wished only that people would take her career choice seriously, rather than see it as a temporary job until she could find what she was "truly" passionate about. And by people, she mostly meant her mother, who loved to tell her that the Bustelo coffee she brewed at home was *far* superior to the six-dollar beverages Núria crafted at the café.

"Hey, Nú. I've got to go to the loo for a minute. Can you hold down the fort?" asked Anh, the Vietnamese-Australian guy who usually took the orders and manned the register.

Núria nodded. "Yeah. Go ahead," she said, keeping an eye on the milk she was steaming. Once the milk was sufficiently hot and foamy, she poured it into a cup with a shot of espresso in it, swirling and whirling until she'd created a fern leaf design. Perfect. For the briefest of moments, she smiled, proud of her work.

"Uh. Excuse me. I mean, good morning."

She glanced over to the customer waiting at the register. "Give me a sec," she said, placing the latte on a saucer with a tiny teaspoon and a complimentary spice cookie before handing it to the customer. "What can I get for you?" she asked, not even bothering to go over to the register since she preferred to stay behind the confines of her espresso machine.

"Ummm . . ." The customer looked indecisive, staring at the blackboard menu.

Núria was used to these kinds of customers—the ones who would take forever to decide unless they were given some guidance. One of her favorite things to do at work was size up these customers and offer them their perfect beverage. So she looked at them, *really* looked at them. The former blur of a customer was a man, tall and solid with shaggy dark hair, a strong jawline, and brown eyes that reminded her of the thick hot chocolate she'd dunked her churros in as a child. Something about him reminded her of those giant, furry Newfoundland dogs she'd see in the dog park from time to time.

"How about an almond mocha latte?" she finally said. For some reason, she sensed that he needed a little something sweet to brighten his day.

"That sounds good. Thanks," he replied.

As soon as Núria began crafting his beverage, Anh returned from the restroom. The man paid for his drink, then shuffled over to the counter to wait.

"We can bring it to your table," she said, seeing that he was anxiously waiting.

"It's okay. I don't mind."

*Suit yourself.*

Truth be told, though, the guy was making her kind of nervous. He had this staticky sort of energy that made her skin prickle. Maybe he was just a creep? Or maybe he *really* needed his caffeine fix.

Núria poured the steaming milk into the cup, once again swirling and whirling, her hands automatically creating three hearts out of foam. She placed the cup with the complimentary cookie on the counter carefully, so as not to ruin her masterfully executed latte art. "Here you go. Enjoy," she said, hurrying off to start her next drink order.

Except the guy just stood there, staring at his almond mocha latte so hard that it was almost as if his eyes were tracing the hearts one by one.

"You need anything else?" she said, hoping he would go away already.

The guy startled. "Oh. Um. No. All good. Thank you," he said, taking hold of his cup and saucer with shaky hands.

Out of the corner of her eye, Núria watched him navigate his way back to his table, where another guy was already seated—a customer she recognized as one of her regulars.

"So, what was he like?" said Anh, sidling over.

Núria furrowed her brow. "Who?"

Anh made googly eyes toward the almond mocha latte guy's table, his spikey eyebrow piercing pointing right at him. "Collin Thackeray? You know, the bestselling author extraordinaire?"

"Oh." Núria's face warmed with embarrassment. It wasn't that she was averse to reading. It's just that she didn't have much time for it. "I don't know. He was kind of weird. But I mean, who am I to judge?"

"He *is* rather cute, though. Don't you think?" said Anh with a chuckle. "I mean, I *definitely* wouldn't kick him out of bed."

Núria rolled her eyes, then glanced at Collin again, hoping he wouldn't catch her eye. "I guess?"

Anh swatted her arm. "Oh, come on. If he walked in here with a cat-print T-shirt and a Petco shopping bag of cat food, you'd be all over that. For all you know he's got a bunch of annoyingly adorable cats at home."

Núria rolled her eyes. "I seriously doubt it."

"You never know!" said Anh, rushing off to take another customer's order.

# SEVENTEEN

# Cat

"I'm telling you, man. That cheeseburger I had last night was hands down the best burger ever. Next time I order, I'll save you a piece," said Cheery Mailman to Cat, who was trotting beside him. Cat glanced at him with sparkling green eyes. *Mmmm.* He could practically taste it.

The mailman halted for a quick second and stared at Cat as if he was about to impart some words of wisdom. "Just between the two of us, Swiss cheese has no business being on a burger. I mean, Carl swears by it. But that's just nonsense. The only cheeses worthy of a burger are cheddar and pepper jack."

*Meeeooowww.*

To be honest, Cat was a bit baffled by this whole burger debate. His experience with cheese was limited to sidewalk pizza, but surely one cheese was as good as another? Cheery Mailman *was* being sort of dramatic about the whole thing. Cat would happily gobble down any sort of burger with any sort of cheese. Though he wasn't a big fan of bread, so he'd probably skip the bun. And the lettuce, tomato, onions, pickles, and mustard. *Gross.*

By the time they reached the bodega, Cheery Mailman was still going on. "I mean, goat cheese? On a burger? Now, that there is a crime. For real."

Cat hopped onto the bench while Cheery Mailman went over to the entrance of the bodega. He frowned as soon as he spotted the CLOSED sign.

*Great,* Cat thought. He'd had to listen to Cheery Mailman's jibber-jabbering about cheeseburgers for a good fifteen minutes, and now he wasn't going to get one of his creamy treats. That there was the *real* crime.

"Huh. It's still closed," said Cheery Mailman, peering through the glass storefront window. "The metal security gate isn't down, though. Maybe the old man forgot when he closed up last night."

Now Cat was worried. He got up on his hind legs and stared longingly into the dark store. Not only was he worried about the possibility of not getting his creamy treat, but he was also worried about Sad Bodega Man. Had something happened to him? Was he okay? *Hmmm . . .* He pulled his ears back and sniffed the air. Everything smelled as it should. His fur remained unruffled, so his gut told him that nothing bad had happened. Somewhere in there was his creamy treat *and* Sad Bodega Man.

He hunched back down, flopping on the bench. Oh, how he wished Cheery Mailman hadn't spent the entire time talking about burgers. Now Cat was officially starving for his second breakfast. It was obvious he wasn't going to get one today.

*Humph.*

Cheery Mailman sat on the other end of the bench and gestured at him with his elbow. "Don't you worry, my man. I'll buy you two treats tomorrow to make up for it. All right?"

*Meow!*

Okay, maybe Cat *would* forgive him. Just the thought of two sachets of creamy treats made him salivate. If Cat could have smiled, he would have.

But what if the bodega was still closed tomorrow? What if Sad Bodega Man was still holed up somewhere in the back of the store, bawling his eyes out like the other day? Cat couldn't allow that to happen. For his own sake. For Sad Bodega Man's sake. And for the sake of his loyalty to Smiley Lady.

Cat sidled up to Cheery Mailman, closer than he'd ever gotten before. Even though he wasn't at all scared of him, he still wasn't comfortable being too near him; usually he preferred a human arm's length. Today, though, he would make an exception. *Okay, let's do this,* he thought to himself, leaning forward before he would change his mind. Cat aimed his right paw at Cheery Mailman's chest and swatted at the pen in his shirt pocket. One swat. Two swats. Three. Cheery Mailman chuckled and pulled a USPS pen out of his pocket.

"You want one of my pens too?" he said, holding it out to Cat.

*Humph. I thought he was smart.* Cat swatted at the pen again and again and again until Cheery Mailman took it back with a frown.

"Well, if you don't want the pen, then what *do* you want, my man?"

Cat craned his neck and stared longingly into the bodega. Cheery Mailman frowned, blinking for a good minute before grinning, like he finally understood the assignment. "I getcha," he said, nodding to Cat, then reaching for one of the old man's bills. He clicked the pen and pulled his lips to the side, thinking for a couple of seconds before jotting a note on the white envelope. Cat stretched his neck as far as it would go so he could take a peek, except there was one problem. He couldn't read. The sticks and curves and dots didn't mean a thing to him. But still, he was curious.

When Cheery Mailman was done, he went back over to the entrance and slipped the envelopes, including the one with the note, under the door, exhaling when he stood back up.

"Mission accomplished." He nodded. "All right, I'll see you tomorrow. Stay safe, Gatito," he said before walking off around the corner with his mail cart.

For a moment, Cat sat there, feeling satisfied with himself. Well, maybe not quite *that* satisfied, since his stomach still grumbled for one of those damned creamy treats.

# EIGHTEEN

# Bong

*Are you okay? Call me if you need to talk or whatever.*
*Omar, the mailman.*

Bong stared at the note with Omar's phone number below it, written on the back of his credit card bill. He'd already read it three times, but he was in disbelief. Omar was practically a stranger, yet he'd cared enough to reach out, something that perplexed Bong. Then, as he read the note again for a fourth time, something occurred to him.

Did Omar think he was suicidal?

Admittedly, he'd been a complete mess when Omar walked in on him the day before. He could only imagine what he must have looked like—a blubbering, snotty pile of sadness. If he'd been the one walking in on himself, he might have come to the same conclusion.

But what made Bong even more perplexed was that he actually wasn't certain how he felt. There were moments when he did want to die—moments that were fleeting but there nonetheless. Other times, he was happy to be alive, hoping for something miraculous to happen so he could enjoy life again. Even if it was without his beloved.

He sighed, his shoulders slumping in defeat. It was late morning and the bodega was still closed. Sure, he'd lost business, but he'd needed the extra sleep since he'd been up most of the night tossing and turning, trying to suppress the overwhelming grief that had taken hold of him. Anyway, Bong was pretty sure that his regular customers would survive one morning without their protein bars or bottled juices or breath mints or lotto tickets. It was Brooklyn; you could throw a stone in any direction and it would land on a neighborhood bodega. Bong's bodega wasn't any more special than the rest.

*Scratch. Scratch. Scratch.*

Bong startled, almost dropping the mail. He'd been so deep in thought that he hadn't realized he'd been standing behind the door of the still-closed bodega for a good ten minutes. Maybe even longer.

*Scratch. Scratch.*

That noise. What was it? He couldn't see anyone outside through the glass door. He stuffed the mail in his back pocket and went over to the door to unlock it. When he pushed it open, there wasn't anyone there.

*Meow.*

Bong startled again. On the pavement by the doorway was Itim, the black cat. It, or he—yes, now he remembered, Conchita had said he was a male cat—stared up at him with green eyes that to him looked a bit scared, a bit curious, and a bit something else that he quite couldn't put his finger on. The cat meowed at him a second time.

"I'm sorry. . . . We're closed. Shoo! Go on now." He waved his hand at the cat, hoping he would go away.

*Meeeooowww!*

It didn't work. Itim didn't budge, only flinching slightly at the sight of his hand. In fact, he seemed even more determined to stay put. Bong was about to try and shoo him away again when a memory materialized in his head.

Conchita had heard meowing from somewhere around the bodega. "Mahal! Do you hear that? It's a cat . . . Come help me find it," she'd said, grabbing his arm. They'd searched the storage room and the basement, outside the front of the store, and then the back. That's when they'd seen Itim for the first time, huddled next to the garbage can. His black fur had been dull and scruffy, and he looked as if he could use a good meal or two.

*Meow.* It had been a soft, somewhat pathetic-sounding meow.

"Mahal! Go get some canned food and put it in one of those take-out containers I keep behind the counter. And some water too. Hurry," she'd said. As he'd walked off, he'd heard her speaking softly to the poor cat. "You can trust me. Okay? I'll give you some food and some water, and then we're going to be good friends . . . Look at that beautiful black fur of yours. In the Philippines where I'm from, we call that color itim. I think that would be a great name for you. What do you think, Itim? Are we going to be friends?"

Bong had grinned, shaking his head because he knew that from then on, she would feed this cat every single day, and he would have no say in the matter, even though the food would probably attract rats and roaches and maybe even other stray cats. And of course, he'd been right. Because that was his Conchita. She was practically a saint.

*Meow.*

Itim gazed up at him, almost daring him to try and shoo him away again. But the memories had plucked at his heartstrings, as if Conchita herself were doing the plucking.

His face warmed. Conchita hadn't been there to witness his actions, and yet he somehow felt guilty. He'd acted unkind. If Conchita could see him she surely would give him a piece of her mind, saying something like, "He is also God's creature, Bong. And all of God's creatures, even strays, deserve kindness."

Bong opened the door wider. "You want to come inside?" he said, stepping aside to clear the entryway.

For a second, Itim gazed into the bodega, stretching his neck to get a better view. Then he looked up at Bong, studying his face, his body language. Bong couldn't really blame him for hesitating. He *had* been mean just moments ago. Of course the cat was suspicious.

Bong would have to earn back his trust.

So he placed a doorstop in front of the door and went over to the aisle where the pet supplies were. When he came back, he was holding out a handful of cat treats. "You want some?"

Slowly, Itim entered, walking low to the ground, as if he was still suspicious of Bong's intentions. Once the cat was a few feet inside, he planted himself in front of the cash register where the candy display was. So as not to spook him, Bong moved in slow motion, grabbing a paper plate from behind the counter and squeezing a couple of the creamy treats onto it.

"Here you go. Enjoy," he said, placing the paper plate on the floor and pushing it closer. Itim stepped back a couple of inches, but as soon as Bong went to the register, he pounced on the plate and gobbled the food up.

For a moment, Itim stayed put, gazing at Bong. Then, when he was seemingly satisfied with whatever he had observed, he licked his paws—a couple of licks on one and a couple of licks on the other—before trotting toward the front door. He looked back at Bong for a second before rubbing up against the doorway once and disappearing into the street.

# NINETEEN

# Collin

Suffice it to say, the casual coffee meeting with Quentin had been a disaster. Collin had been defensive the entire time, even though he knew that his agent meant well. But Collin hadn't been able to help it. The excuses had spewed out of his mouth non-stop. Frankly, it had been an embarrassment. Weren't authors supposed to be thoughtful with words? In spite of all that, they had ended the meeting amicably, with Collin promising that he would share some ideas in the coming weeks. At least for now, Quentin's concerns were allayed.

Collin hurried down the block, eager to get back home. Not only because the meeting with Quentin had frustrated him, but because the exchange with the woman who fed the cat had drained him of any pride he'd had left. He'd acted like a total fool, a clown, a blabbering idiot. The only part of their exchange that had seemed remotely positive was the hearts she'd meticulously designed out of foam. Even that, though, was grasping for straws. Only an awkward eighth-grade boy would swoon over latte hearts. Yet there he was, strolling down the street, daydreaming about those hearts as if they'd been some declaration of love.

God, he truly *was* a hopeless case.

For a moment, he halted. All the stress and overanalyzing and the heat had made him a bit light-headed. *Breathe, Collin. Breathe.* And as he breathed and tried to calm himself, he caught sight of the black cat across the street. It was prancing down the block with a satisfied look about it.

Seeing the cat reminded him about the incident in the alleyway the night before. If only he could do something, even just a small thing, to make the cat's life better.

What did the cat really need?

It had food. It kind of had companionship. But what about a home? Collin wasn't about to catnap the creature and bring it inside his house, but maybe he could do something else. He looked around, mulling it over, while sweat trickled down his forehead and neck from the oppressive humidity. Then, voilà! He spotted the Foodtown and suddenly had an idea. A rather brilliant one, actually.

Collin marched to the supermarket with long strides, the whole embarrassing situation at the café temporarily forgotten. When he passed through the entrance, he paused to catch his breath. It was imperative that he prepare himself for the overwhelmingness of the store—the bright lights, the endless aisles of products, the smells, the people, the sounds. Collin usually ordered groceries online so he could avoid everything surrounding him at that very moment. But he was too excited to wait.

He grabbed a cart. It was just before the weekend, so the place was pretty busy. The only way he could cope was to not look at anyone, instead keeping his gaze straight ahead.

After making a few wrong turns, he finally found himself in the pet supplies aisle. The rows and rows of colorful canned foods and bags of kibble and cat litter assaulted his eyes. But he tried to focus, knowing exactly what he needed. He grabbed six cans of salmon-flavored cat food, because everyone loved salmon, right? Then he got two metal bowls for food and water and a cat bed covered with plaid fabric, the most logical choice since he was pretty sure a cat wouldn't appreciate a leopard or cow print. After that, he hurried off to the office supplies section to pick up some nontoxic glue and markers.

He spotted an open register and headed straight for it. The cashier girl was staring off into space. As soon as he plopped the stack of canned cat food onto the conveyor belt, she startled and began cleaning the area with a rag. "Oh, good morning," she said.

"Uh. Morning." Collin unloaded the rest of his stuff, pushing the empty cart through when he was done.

While the cashier girl checked out his items, he stood there watching her hands move. For some reason he fixated on her fingernails, which were painted with pink nail polish that was mostly chipped off. These were the kinds of details he liked to use in his stories, the imperfections that made characters more real.

"That'll be thirty-eight dollars and thirty cents, please," said the cashier girl.

He flinched and looked up at her, unfortunately landing right in her gaze. *Crap*. She batted her eyelashes. When it came to women, Collin was pretty clueless. Was she flirting with him? Oh God. Maybe she was. She looked like she was practically a teenager. He was quite sure his neck was starting to break out in a rash.

"You need something else?"

As much as he wanted to just pay and get out of there, he did need something else. "Yeah, actually. Do you have a couple of empty cardboard boxes? Large ones?" he asked while fumbling for his wallet.

"Sure thing." She went off toward the back of the store and, a couple of minutes later, came back with two flattened boxes. "Are these okay?"

"Yes, perfect. Thank you," he said, handing her his credit card.

The girl handed him his receipt, her fingers lingering on his. "Are you moving or something?"

But Collin was done. Like *done* done. So he didn't reply, hastily grabbing his groceries and running off before the cashier girl could interrogate him further.

# TWENTY

## *Lily*

*hat the actual fuck.*

Lily watched the customer rush off toward the store exit. It was always kind of annoying when grown-ass men assumed she was flirting with them just because she was being friendly. Sure, the guy was pretty cute. Rich too, by the looks of it. She could tell by the quality of his clothes and watch and wallet that he was probably rolling in dough, the kind of dough she so badly needed. Lily might have been desperate, but she wasn't that desperate. She still had morals and values.

Though, truth be told, she wouldn't have minded having a boyfriend in this town. Someone a couple of years older who could treat her to dinner from time to time. Someone she could confide in and cuddle with after a hard day's work. So far, though, she hadn't met anyone. New York City must have been teeming with young single guys, but she wasn't meeting any of them working as a supermarket cashier. Maybe it was for the best. Because she wasn't here to snag herself a nice, cute boyfriend. She was here to meet her long-lost half sister.

All she'd done so far, though, was stalk her. For months and months, she'd fantasized about that joyous day when they would finally meet, and Lily would find the words to tell Núria who she really was. There would be balloons and streamers, and a cake with pastel-pink frosting, and right after they hugged with happy tears in their eyes, there would be fireworks up in the sky. In her mind, it was magical. But in reality, their first encounter had been nothing but a meaningless exchange of words at the checkout counter. Real life was nothing like the movies.

Lily sighed. She was deeply ashamed of her childish fantasies. She glanced down at her hands, at the once-pink fingernails she'd scraped with her teeth. A nervous habit. At night, while her roommates were in the living room drinking margaritas and watching *90 Day Fiancé*, she holed up in her room, thinking about her dad and how much she missed him, thinking about whether Núria would even want to have a relationship with her, thinking about how disappointed her mom was that she hadn't ended up like the other girls in her cheerleading squad—with the perfect boyfriend, in the perfect college, with perfect grades and a future with a perfect job and a perfect house and four perfect little kids.

Her life was shit. And she knew it.

Sometimes, she wondered what her life would have been like if she'd never found out about her sister. But who was she kidding? Eventually, she would have stumbled onto her father's secret. It had just happened sooner rather than later. Lily was a snoop; she always had been. After her dad had tragically died in a car accident, she'd gone through all his old stuff that was stored in boxes in their dusty basement. Most of it had been knick-knacks, trophies and awards from his youth, his police badge from when he worked as a cop in Florida, some albums of black-and-white photos, stacks of baseball cards, and a bunch of random books. But there had also been a semi-rusty cookie tin tucked into the corner of one of the boxes. Lily had opened it. Inside had been a children's book, one that didn't belong to Lily. Its title had been *The Cat Who Went to Heaven,* and inside had been an inscription that read:

> *Happy birthday to my dearest daughter, Núria.*
> *Papa misses you very much.*

At first, she'd assumed that the book must have belonged to someone else. But as she'd flipped its pages, somewhere toward the middle she'd discovered a discolored family photo that looked to be from the 1990s. There was a father and a mother and a daughter standing out on their front lawn next to some pink plastic flamingos. They were huddled together, eyes squinting from the bright sunlight. Lily had stared at the family, her heartbeat fluttering in her chest. Because the man in the photo was her father. The woman, however, was not her mother, and the daughter was most definitely not her.

There had also been a bundle of letters, the envelopes yellowed with age. They had been stamped RETURN TO SENDER. All of them had remained unopened. At the very bottom of the cookie tin, there had been a rolled-up magazine. Lily had unrolled it and stared at an issue of *Barista* magazine. On the cover had been a smiling, freckled woman next to an espresso machine. The header had read "Núria Rey Andreu of Brooklyn Brew Talks Cappuccinos and Cats."

In that moment, she'd known that the little girl in the old photo was the woman on the magazine cover all grown up. She had Lily's father's eyes, his jawline, his smile. This girl, this woman was her sister—the sister she had longed for her entire life.

## TWENTY-ONE

# *Núria*

Churro, Gazpacho, and Miel sat by Núria's bare feet, waiting like a pack of thieves eyeing their loot. Núria took the last bite of her Fatboy's vegan burger and glared back at them.

"You know the vet said no more table scraps. Besides, it's not even meat," she said, wiping her mouth with a paper napkin.

The three cats meowed in unison, circling and rubbing her legs. In spite of their antics, Núria stood her ground because the last thing she wanted was another lecture from the vet about their chonkiness.

"Sorry, guys." She picked up her phone and opened up her photo album. There it was. The selfie of her and Omar, aka Charles. With all her running around and a busy day at work, she hadn't had time to send it to her mom yet. Now she was home. She'd fed the ingrates *and* herself. All she had left to do was find the courage to actually send the damned photo and brace herself for her mom's endless questions.

*Is he Puerto Rican? Dominican?*
*How old is he?*
*Is he really a mailman or is that one of those hipster looks?*
*Have you met his parents?*
*Does he have all his fingers and toes?*
*Is he a Democrat or a Republican?*

And most important . . .

*When is he going to propose already?*

Núria went to the fridge to get herself a beer. She would need the alcohol to soothe her nerves. As soon as she sent the photo, she was 100 percent sure that her mom would call her in two minutes or less. Guaranteed.

She sat back down and chugged half of her beer. Then she took a deep, deep breath, one that filled her lungs to full capacity, before exhaling it all out.

"Okay, here goes nothing," she mumbled. Before she could change her mind, she tapped on her phone and typed out.

**Hello from me and Charles.**

She attached the selfie and pressed send. There. She'd done it and she couldn't take it back. Núria put the phone down and waited, staring at the walls, the ceiling, her lap, her hands, her cats, who were nibbling at her toes as if they were leftover kernels of popcorn.

*Twinkle-twinkle . . . Twinkle . . . Twinkle-twinkle.* One minute and forty-eight seconds. Not even two whole minutes had passed. Núria let the phone ring for a bit longer, the most torturous thing she could do to her mother. If she was going to be on the receiving end of her interrogation, her mother could surely take a bit of torture herself.

Finally, she answered, "Hola, Mamá."

"Oyé! What took you so long?" she said in a voice so shrill that Núria had to pull the phone away from her ear.

"Sorry. I was busy."

"Busy doing what?"

Núria gazed around her studio apartment. "You know, eating dinner, cleaning the litter boxes, reading bridal magazines—"

*Silence.*

"I don't appreciate your jokes, mija," her mother said, her voice several octaves lower.

Núria slumped in her seat. "Fine."

She could hear her mom trying to control her breathing on the other end. Either she was *really* pissed off, or *really* ecstatic.

"So, dígame. This Charles. Is he really a mailman or is that one of those hipster fashion statements?" she asked.

Núria had to hold her breath to stop herself from cracking up. God, her mom was so predictable. "He is in fact a mailman," she replied. At least *that* wasn't a total lie.

"*Humph.*" There was a long pause. "Well, at least he has benefits," she added flatly.

It was obvious she would have preferred a doctor or a lawyer or a Wall Street stockbroker. But at this rate she was in no position to be picky.

"He's a great mailman, and he's *really* nice, and—and he loves cats," said Núria, not knowing what else to say about a man she barely knew.

"Well, thank God for that!" her mom said dramatically. "Those cats are like man repellents."

Núria furrowed her brow. "They are *not*. For your information, loads of guys like cats."

"*Humph.*" There was another pause. Núria was sure she'd pulled the phone away so she could get another look at the photo. "He's quite tan, mija. And that curly hair . . . Is he Dominican? Does he at least speak Spanish?"

"He's not tanned. He's brown, okay? And yes, he's Dominican *and* speaks Spanish *and* he can cook the most delicious mofongo in the world," said Núria, biting her lip.

"Mofongo has pork in it," her mom said matter-of-factly.

Núria rolled her eyes. "Okay, okay. He makes the most delicious *vegan* mofongo in the world."

"Well, I do like a man who can cook. But stay vigilant, mija. I hear plenty of stories on the news about those people who work for the USPS. Rapists, murderers, thieves. You know, they don't call it 'going postal' for nothing," she warned.

Núria could feel her face getting hot with anger. "I'm going now, Ma. Maybe I'll talk to you some other time. Unless I get murdered by my boyfriend first."

Then she hung up and chugged the rest of her beer in one go.

# TWENTY-TWO

# Collin

Collin was in his study. It was dark except for the light from his computer screen. He should've been busy making a list of story ideas for his agent. But no, he was watching YouTube tutorials on how to craft a DIY cat house.

Was it another outlet for his procrastination? Perhaps. To Collin, though, it didn't feel like it. The creative juices were flowing, but in an altogether new and different way. He was on a mission and he wouldn't be able to sleep until he'd accomplished it.

*Aha!* Finally, he found a design that he could pull off with his limited crafting skills. It was a simple structure made of one large box with an A-frame roof, a couple of cut-out windows, planter boxes drawn with marker, and ample room inside for the cat bed he'd purchased. Collin knew that a cardboard box house wouldn't last too long outdoors, but it seemed like a cop-out to order something expensive online, which was something his mother would do. For her, everything *had* to be designer, limited-edition, one of a kind. She wouldn't step into a Target or a Walmart if someone paid her. That might have been a part of why he was so attracted to the woman who fed the cat. She was the polar opposite of his mother. Not that he didn't love his mother. He did, but it was a love filled with boundaries. When it came to romance, though, he yearned to love without limits. It was something he'd been searching for his entire adult life, but had yet to find. Maybe he would have that chance with the woman who fed the cats . . .

*Ping!*

He glanced at his watch. It was eight P.M. Was it a coincidence that he'd been thinking about his mother? Perhaps not. Clearly his mind was trained to expect her weekly missive, which arrived in his inbox every Friday at eight. In the past, she would send him hand-written letters on cream-colored stationery with a chartreuse border. However, she'd shifted to emails when she figured out he was more likely to read them and respond.

As much as he would have preferred to continue his DIY project, he clicked over to his inbox to get it over with. There was nothing quite as excruciating as reading the criticisms she disguised as small talk and niceties on a Friday night. He breathed deep as he opened the email, whose subject line read *Onward and Upward.*

My dearest, darling Collin,

   Tonight, as I drink my chamomile tea, I find myself reminiscing about you and your sister, in particular about the days in your youth when anything and everything seemed possible. I often daydreamed about both of your lives; Caroline would graduate valedictorian, and then go to Brown, where she would meet a young man from a good family—a man who would one day become a U.S. senator, perhaps even president, whereas you would go to Harvard Medical School, where your research on cancer or Alzheimer's would lead you to one day receiving a Nobel Prize for medicine, which you would rightfully dedicate to me and your father. Of course, I always envisioned at least four or five grandchildren; any more would be considered gauche by today's standards. But you have both chosen different paths. Alas, such is life. I've come to peace with it. Your lives are yours, after all. And so, on this Friday eve, I say, onward and upward with whatever it is that you wish to accomplish.

*With affection,*
*Mom*

P.S. Your father wants to know if you have any interest in his platinum and mother-of-pearl cuff links since he's become rather unfond of them.

Collin exhaled, allowing his shoulders to relax. He could almost picture his mother tapping away at the keyboard of her laptop with her perfectly manicured nails, resting her hand on the surface of her polished walnut antique desk or on the silk Hermès scarf around her neck as she considered her words. Her vermillion lips would've curled into a slight smile while she typed the words "onward and upward," as she was proud of the encouragement she was imparting. She certainly wasn't the warmest of mothers, not by a long shot. But she was *his* mother. Years ago, he'd come to terms with that.

Later, he would compose his reply to her. At the moment, he was way too excited about finishing his little project. *"Onward and upward,"* as his mother had proclaimed.

Collin turned on the overhead lights and blinked for a second, his eyes reacclimating to the brightness. He retrieved the largest of the two cardboard boxes, glue, markers, tape, some binder clips, and a box cutter he kept in his desk drawer for packages.

On the wooden floor in the middle of the room, he set up his working station. He sat down and began cutting, trimming, and folding the box as the video had instructed. When the base of the house was done, including the door and windows he'd made with the box cutter, he applied the glue to the roof pieces, using a couple of binder clips to hold them together until it dried. While waiting, he cut a bunch of rounded shingles with the extra cardboard and used the markers to draw some planter boxes with daisies under the windows and a sign over the door that said HOME SWEET HOME. After that, he sat back and evaluated his handiwork. *Not bad.* Drawing wasn't something he excelled at, but at least it looked somewhat better than what a kid would have done. The finishing touch was gluing on the shingles so that they covered the roof, giving it a rustic country home vibe.

But wait! He'd forgotten all about the cat bed. On all fours, he crawled over to the shopping bag and grabbed the fluffy pillow. He plopped the cardboard house over it, then taped the bottom flaps closed. There. It was done. He'd managed to pull it off. For a moment, he sat there grinning. His cheeks and chest were warm with pride. It was the same feeling he'd had both times he'd typed *The End* when he finished a manuscript. Except this had taken him only less than an hour. Perhaps, if he ended up becoming a washed-up author, he could transform himself into *the* king of cardboard box cat houses. He chuckled at the idea.

In his mind, he told himself he was doing this to impress the woman. But as he carried the cat house downstairs and into the alley, he couldn't help but notice how happy he felt, as if the weight of all the stress he'd been feeling had been lifted. Maybe the key to a happier life was doing things for others. Other people. Other beings. Maybe that's what had been missing in his dreary life. Maybe he'd just been too focused on himself.

Onward and upward indeed!

Outside, the alleyway was quiet. No sign of the cat. Collin wondered if the cat would even know that the house was for him. Perhaps he should get the food and water bowls and leave those too. The scent of canned cat food would surely lure him out. He situated the cat house near his composting area, underneath a large, leafy oak tree, and then went back inside to fill the bowls with water and food.

The salmon-flavored pâté smelled awful, nothing remotely close to the fillets of wild Alaskan salmon he cooked for himself. No matter. Surely the cat would think otherwise. Collin went back out and left the bowls by the cat house. Then he left to go back inside. But just before closing the door behind him, he gazed over his shoulder at the cardboard house he'd constructed. Suddenly, a rush of emotion—anticipation and hope—made his skin tingle in the best possible way.

# TWENTY-THREE

# Cat

Cat was curled up at his usual spot under the hedge where nobody bothered him. He heard movement—rustling and footsteps. He lifted his head so he could hear better. It didn't sound dangerous. After a couple of minutes, he smelled something fishy, something that made his mouth water.

*Food?*

Was there someone out there at this late hour? Rainbow Lady usually came only in the mornings—except for a couple of times when she'd come in the afternoon, mumbling apologies and feeding him a double helping. At night, he'd stave off hunger by scrounging around garbage cans, unless some unlucky bastard accidentally dropped half their sandwich or pizza or ice cream on the sidewalk. The streets were like a mystery buffet; one never knew what the evening's offerings would be.

This aroma, though, wasn't from some random sidewalk snack. It smelled just like the canned food that the Rainbow Lady fed him. Cat poked his head through the foliage, looking right and then left. There was nobody there. He crawled out and sniffed the air again. A gentle breeze blew by, and that's when he figured out that the smell of fishy goodness was coming from the guy's alleyway—the awkward neighbor guy.

Cat was intrigued, because he was almost 100 percent sure that

Awkward Neighbor Guy didn't have any pet cats, otherwise he would have seen them through the windows. Slowly, he sauntered over, slipping through the gate just like he'd done the night before. There was still no one around. The smell was stronger.

*Hmmm.* Everything looked more or less the same. Or did it? Cat suddenly noticed something peeking from behind one of the bins. He took a couple of low-lying steps. Then a couple more. Until he saw it. Behind one of the bins was a cardboard box house with two metal bowls beside it.

*Is this for me?*

Again, he looked right and then left and then straight ahead to make sure there wasn't another cat around. But there *really* was nobody there. Cat wanted to act unimpressed. He was a cat after all. Anyone who knew anything about cats knew that they weren't easily impressed. As much as he wanted to stick his nose up in distaste and march off like it was nothing, he couldn't help feeling a bit warm and fuzzy. His insides began to vibrate, and this intense desire to rub up against the cardboard house overtook him.

*Purr . . . Purr . . . Purr . . .*

He went over and sniffed the corner. There were layers of scent—dust, tortilla chips, glue and marker, and something clean, something subtly citrusy and herby, maybe the guy's soap. On top of all those smells, he also sensed warmth and kindness and the desire for connection. Cat could sense these things. It was part of his natural instinct—the instinct that had kept him alive on the streets for so many years.

Awkward Neighbor Guy may not have been on the same level as Rainbow Lady, but he was trying to make an effort. And an effort was *way* more than what most people gave him. So, in a gesture of appreciation, he curled his tail and rubbed his face and neck and the side of his body against the cardboard, claiming the mini mansion for himself. He did the same with each corner until his scent was scattered all over. Once he was satisfied, he hurried over to the bowls, first sniffing the food to make sure it wasn't laced with poison. He may have been hungry, but he still had street smarts. It smelled good. *Really* good.

Was this real? Was he dreaming? Was it a trick?

Once more for good measure, he looked around. The coast was clear. *Woohoo!* Cat crouched down in front of the food bowl and gobbled up the fishy goodness, grumbling in satisfaction every few seconds. As his belly filled, he couldn't help but think of all the luck he'd had lately. Not only was he being fed by Rainbow Lady, but there were also the snacks from Cheery Mailman, Sad Bodega Man, and now Awkward Neighbor Guy. Clearly his days of slumming it in the hedges were over.

When all the food was gone, he lapped up some fresh water, then did a cat stretch. It was time to check out the inside of his house. Cat went over to it, sticking his head in first, then half of his body, turning around and stepping back out again. So that's how the door worked. *Huh.* Time to check it out again. Head. Neck. Torso. Flank. Tail. This time, he was fully inside. It was roomier than he'd imagined. There was even a cushiony bed in a tasteful plaid pattern. As much as he wanted to plop down on it and take a catnap after the delicious meal he'd just had, there was some testing that needed to be done first. One paw, then another paw. A little kneading here and there. *Good. Nice and soft.* A third paw. A fourth paw. Cat was standing on it. One last test. Round and round and round he went until he found the right spot. *Plonk.* He curled into a ball, facing one of the cut-out windows. This bed was probably the comfiest thing he'd ever experienced.

Was this how inside cats lived? Regular meals in shiny metal bowls, comfy beds, walls that made them feel safe? It was a bit of a revelation, really. Cat had always assumed that inside cats were like prisoners. But maybe he'd been wrong all along.

Before leaning his head down to close his eyes, he gazed out the little window, up at Awkward Neighbor Guy's house. There was a light on in the second floor. Maybe he was still awake, wondering if Cat had found his gift.

# TWENTY-FOUR

# *Omar*

Omar was earlier to work than usual. Not because he was all eager-beaver to get to his job, but because he hadn't been able to sleep well thinking about Bong, who hadn't called. While eating dinner, he'd checked his phone. While watching TV, he'd checked again. While trying but failing to fall asleep, he'd checked one last time.

Was Bong okay? Was he depressed? Suicidal? Was there something Omar could do to help?

His abuela, Rosalinda, had always said that his empathy was one of his best qualities. Carl, on the other hand, always said that he cared *way* too much about others. That people would take advantage of his niceness. But Omar was just being Omar. He didn't know any other way to be.

So at four thirty A.M., he quietly crawled out of bed so as to not wake Carl and started his day with a strong cup of coffee and a cold shower. He would need the caffeine and the blood flowing vigorously through his veins to get by on barely any sleep. He decided that maybe he could ask Mrs. Lewis for some advice. She was a widow, after all. He was sure she'd have some nuggets of wisdom to pass along.

When he got to her brownstone, he opened the no-longer-squeaky gate and parked his mail cart by the potted herbs. He reached out, pressed his finger on a basil leaf, and inhaled the scent. It reminded him of his abuela and the abundance of basil she'd grown, which she'd used to make pesto and tomato sauce to share with neighbors. He could almost taste the kipes she used to make for his after-school snack, the hint of basil always lingering on his tongue.

Omar pushed the memory aside. The last thing he needed was to be bogged down by his own sadness when he was trying to help someone else. He climbed Mrs. Lewis's front steps and rang the doorbell.

*Yap! Yap!*

Mrs. Lewis opened the door and out ran Sinatra.

"Good morning, Omar." Mrs. Lewis had on one of those old-fashioned Hollywood-style turbans, a pale-pink one to go with her cherry-blossom-patterned silk robe.

Omar bent down to scoop Sinatra up. "Good morning to the two of you," he said with a smile.

Mrs. Lewis opened the door wider. "Since you're so early today, would you like to come in for some tea? I've got those fresh blueberry scones you like so much."

"Sure, I'd like that." He followed her inside to her sitting room, where she'd already set up the tea and scones with two place settings, as if she'd known he'd have time for a chat that day. Sometimes, Omar thought she had a little brujería in her. Mrs. Lewis sure had a knack for knowing what he would say and do even before he did.

Placing Sinatra on his lap, he sat while Mrs. Lewis poured the tea. He gazed at all the beautiful antiques around the room, each with a unique story, some of which Omar had heard over the years. Mr. Lewis had been an antiques dealer, and in their younger days, he and Mrs. Lewis had traveled the world, scouring flea markets and estate sales for the most unique items. Omar's favorite was the pristine hand-painted green-and-gold porcelain Sèvres tea set they'd found in the dusty garage of an old woman in the south of France. It certainly wasn't the most valuable, but the memories attached to that tea set, all the stories and chats he'd shared with Mrs. Lewis, made it priceless in his eyes.

"You seem a bit preoccupied, Omar," said Mrs. Lewis, dropping two sugar cubes into her tea and stirring.

Omar couldn't help grinning at her keen observation. "I can't get *anything* past you, Mrs. Lewis."

She served him a blueberry scone with just a hint of a smile in her eyes. "It's not witchcraft, my dear Omar, it's called getting old." She giggled and then winked. "I've been around the block, if you know what I mean."

Omar laughed. Sinatra gazed up at him from his lap, annoyed that his human dog bed had moved. "One of these days, you have to finally write that memoir of yours."

"Perhaps . . . So what's on your mind, Omar? You know nothing much interesting happens around here, unless you count Sinatra peeing in my slippers."

"Naughty, naughty boy," said Omar, patting Sinatra's head. "Well. I *am* a bit concerned. But don't worry, it's not about me. . . . There's this man on my route who lost his wife several months ago. And from what I can tell, he's still pretty devastated about it. Not that I'd expect him to get over it or anything. But . . . I don't know. I just feel like maybe there's something I can do for him. Except I really don't know where to start."

Mrs. Lewis put down her teacup, and reached out to put her hand on his. "Omar, my dear. Do you remember when Stanley first passed? My daughter was here to help me with all the arrangements. But when she went back home to Boston, that's when it really hit me. I felt so alone, even with friends stopping by with casseroles and cakes and bouquets of flowers. It was a constant reminder that Stanley was gone. I'd become a widow, and sometimes it felt like that's all I was. But you know what *really* helped me?"

Omar leaned in closer.

"You, my dear boy! Your visits were a godsend! All those minutes we chatted and drank tea and lemonade, all those pastries we shared, all those times you helped me finish the *New York Times* crossword puzzle, all those times you took care of Sinatra so I could go visit my grandkids. You never treated me like a widow. You never walked on eggshells when you were around me. You weren't afraid to make a joke, to make me laugh, to make me remember that I could still have fun even if Stanley wasn't around."

Omar was stunned. For a moment, he just sat there, trying to ignore the stinging in his eyes.

"Thank you for everything you do for me, my dear Omar," she said, squeezing his hand.

"Anytime, Mrs. Lewis."

"Now, I know you have to go in a minute, but hold on a second." She got up and went off to the hallway leading to the kitchen, then came back with a brown pastry box. "I want you to give the man some of these scones. A little sugar always makes the day a bit brighter," she said, carefully placing four of the pastries in the box. She closed up the box and handed it to him. "Go on now, Omar. Go on and do your magic."

Omar grinned from ear to ear, not because of the compliment Mrs. Lewis had just paid him, but because all of a sudden, he knew. He knew exactly what to do.

# TWENTY-FIVE

# *Núria*

The bodega was closed again. At least this time, though, Núria'd had the hindsight to bring some backup plastic containers. She walked down the block so fast that her neon-yellow tank top and tie-dye yoga pants were a blur.

By the time she got to Cat's hedge, her messy top-bun was even messier, leaning to the side like a frazzled cactus. *Pssspssspsssspss,* she called, bending down to scoop the canned food into one of the plastic containers.

*Meeeooowww!*

Núria looked over her shoulder at the hedge, but Cat wasn't there.

*Meeeooowww!*

She turned the other way, and there he was, slinking through the metal grates of the alleyway gate. *Huh.* It was the first time she'd seen him come from that direction.

"What have you been up to, little devil?" she said to Cat, who was regarding her with his wide-open green eyes. Usually, he would have been circling her legs with his tail twitching. But today, he just sat there rather calmly.

Núria poured some fresh water into the second bowl, then stood and backed up a couple of steps. She fully expected him to pounce on the food and gobble it up like he usually did. Instead, though, he sashayed over and ate daintily, as if he were a gentleman enjoying finger sandwiches at a Victorian-era tea party.

Was someone else feeding him? That had to be it. But who?

Out of curiosity, she went over to the alleyway gate and peeked through. There was nothing there other than some bins for trash and recyclables, a composting area, and some potted plants. Nothing out of the ordinary, really. For a second, Núria considered ringing the doorbell and introducing herself. That second quickly passed.

"Hey! How did it go with your mom?"

Núria whipped her head around. It was Omar, with his bright smile, mail cart, and a pastry box precariously balanced in his left hand.

"Oh! I wondered if I'd run into you again," she said.

He put the pastry box down on top of a huge stack of manila envelopes and catalogs. "So? Are you gonna spill the tea or what?"

"Well, there isn't much tea to spill," she said with a frown.

"As your fake boyfriend, I think I deserve *all* the tea, even if it's just a scant cup."

Núria bit her lip. "Um. I guess it went okay. I mean, she *was* happy about you and all. But she wasn't all that jazzed about your career choice. No offense. And . . . well . . . I might have made up a bunch of stuff about you. Like how you speak Spanish, and make the best vegan mofongo in the world."

There was a moment of silence as Omar absorbed everything she'd said. His face sort of looked as if he'd sucked on a lemon. But then his forehead smoothed out, his jaw relaxed, and he laughed so hard he had to clutch his stomach not to lose it. "Girl. Don't sweat it. That's just your mom being a mom. Nothing wrong with being a mailman. I get it, though. It's not exactly every mother's fantasy for her future son-in-law. I mean, if I could figure out what else I could do with my life, I'd probably quit. . . . But hey, you were right about the Spanish *and* the mofongo. My abuela taught me well."

"Your abuela was vegan?"

Omar chuckled. "Nah. She was all about the chicharrones. But I got skills. My boyfriend, Carl, works as an assistant to one of those chichi interior decorators, so once in a while I cook for some of his chichi coworkers. Vegan, gluten-free, keto, you name it, I've done it."

"Well, I'm impressed," said Núria.

*Meeeooowww!*

Cat sharpened his claws on Omar's mail cart bag, as if he was annoyed to be left out of the conversation. "All right, my man. We can go now," said Omar.

Núria looked at Cat and then at Omar. Truth be told, she was a tad jealous of how Cat seemed so bonded with him. More than that, she was fascinated, because Omar wasn't even trying; his magnetism seemed so effortless, so natural. She totally got why Cat liked him so much. She herself was drawn to him. He was just the type of person she yearned to be friends with.

"Okay, well, it was nice seeing you again," Núria said with a wave. She turned to walk off in the opposite direction.

"Wait, hold on."

Núria halted.

Omar reached for his pocket and pulled his phone out. "You want to come over for dinner? I think it's only fair for Carl to meet my fake girlfriend," he said.

Núria's face warmed, and she was pretty sure her cheeks were as red as her mom's famous gazpacho soup. "Really?"

"Yeah. Why not? Then I can cook you some vegan mofongo for real. You can even send your mom some photos," he said with a wink. "Give me your number and I'll text you the deets."

"Okay." She went over and saved her number on his phone.

And then they went off on their respective ways, no longer acquaintances, but friends.

# TWENTY-SIX

# Collin

As soon as he awakened, Collin propelled himself out of bed. Usually, it would have taken him thirty minutes to an hour to convince himself to crawl out of his nest of bedsheets. But not today. He was too excited to see if the cat had slept in the cardboard house he'd made. The anticipation was so great that he forgot all about his slippers, jogging down the stairs with bare feet.

When he got to the back door, he opened it as quietly as possible in case the cat was still around. Collin only realized he was barefoot when his feet touched the warm concrete floor outside. No matter. Going back inside to fetch his cozy slippers would only ruin the moment. As an author, he knew the essential rule of "moving the plot forward." So that's what he did, tiptoeing toward the cardboard house with as much grace as a newborn giraffe.

From what he could gather, the cat wasn't inside. He could already see through the cut-out windows. The cat bed was empty. For a moment, he was disappointed. Then he caught sight of the empty food and water bowls. The cat *had* been here after all. Collin grinned, the disappointment quickly forgotten.

He got down on his hands and knees so he could peek through the cardboard house's doorway, which was awkward to say the least, since he was so tall, and the house was so small.

*Hmmm* . . . Was that fur on the cat bed? Collin inched in even closer, so his head was almost entirely through the doorway. He could practically count the strands of black fur stuck on the plaid fabric. The cat had slept on the bed. Without thinking, he pushed himself up, eager to do some sort of celebratory fist-pumping, but instead, he lifted the entire box a foot off the ground with his head. He pulled it off and set it back down.

Suddenly, he heard voices nearby.

"Come over here. Give me your number and I'll text you the deets."

Collin frowned. Was that the mailman? He sidled closer to the gate, but not close enough that anyone would see him. It *was* the mailman. And unfortunately, he was talking to *her.* The woman who fed the cat. The woman who made the most adorable coffee foam hearts. The woman who had somehow managed to awaken the kaleidoscope of dormant butterflies in his stomach.

*That* woman took the mailman's phone and presumably saved her number in *his* contact list. Collin slumped against the metal fence behind him. His jaw tensed. There were flutters in his chest, which he was trying hard to ignore. He desperately wanted to look away. But he couldn't. He wouldn't. If only he'd had the courage to speak to her sooner. A wave of regret radiated from his face all the way down to his toes.

The mailman. Why him? Now that Collin thought about it, he was actually not a bad-looking guy. Friendly. Dependable. Employed. Maybe even somewhat charming. Those were traits that were attractive to women. So why *not* the mailman?

Was it too late? Had he lost his chance with her?

*Fuck.*

## TWENTY-SEVEN

### Bong

Bong had slept in. Again. At least he'd managed to roll out of bed in time to open the bodega by nine. He'd missed out on some of the early business, but the entire morning hadn't been lost. Later in the afternoon, he would close the store again for an hour or two so he could go visit with Conchita at the Holy Cross Cemetery.

He used to have an employee named Jun to share shifts with, but Jun had quit a couple of months ago, and Bong hadn't gotten around to hiring a replacement. It seemed like more of a bother to find another employee when he could just do most of it on his own. Sure, he had to sacrifice some business when he couldn't be at the store, but at least he didn't have to depend on anyone but himself. It was easier that way. More work also meant he'd have less time to wallow in sadness. At least, that was the idea, though he wasn't certain it was working very well. Everything around him reminded him of Conchita. Not just the grapefruit-flavored seltzer, but also the little packs of smoked almonds and salted sunflower seeds she'd loved to munch on, the globs of red nail polish on the counter from when she'd tried to touch up her nails right when the fire alarm had gone off, and the racks of magazines and gossip rags she'd ooohed and ahhhed at on a daily basis. Even the air freshener he used—hibiscus vanilla—was something Conchita had picked out. When he spritzed it in the air, he could almost hear her say, *"See? Doesn't it smell just like that bakery we liked so much in Honolulu?"*

All Bong really wanted was to sit by Conchita's altar and then go to bed. But he knew his beloved was watching and wouldn't approve. Life was more than just grieving those who had passed on. Father Luis at his church liked to remind Bong that God had bigger plans for him, that he hadn't yet accomplished what he needed to do in this world. Still, he found it increasingly difficult to go on.

If God *did* have a plan for him, then what was it?

"Good morning, Bong."

Bong startled from his thoughts, then looked up at the entrance. It was Omar. Suddenly, he remembered the breakdown Omar had witnessed, and the note he'd left for him with his phone number. His face stung with embarrassment. Being exposed like that in front of a relative stranger made him feel deeply ashamed.

"Oh. Hello. Good morning," he replied with a forced smile.

Omar approached the register with a couple of envelopes and a small brown box. "How are you doing today?" he asked, handing him the mail.

Bong squirmed, fiddling with the buttons of his shirt. "Good. I mean, much better. Thank you."

"I'm glad to hear that."

Bong could tell that Omar wasn't convinced. His brown eyes wandered, looking for telltale signs—dried tears on Bong's cheeks, dark under-eye circles, swollen eyelids, sagging shoulders. By the time Omar's gaze landed in the middle of his chest, where he'd misaligned the buttons, Bong's cheeks were hot. *Great.*

"By the way, do you like blueberry scones?" he asked.

"Scones?" Bong was taken aback, raising his eyebrows in surprise. "Yes, sure. I like scones."

Omar placed the brown box on the counter and slid it toward him. "A friend of mine, Mrs. Lewis, makes the best scones with French butter and Maine blueberries. She gave me some to share."

Bong stared down at the box. "No. I couldn't . . ."

"Of course you can." Omar opened up the box so Bong could see the most perfect scones on the planet. The scent of cream and butter and blueberries wafted into the air.

Bong's mouth watered. He hadn't had breakfast yet. "Okay. Thank you. They do look good," he said with a nod.

Omar grinned. "Now, you can have them with coffee. But I highly suggest you pair them with some tea, preferably Earl Grey."

*Earl Grey?*

"How about Lipton?"

"All right. Lipton will do." Omar chuckled and closed the pastry box back up. "Oh. And one more thing."

Bong frowned. He did not like the sound of "one more thing," as if the scones were being used to butter him up.

"If you're free on Sunday, I need your help with something."

In one second, Bong's expression went from surprised to confused to curious to suspicious. "Help? With what?"

Omar leaned in closer. "It's kind of embarrassing. So, maybe I can just fill you in on Sunday? I promise it's totally innocent. We're not going to rob a bank or anything."

"I-I don't know." Bong glanced at the pastry box, then at his hands on the counter, and then up into Omar's steady gaze.

"You can trust me," Omar said.

*Scratch. Scratch. Scratch.*

Bong and Omar looked over at the storefront window. Itim was on the bench outside, standing on his hind legs and scratching the glass with his claws.

"Why is that cat always following you around?" asked Bong.

Omar shrugged. "I guess he's a friend, you know. And friends like to hang out."

*A friend.*

For the first time in a long time, Bong smiled a real smile. He straightened his back, lifted his shoulders, and went over to the back of the store. When he came back, he was holding half a dozen creamy treats in his hand. "For your friend," he said, handing them to Omar.

"Thanks. I'll see you on Sunday, then? I can swing by here around ten in the morning, if that's okay with you."

"Yes. Of course. I'll help."

Conchita had sent him a sign.

And Itim had been the one to bring the message to him.

# TWENTY-EIGHT

## Lily

Lily was late for her morning shift. *Really* late. Still, she strolled down the block at a leisurely pace, stopping to peek through storefront windows so she could ogle all the expensive clothes and expensive jewelry and expensive pastries she couldn't afford. She secretly hoped she'd get fired one of these days, but deep down, she knew it was unlikely. Bill, the store manager, was too sweet on her. Every time she messed up at work, he would shrug it off and say something like "Everyone makes mistakes" or "You'll get it right next time."

Whenever he'd say those things, she would catch him staring at her glossy pink lips, as if he were salivating over a shiny, sweet lollipop. Many times, she'd been tempted to hand him a napkin in case he needed it for his drool.

Up ahead, Lily spotted the café where Núria worked. Plenty of times, Lily had wanted to go inside and order a coffee while Núria was on shift. But every single time, Lily had chickened out. Besides, she couldn't afford the pricey drinks there. She was already late on rent, and if she didn't pay up soon, her roommates would kick her out. Unfortunately, they weren't as charmed by her good looks as Bill was.

Whenever she passed the café she would linger out front for a couple of minutes, and if Núria was there, she would watch her. She would study her facial expressions and mannerisms to see if they reminded her of her dad, or even herself. She would try to read her lips.

Truth be told, it made her feel icky to spy on her sister like that. Until she drummed up enough courage to confront her about who she was, though, spying would have to do.

When Lily reached the café, she halted at the exact spot where she knew she'd have a bird's-eye view of the espresso machines. There was already a line of customers waiting to order—the usual crowd of people trying too hard to be hip while sporting five-hundred-dollar shoes, sixteen-hundred-dollar tattoos, and two-hundred-dollar haircuts.

Núria was nowhere in sight.

Lily walked off, a bit faster this time, since her stomach was growling so loud that it seemed to echo. Most of her meals were purchased at work because it was cheaper with her employee discount. Since moving to Brooklyn, she'd pretty much survived on ready-made tuna sandwiches, chef salads, frozen burritos, pizzas, and rotisserie chickens, with a banana here and there. It was pathetic, but hey, at least she was getting by.

Her mother had sworn that she would last in the Big Apple for only a week, tops, then come crawling back home. Lily grinned. Not only had she managed to survive longer than that, but she'd also not needed to beg her mother for money. She may have been slumming it, but at least her pride was intact. And *that* was something.

One day, hopefully, in the not-so-distant future when she'd finally found some success, she would go home and *really* rub it in her mother's face. The mother who had told her time and time again that all she had going for her was her beauty. The mother who'd never believed she'd amount to anything.

Lily could feel tears stinging her eyes. *Great.* All she needed was to show up to work with runny mascara and puffy eyelids, giving her coworkers ammo for gossip. They all hated her, except for Bill. She stopped and searched her purse for a napkin to dab her eyes with. *Nothing. Crap.* Instead, she used her ring finger to gently wipe the tears away. When she'd finally composed herself, she took a deep breath.

She zipped her purse up and set off again, except something caught her eye. In front of the bodega across the street was a black cat on its hind legs, scratching at the glass storefront window. In between scratches it stared inside longingly, as if it was desperate. Lily frowned. Was that what she looked like when she gazed through the café's window? At least the cat had the guts to scratch the window and get the attention of whoever was inside. All she did was stare.

From here on out, she promised herself, she would no longer shy away.

Somehow, Lily would find the courage to finally meet her sister.

# TWENTY-NINE

# Núria

Núria couldn't help but wonder why Omar had invited her over for dinner.

Was he going to try to lure her into a cult?

Did he have a Ponzi scheme that needed more victims?

Would he try to drug her and sell her organs on the black market?

Or did he simply feel sorry for her?

Ever since she was little, she'd had a hard time making friends. She wasn't exactly introverted. For whatever reason, though, she found it difficult to open herself up to people. Her childhood had been spent mostly alone. She'd eaten lunch all by herself at school. She hadn't had anyone to play dollies with at home. She had sat out on the lawn while the neighborhood kids played hopscotch, tag, and hide-and-seek. Not much changed since she'd become an adult. There had been no Cinderella moment—no fairy godmother to transform her into a beautiful princess with a kingdom full of friends and a handsome prince to sweep her off her feet. Instead, she had cats. And Rocky. For the most part, that had been enough.

As Núria wandered the streets feeding the strays, she could feel herself sort of floating. The phrase "walking on air" came to mind. She hadn't felt that way in a long while. Not since Rocky had waltzed into the café one day and decided that Núria, the barista who had crafted her extra-sweet chai latte, was going to be her new BFF. Back then, she'd had doubts too. Why would an outgoing, successful, and beautiful woman want to be her friend? As she got to know Rocky, she realized that they *did* have something in common. Núria's calling was taking care of stray cats. And Rocky's calling was taking care of stray people.

Maybe she was just overthinking it.

Núria stopped in front of Cat's hedge. Her feet suddenly felt solid and grounded. She decided that she would go with the flow and stop worrying so much. She would get dressed up and go to Omar's dinner with a bottle of wine and have some fun for a change.

Screw all those kids who had ignored her.

Screw all those people who thought she was weird.

Screw all those guys who had called her a "crazy cat lady" and run off.

She reached up to adjust her lopsided top-bun, and from the corner of her eye, she spotted a neon-pink Post-it note tucked inside the empty plastic feeding container. *Huh.* With everything going on, she'd almost forgotten about the mysterious stranger. She bent down to retrieve the note and read it.

*Do you ever wonder if the cat misses you when you're not around?*

Núria smiled. But then she quickly covered her mouth in case the mysterious stranger was watching. It was an odd question. However, she had to admit that the thought had crossed her mind. If she stopped showing up one day, would the cats miss her too? Or would they just miss the food? People always joked that if a cat owner was murdered, their cat wouldn't care; their dead body would become just another piece of furniture or a scratching post or, even worse, cat food. Núria disagreed, though. Cats did form bonds. Every time she went somewhere for just a couple of days, her cats would rush her as soon as she got home.

From what she could gather, this rando was not a cat person. Which was fine and all. It certainly made her even more curious about the person's intentions. In spite of Rocky's teasing, she still wasn't sure that this was a romantic gesture. One, because she looked like an absolute slob whenever she made her rounds. Two, because men were generally not shy about approaching women they were interested in. At least, that's what she'd experienced in the bars that Rocky had dragged her to. Could it be a woman, though? Or a non-binary person? *Huh.* The possibility hadn't crossed her mind until now.

Núria stared at the handwriting on the note, trying to analyze every letter—their curves and lines and dots. Well, not really dots, since the dot over the "i" looked more like an accent. Also, the letters were neater than most guys' penmanship, but it didn't scream "girly," either. Then again, maybe that was stereotyping. The more she stared, though, the more confused she got. Did it even matter who this person was? Was she even interested?

As much as she wanted to toss the note in the trash and forget all about it, she couldn't help feeling intrigued. Maybe even flattered. It wasn't often that someone was interested in her like that. The handful of relationships she'd had in her life had ended disastrously. Looking back, they hadn't even been real relationships, not in the give-and-take sort of sense. It had been Núria doing all the giving and the men doing all the taking. That's probably why she preferred the company of cats. There was no pretense when it came to her feline companions. When they were being sweet, they were being sweet. When they were being assholes, they were being assholes. When they wanted to ignore you, they ignored you. Cats didn't have a hidden agenda.

Núria sighed and stuck the note in her pocket. She needed a double shot of espresso and some words of reassurance from Rocky before deciding whether to write back.

# THIRTY

∽

## *Collin*

ollin was a creep. At least, he felt like one as he watched the
woman from his second-floor window. From that angle, he
couldn't see her face, only the bun on top of her head that
looked like a giant cinnamon roll. But it was safer from a distance.
He'd nearly lost it earlier from a few feet away. What if she'd seen
him and immediately figured out that he was the author of the Post-
it notes? It was too soon. Way too soon. He needed time to observe
her, to get to know her from afar before jumping in headfirst.

The woman stuck his note in her pocket, then cleaned up the
feeding bowls and took off down the street. He smooshed his cheek
against the glass to keep sight of her, and when she was almost gone,
he opened the window and stuck his head and torso out, watching
her until she turned the corner.

Collin was breathless. His heart fluttered. As much as he tried to
deny it to himself, he was clearly enamored with this woman—
a woman whose name he didn't even know. Watching her made him
feel like an awkward, nerdy middle-schooler all over again. Never
mind that he was six-foot-three, forty years old, and a successful author. It was as if the years had rolled back and he was twelve again,
sitting in Mrs. Colby's classroom, staring at Selena Martinez's wavy

ponytail in front of him. It had reminded him of a cascading water-fall, the wisps on her neck like delicate ferns. He'd admired her from afar, writing sweet little poems about her in his notebook. Unfortunately, she hadn't really known he'd existed. That is, until Rob, the class bully, stole his notebook and read every single poem out loud in the cafeteria. Just thinking about it made his face flush.

Collin was eager to keep seeing the woman, even if it made him feel like that awkward kid all over again. He closed the window and sighed. What he really should have been doing was writing. But the inspiration wasn't there. Maybe what he needed was a change of scenery. *Yes.* The café. His laptop. Coffee. The woman. As much as he hated crowds, and often scoffed at writers who worked in cafés, maybe it really was what he needed. Perhaps the inspiration was somewhere out there, rather than inside his study. It wouldn't hurt to try it. Right?

So off he went to his bedroom to change out of his pajamas into something casual, unassuming—khaki joggers, a white T-shirt, and checkered Vans. He wanted to blend in, not call attention to himself while he observed her. He ran his fingers through his hair, then went to his study to pack his laptop, notebook, and pens into his messenger bag, even though he was certain not much work would get done.

Collin was nervous. *Really* nervous.

It was only a neighborhood café, but for whatever reason, it felt as if he were getting on an eighteen-hour flight to a far-flung country.

The café was even more crowded than before. Still, Collin managed to find a seat at a long wooden counter facing the window, which was far from ideal, since he would have to look over his shoulder to get a view of the barista counter. He left a hoodie on the chair and then got in line to order. There were five people ahead of him, and as he inched forward, he could see bits and pieces of the woman—an arched eyebrow as she tiptoed in front of the espresso machine to reach for a cup, a sharp elbow as she frothed some milk, a hazel eye as she passed a finished drink to a customer. The closer he got, the more nervous he became. Would she recognize him from the day before? Would she adorn his coffee with more hearts?

"Hey, what can I getcha?" The guy behind the register raised his pierced eyebrow at Collin.

Collin had been waiting in line for around ten minutes, yet not once had he considered what he would order. "Uhhh." He glanced up at the menu. The words blurred, jumping from one line to another. Despite the arctic-level air-conditioning, he could feel a bead of sweat falling from his temple to his cheek.

"You want the same drink as yesterday?"

It was her. The woman. Speaking to him. He glanced over, focusing on her freckles instead of her eyes. "Yes, thank you. And-And—"

"An almond croissant?" she guessed again.

This time, his gaze traveled up to hers. She regarded him quizzically, as if he were a living, breathing Rubik's Cube. "Yes. Perfect. Thank you," he replied.

The woman nodded and went off to make his drink. Collin paid and scooched over to wait. He tried hard not to stare, but he found it impossible. She worked with so much precision and speed and grace that she could have easily been an athlete or a scientist or a dancer. It was the complete opposite of how she was during her feedings. Collin was fascinated by the transformation. So fascinated that he hadn't even noticed that she was standing there with his coffee and croissant.

"Anything else?" she asked.

He glanced down at his coffee. Instead of hearts, she'd made a four-leaf clover.

"For some luck," she said, her lip curling into a barely there smile.

"Thank you. I'm good," he replied.

*Thank you. I'm good?* For Christ's sake. That's the best he could come up with?

For a second, the woman watched him as he picked up his coffee and croissant with shaky hands. Collin tried to avoid her eyes yet again. Instead, his gaze landed on the name tag on the left side of her chest. Her name was *Núria*, with an accent over the "u."

Collin went back to his spot by the window, almost spilling his coffee while dodging customers. The narrow counter was a joke, with barely enough room for his cup, saucer, plate, and laptop. Not to mention that his knees hit the storefront window every time he adjusted himself on the uncomfortable high chair. He was willing to suffer, though. Just being in the same room as her made him feel energized—as if he'd already chugged half a dozen espresso shots.

After a sip of coffee, which was even more delicious than he'd remembered, and a bite of croissant, he turned on his laptop and opened a blank document. The white screen glared at him. It was pretty obnoxious, actually. So obnoxious that he pulled up Google to get away from it. His fingers hovered over the keyboard. A couple of seconds passed and then he quickly typed "Núria name origin." According to the *All Things Baby Names* website, "Núria" was of Spanish, more specifically Catalan origin, and, based on its Latin roots, meant "fire" or "bright." *Huh.* How appropriate. He looked over his shoulder, twisting his torso to get a good look at her. There was no longer a line of customers. Núria was standing really close to the espresso machine, using its shiny surface as a mirror as she tucked a rogue curl back into her bun. It was ridiculous but also adorable. At that moment, every single person in the café disappeared, except for her—Núria—bright as a glowing candle in a pitch-black room.

*Beep! Beep!* His cellphone vibrated, almost falling off the counter. He caught it and squinted at the screen. It was his sister, Caroline.

*Beep! Beep!* It was tempting not to answer it. He was certain she was calling to bitch about their mother's email, the same one he'd gotten because their mother couldn't be bothered to write them separately. Most of the time, Collin didn't know what to say when she unloaded her feelings on him. While he never fully got along with their mother, he'd somehow found a way to coexist with her. She and Caroline, on the other hand, were like two magnets repelling each other.

He inhaled deeply, preparing himself for the unpleasant conversation he was about to have.

"Hey, Caroline," he said. "Sorry I almost missed you. I'm in a coffee shop, working. It's kind of loud in here."

"What the actual fuck, Collin," she growled.

He winced. "Uh. Well, hello to you too, sis." He glanced over his shoulder at Núria, who was once again busy whipping up drinks. He opened his mouth to say something else, but Caroline beat him to it.

"Onward and upward, *my* ass. You know if I called and told her I was leaving Alesha because I'd fallen in love with some Kennedy dude, she would piss all over her Ferragamo shoes in excitement."

"So I guess you read her email, huh?" he said, trying to sound as neutral as possible.

She sighed. "Yeah. I'm sorry. It's just frustrating, you know? Like why can't she just move on already?"

"Well, you know Mom. It takes her a gazillion years to get over anything. I don't think she's forgiven me for not going to med school yet." His jaw tensed at the thought. "But, hey, at least she's *contemplating* moving on? Maybe in another decade she'll have completely forgiven us. That's something to look forward to, huh?"

"I guess." She sounded deflated. "It's just not the same. I mean, a parent being disappointed over their child's chosen profession is one thing, but being disappointed about who they *are* is another thing altogether. As if me being a lesbian is something I chose for myself."

Collin's shoulders slumped. His chest tightened. The situation saddened him. He could only imagine how much Caroline was hurting. "I know. I'm sorry. But I'm here for you, okay?"

For a moment it was silent, the siblings entangled in their own thoughts. Collin opened his mouth, then closed it. How could he possibly make his sister feel any better?

"Thanks, Collin. Thanks for listening," she said softly.

He relaxed into his seat, relieved. "Anytime, Caroline. I'm just a phone call away."

She breathed in and out raggedly, as if she was trying her best to stop herself from crying. Then she coughed a couple of times and said, "All right, enough with the pity party. I have to get back to work, and so do you. How much longer do I have to wait for that next book of yours?"

"Um. Not too long, I hope," Collin mumbled.

"Good. Why don't you come over for dinner soon?"

"Sure," said Collin. "You take care, big sis."

"You too, little bro."

Collin held his phone to his ear, listening to the silence. Even though he dreaded these talks with Caroline, he also missed her dearly. Ever since she'd left the city and moved to Hudson, New York, with her partner, Alesha, he hardly ever saw her. As much as he preferred his own company, there was this teensy-tiny part of him that wanted someone by his side to unload all his feelings to, someone who would listen to all his nonsense, someone who would dole out advice when needed. These days, it seemed like his sister was too busy for any of that. And, well, he really didn't have any close friends anymore. One by one, they'd gotten married and disappeared from his life.

When would it finally be his turn to find that special someone?

He gazed at Núria once more from over his shoulder, catching her in the midst of a giggle. It was obvious that the cashier had said something funny. He just hoped the joke wasn't at his expense. Quickly, he turned back around and stared at the blank computer screen in front of him. Maybe it was hearing his sister's voice. Maybe it was the glimpse of Núria's beautiful face. The face that made him feel so alive.

Collin reached out and typed:

*Untitled*
*By Collin Thackeray*

It was four words. Only four fucking words. But it was a start.

# THIRTY-ONE

# Bong

It was a hot and humid afternoon, but at least the ferocity of the sun was starting to wane. Rather than take the bus, Bong preferred walking to the cemetery. The heat didn't really bother him. In fact, he kind of liked it. It made him feel alive, cleansed, as if the sweat pouring from his pores was actually holy water straight from the stoup at his church.

When he arrived, he was relieved to see the double-arched entrance with its green roof and cross on top. It had been a whole week since he'd visited, and the guilt had been gnawing away at him. He felt like a bad husband, because in his eyes, the "'til death do us part" bit of the marriage vow was totally incorrect. Marriage was forever, whether you were alive or dead.

He strolled past the various headstones, mausoleums, and statues, past the lush green trees and grass and the occasional wilted bouquet left by visitors. Bong wasn't one to bring flowers. He saved those for the altar at home. Instead, he brought a handful of Conchita's favorite snacks, because he knew she'd want to share them with the squirrels.

After fifteen minutes, he reached his destination—the simple white marble slab where his beloved rested. It was under a large maple tree that, in the fall, turned from bright yellow to bright orange to bright red, just like the beautiful sunsets back in the Philippines. He touched the cool marble with his hand before kneeling on the grass.

"Kumusta na, mahal ko?" Bong said out loud.

Closing his eyes, he imagined Conchita sitting on the grass beside him, wearing her favorite sundress and blue straw hat. She would smile at him. He'd reach out and poke her right dimple with his finger like he always did. In return, she would pinch him on the arm or, if she was feeling particularly flirtatious, on the butt. But only when nobody was around.

Bong chuckled and opened his eyes. One by one, he took out the snacks from his pocket—the smoked almonds, sunflower seeds, and Ritz crackers. He swept the dried leaves and twigs off Conchita's grave, all the while chatting about the strange things that had been happening in his life.

"Alam mo, mahal? The other day, Itim, that stray black cat you used to feed, came by the store. I let him inside and gave him something to eat. And this morning, I discovered that Itim is friends with the mailman. Imagine that!"

Bong unwrapped the snacks and made neat little piles in front of the headstone. "But I have a feeling you already knew that. You sent Itim and that mailman to me for a reason. I'm not yet sure why. But I trust you, mahal. I trust that this is part of God's plan," he said, making the sign of the cross.

He tried hard to ignore the ache in his heart, the echo of his voice, the silence that lingered after he spoke. Kneeling down even farther, he kissed the grass on the exact spot where he imagined Conchita's face was. "Naniniwala ako na balang araw, muli tayong magkikita."

There were tears in his eyes, but he didn't bother wiping them away. Bong knew he would see Conchita again one day. He was certain of it. Saying it out loud, though, made it feel as if it was in the distant future. That was just too long for him to wait.

Bong pushed himself off the ground and swept the traces of dirt and remnants of grass off his pants. It was time to go back to work. He turned toward the same way he'd come. But standing there on the pathway staring at him was a girl. She couldn't have been more than eighteen or nineteen years old. The way she stared at him reminded him of a baby deer he'd once seen in upstate New York. It had wandered along the edge of the forest by the road, seemingly lost, until the mama deer appeared through some bushes.

This girl was like that baby deer. Lost. Alone. Searching for something.

# THIRTY-TWO

# Lily

"Is that your wife?" Lily asked the old man.

At first, he seemed confused, as if he hadn't heard what she'd said. After an awkward silence, he looked over his shoulder at the headstone and said, "Yes. My wife, Conchita."

Lily had been watching him for a good ten or fifteen minutes. She'd heard him speak in a language she hadn't recognized. She'd seen him lay out the little piles of snacks. She'd seen him bend over and kiss the grass. She'd seen the tears in his eyes.

Even though he looked nothing like her dad, something about him reminded her of her father. Maybe she was just imagining things, willing something to be there that wasn't.

He approached her, slowly, then stopped about four feet away from her. "Are you here visiting someone?" he asked.

It seemed like an innocent enough question. Especially since Lily had already poked her nose where it didn't belong. She was fully aware of how rude she could appear at times. But she was from Georgia, after all, and Southerners had a knack for being meddlesome.

"Yes. Well, no. Actually, not really," Lily replied.

The old man furrowed his brows but didn't say anything. So she felt the need to explain herself.

"My dad died in a car crash. He's buried back home in Georgia.

Sometimes, I like to come here and pretend he's buried in one of these graves. . . . It makes me miss him a little less."

"I understand," he said with a nod.

Lily noticed that he was tearing up again. She understood how hard it was to push the tears away once they showed up. The first few months after her dad had died, she'd cried at the drop of a hat. Because *everything* reminded her of him. The carpeted stairs at home they'd sledded down with pool inflatables. The ice cream truck that came around every day; she had always ordered a vanilla soft serve with rainbow sprinkles, and her dad had ordered a Choco Taco. The coffee mug in the cupboard with "Best Farter Ever" written on it that she'd given him as a joke on Father's Day.

"You live around here?" said Lily, attempting to change the subject.

The old man pointed toward the cemetery entrance. "Yes, in the apartment on top of Bong's Bodega."

"Oh. I know that place. I live a couple of blocks east of there," she said.

The old man smiled. "Oh. Well, that's me, Bong."

Lily giggled. "That's your name? For real? I thought the person that owned it was really into smoking weed or something."

Bong's face became serious. For a second, Lily thought she might have offended him. But then he grinned and said, "My wife said people would think that. I didn't believe her. She was right, though. She was *always* right."

"I'm Lily, by the way," she said, reaching out to shake his hand. Then something curious happened. As Lily and Bong continued to chat, their legs started to move, their feet taking them toward the neighborhood where they both lived.

For once, Lily had been right. The old man was a lot like her dad. He was mild-mannered and thoughtful and expressed interest in her without being creepy. She was comfortable around him, even though they'd only just met.

"So, how long have you been living here in Brooklyn?" he asked as they strolled down the street.

"Not long. I still feel like I don't know what I'm doing, or where I'm going. . . . It's *really* different from my hometown."

Bong nodded. "Ah, yes. I know what you mean. When Conchita and I first moved here from the Philippines it was quite a shock. Manila is also a big city, but still so very different. The weather. The way things move so fast here. The people. *Especially* the people. It is very hard to make friends here. Everyone just wants to mind their own business, to look the other way. In the Philippines, we are friendly and warm and polite."

Lily smiled. Finally, someone understood. Whenever she said these things to her roommates, they rolled their eyes and called her a "hick" and a "country bumpkin."

"Yeah. I don't really have any friends here. My roommates hate me. My coworkers hate me. Sometimes, it feels like it's me against the world," she said with a sigh. "I mean, I'm not exactly the easiest person to get along with, but still, you'd think I'd have made at least one friend here."

They both halted at the curb, waiting for the pedestrian light to turn green. Bong pulled a handkerchief from his pocket and wiped the sweat off his forehead and neck. Lily couldn't help but notice the deep frown on his face.

"Why did you move here? For college? For work?" he asked.

She chuckled. "Uh, definitely *not* for college. I barely graduated high school. And as for work, I'm just a part-time employee at the Foodtown. It barely pays the bills. There's a good chance my roommates are going to kick me out at the end of the month."

When they got to the other side of the road, Bong stopped in front of a juice place on the corner and said, "You want a lemonade?" Lily glanced at the sidewalk menu. As if reading her mind, he pulled out his wallet. "My treat."

"Okay, thanks."

Bong went inside to order while Lily saved them seats on the bench outside. The walk, the chat, and now the lemonade. It really did feel like she was on an outing with Dad, just like they used to have every Sunday afternoon. She found herself wanting to pour her heart out to him. Ever since she'd found out about her half sister, she'd wanted so badly to tell someone. But there was nobody to tell. Not even her own mother, who would have only made Lily more insecure about her quest by spewing negativity in between sips of whiskey. So the secret had stayed inside her, bottled up like the cheap perfume she used to buy at the mall.

After a couple of minutes, Bong emerged holding two large lemonades. The one he was sipping was a regular one, and the other a light pink that matched her dress. "Here," he said, handing it to her. "I thought you'd like the pink one."

"Thanks." She took a long sip. The tangy sweetness brought her back to the Georgia summers of her childhood.

"So, why did you come to Brooklyn then?" Bong asked.

Lily took another sip. Then she sat up really straight and pulled her shoulders back as if she were about to launch herself into a complicated cheerleading maneuver. "I came here to meet my sister . . . except, um, well, she doesn't even know I exist."

Bong turned so his gaze could meet hers. Unbeknownst to Lily, there were already tears rolling down her cheeks. Her face was numb, but her heart ached. She was certain he would offer some words of wisdom, maybe a sentence or two to comfort her. Instead, he moved closer to her just as her body crumpled in despair. She burrowed her face where his shoulder met his chest, crying all the tears she'd been holding in for months.

# THIRTY-THREE

# *Núria*

Núria sat on her bed with a towel wrapped around her freshly showered body. She stared at her phone, waiting for Rocky to text back while the ingrates pawed at her feet, her towel, and her sopping wet hair. It had been hours since she'd texted her about the mysterious Post-it note person. Why was she taking so long to reply? Núria was *this* close to calling her, but they had a no-call agreement. Calls were for emergencies.

Finally, her phone vibrated. She tapped on Rocky's message.

> Girl . . . I don't even know why you're asking for my advice.
> It sounds like you've already made your mind up. Keep on
> replying to your mystery admirer. What have you got to
> lose? For all you know, they're just as crazy as you are. A
> match made in heaven! LOL. Keep me posted, okay?

Núria grinned. Rocky knew her *oh so* well. For whatever reason, Núria always sought out her approval, even though, at the end of the day, she would do what she wanted. The next time she went on her feeding rounds, she would reply. But what the hell would she say? Flirting wasn't really something she excelled at. At the café, Anh would sometimes elbow her and tell her that some dude was flirting with her, because Núria was always completely oblivious. The idea of flirting with someone made her want to crawl under the counter and hide until every single customer was gone.

There was something about this Post-it writer, though. Núria was drawn to them. Maybe they were just as clueless as she was when it came to relationships. Was there actually someone out there like her? Clueless. Awkward. Lonely.

Speaking of which, it was time to get dressed for dinner at Omar's. It wasn't often that she was invited to a meal at someone's home, so Núria went the extra mile, showering, shaving, and moisturizing, even though Omar and his partner, Carl, probably wouldn't care one bit about her hairy legs and armpits. She felt like a new woman, smooth and clean and smelling of the lavender soap that her mom had gifted her last Christmas.

She went to her teensy-tiny closet and went through every single item of clothing, which wasn't really all that much: mostly colorful yoga pants, some joggers, a couple of pairs of well-worn jeans, oversized T-shirts from thrift shops, and her work uniform. All the way at the very end, next to the bin where she stored her winter clothes, she had a couple of dresses. One was a multicolored striped linen dress that was a hand-me-down from Rocky, and the other two were floral monstrosities that her mother had forced her to buy at the mall the last time she'd visited Florida. Núria grabbed the linen dress and laid it out on the bed while she put on a mismatched pair of underwear and bra. She didn't like bras all that much, but she kind of felt obligated to wear one for the sake of the dress, which was a tad low-cut.

Of course, the minute she wasn't looking, Miel plopped on top of the linen dress and rolled around, getting fur all over it. Since there wasn't a lint roller in sight, she simply did her best to dust off as much of the fur as possible. *Good enough.* Once she was dressed, she applied some leave-in conditioner to tame her curls and dried her hair until it bounced like freshly cooked fusilli noodles. A bit of lipstick and mascara and she was good to go.

*Meeeooowww!*

The ingrates screeched and followed Núria to the door, almost causing her to trip and fall flat on her face. All she needed was to show up to dinner with a black eye.

"You guys behave, okay?" she said, closing the front door behind her.

She tried to ignore the flutter of guilt in her stomach. She hardly ever went out, unless Rocky forced her to tag along on one of her overly optimistic *don't-worry-it's-going-to-be-a-blast* adventures. Newsflash: It never was. Though Núria had to admit that an intimate dinner in someone's home was way more appealing than a crowded bar. *Who knows?* She might actually enjoy herself.

She fast-walked down the street, heading to the nearest liquor store, which was a few doors down from the bodega. It wasn't one of the new fancy-schmancy wine shops that were popping up all over the neighborhood, but she knew they had a decent selection of Spanish wine.

*Cring, cring.* The bells above the door announced her arrival. There was nobody inside other than Moshe, the dude who owned the store.

"Hey," she said to him before heading straight to the wine aisle. He nodded, clearly not recognizing her without the sweat and grime and the layer of cat fur on her clothes. It was kind of fun, actually. She could pretend to be some other woman—a more beautiful and sophisticated version of herself. What kind of wine would this woman buy? *Hmmm . . .*

Perhaps a refreshing sparkling wine? Her eyes perused the Spanish whites, bottle after bottle after bottle. Then she saw it—a 2020 sparkling wine called Nieva York. Its label was adorned with a black-and-orange illustration of the Brooklyn Bridge. Núria was a sucker for a nicely designed wine bottle. In fact, it's how she had usually selected most of the wines that she'd bought over the years. There was only one thing. At thirty-eight dollars, it was way more than she usually spent on wine. But why the hell not? For once she would splurge.

*Cring, cring.*

Instinctively, Núria glanced at the store entrance. A tall guy walked in, wearing what looked like pajama bottoms, a white T-shirt, and sneakers. She chuckled because that's what she usually looked like when she left her apartment.

But wait. He looked kind of familiar. Núria craned her neck and squinted at him as he headed for the red wine section. The shaggy dark hair. The awkward gait. The lopsided smile. *Ahhh.* It was the bestselling author guy from the coffee shop. He was alone, buying booze with his pajamas on. A little part of her felt relieved that she wasn't the only loser in town.

She brought the wine to the register so she could pay. As she reached for her wallet, she could sense the author guy's presence behind her. It was pretty impossible not to. There was a certain warmth surrounding him, and he smelled of lemons and soap. Núria looked over her shoulder, higher and higher and higher, until she met his gaze. "Oh. Hey!" she said, feeling unusually friendly.

The guy almost dropped the bottle of wine in his grasp. For a moment he seemed confused, which, come to think of it, wasn't all that strange, considering how different she looked.

"I work at the café," she added.

The lopsided smile was back. "Yes-Yes, of course. Hello. I mean, good evening," he stammered.

"Anything else?" said Moshe, grumpy and impatient as always.

Núria opened her wallet to pull two twenties out, but before she turned back around to focus on paying and getting out of there, she took one more glance at the author guy. Specifically at his chest, where she could have sworn she spotted one lonesome strand of black cat fur.

*Huh. Interesting.*

If she hadn't been in such a rush, she might have asked him about it. Maybe some other time. She grabbed her change and her bottle of wine and ran off like Cinderella. Except, instead of leaving behind a glass slipper, she left a fully grown man with his jaw on the floor.

# THIRTY-FOUR

# Cat

Cat watched the light fade from his cardboard house window. His eyelids were heavy. Every inch of him was relaxed. This time of day was always the quietest. There was less action on the streets. Whenever he peeked into people's homes, he would see them preparing a meal while the kids watched moving pictures on the flat box on the wall. Often there would be a cat or a dog napping nearby, oblivious to his presence.

But he was too tired for that today. Instead, he decided to pretend he was one of those inside cats, curled up on a cushy cat bed. Maybe he was getting older, but he increasingly found it exhausting to wander the streets at night. More often than not, he would just let his stomach grumble until morning. He'd never really desired to be owned, but he had to admit that he was starting to rely on the cardboard house and the meals from Rainbow Lady, Cheery Mailman, Sad Bodega Man, and Awkward Neighbor Guy. Cat was becoming less wild in his old age, though he still had a hard time admitting it to himself. Denial wasn't an emotion exclusive to human beings.

*Ahhh* . . . He leaned the side of his head on the cushion and curled until his body was rounded, like those loaves of bread he saw displayed in the neighborhood bakery's window. It seemed that most people loved bread, but Cat wasn't a fan. Well, except for the one time when he'd found a partially eaten tuna sandwich on a park bench. That sure had been a good day. As he dozed off, he fantasized about the creamy tuna and the crunchy bits of celery and the soggy bread, which had soaked up the dressing. He could almost smell the delicious aroma.

*Squeak. Thud.*

Cat's head jerked. It sounded like his neighbor's door opening and closing. There were footsteps, not the heavy kind caused by hard-soled shoes, but the softer kind that sounded like dried leaves sweeping against the sidewalk. He stretched his neck as far as it would go and peeked out the window. From the corner of his eye, he spotted plaid pajama pants and slippers. It *was* his neighbor.

Awkward Neighbor Guy cleared his throat. "Hey, little guy. Are you hungry?"

Cat could have sworn he smelled the pungent scent of salmon pâté. *Food?* He crawled on his haunches toward the door and stuck his head out. A couple of feet away stood Awkward Neighbor Guy, holding two bowls, one with food, the other with water. Something about the way he looked reminded Cat of some of the kids he came across; they so badly wanted to reach out to pet him, to be his friend, yet there was this tiny bit of uncertainty holding them back. Perhaps it was the fear of getting scratched or bitten. Little did they know that Rainbow Lady had managed to catch him one day, bringing him to a place with lots of cages and a person with a white coat who poked and prodded him until he fell asleep and woke up with a notch in his ear and a sore muscle. He'd heard the white coat person explain something to Rainbow Lady, using words like "rabies," "deworming," and a "five-in-one shot." A few days later, he'd been returned to his hedge as if nothing had happened. Cat had known something was different, though. His desires had shifted. He mellowed. Wandering no longer seemed like a necessity.

"C'mon. You *must* be hungry," said Awkward Neighbor Guy.

Cat slowly emerged from his house, keeping an eye on him. Though he seemed nice and all, you could never be 100 percent sure about a person's intentions.

*Meow.* Cat didn't want to appear too needy. He didn't want the guy to think he had the upper hand. When Cat gazed up, he saw his neighbor lowering the bowls. The aroma of salmon wafted into his nose.

*Meeeooowww!*

Cat threw all subtlety out the window, circling Awkward Neighbor Guy's legs as his tail twitched. As soon as the bowls landed on the ground, he pounced. In between bites, he glanced up at Awkward Neighbor Guy to make sure he kept a safe distance and was startled to see the man sitting on the ground with his knees pulled up to his chest. For a second, Cat considered darting back into the box. Then he noticed the wetness in Awkward Neighbor Guy's eyes, the softness of his jaw, the way he stared at Cat.

"Why didn't I just talk to her? Like, *really* talk to her? She was right there in front of me, and I screwed it all up," he whimpered.

Cat had this sudden urge to go and rub himself against the man's legs. But the urge was just that—an urge. He wasn't *that* kind of cat. Instead, he went back to gobbling his food while he listened.

"Do you think I even stand a chance? Or am I just barking up the wrong tree?" Awkward Neighbor Guy sighed. "I'm sorry, excuse the dog reference. What I should have said is . . . Do you think she could ever think I'm the cat's meow? Or am I just wasting my time?"

Cat finished his meal. He straightened back up and licked the fur around his mouth. Awkward Neighbor Guy leaned his head against his knees, grabbing clumps of his shaggy hair in frustration. Cat wasn't at all sure why he was so upset, but he somehow sensed that the guy needed some reassurance. How could he do that from a safe distance? How could he express himself without touching the man?

*Hmmm . . .* Cat pondered the situation. He took a couple of licks from the water bowl, then pondered some more. And then he remembered a dog he'd once seen in the park, one of those flat-faced ones with rolls of skin around its neck and back. The ridiculous-looking dog had flopped on the dirt, stretching its legs as it rolled back and forth, covering itself with dust and leaves and bits of grass as his owner laughed and smiled. It had been a genius move for such a dumb dog.

Before he could change his mind, Cat took a couple of steps closer.

When he was an arm's length away, which was pretty far since the guy had really long arms, Cat flopped on the ground. In his most convincing dumb dog imitation, he wiggled from side to side, trying his best to look as cute as possible.

Was it working?

He chanced a quick look at Awkward Neighbor Guy's face. What he saw almost made him get back up and rub up against his long, protruding legs. Because the guy—his neighbor, his roommate, his newly appointed nighttime food server—was smiling, his entire face lit up from his forehead down to his chin.

# THIRTY-FIVE

## Omar

O mar loved a challenge. And cooking vegan versions of his family favorites was definitely a challenge. The plantains were already fried and ready for mashing in his pilon, along with some garlic, onions, vegan bacon, and some mushrooms for extra umami. On the stove, he had a saucepan of mushroom gravy to go on top of the mofongo and a cast-iron pot of habichuelas guisadas. There was also a rice cooker full of fluffy white rice and, in the fridge, a vegan flan that he'd made with agar powder.

Carl had been somewhat confused by Omar's inviting a random woman he had met on the street to dinner, even if she was his pretend girlfriend. After Omar had reminded Carl that *he'd* invited plenty of pseudo-random coworkers over the years, sometimes without much notice, Carl had shrugged, leaving Omar to do all the cooking while he freshened up. This arrangement wasn't all that unusual. They split the bills evenly. Omar did all the cooking and shopping, and Carl did all the cleaning and laundry. For the most part it worked, even though Carl would silently grumble about the amount of pots and pans Omar used to cook.

"Ugh. I'm starving," said Carl, his arm poking out of nowhere to swipe a fried plantain.

Omar swatted him with a spatula. "Out! Go tidy up the living room while I finish up."

Carl rolled his sparkling blue eyes—the ones that Omar found so irresistible. "I swear you missed your calling as an army drill sergeant."

"Ha!" Carl knew that the *ha!* was like a period at the end of a sentence. Omar wanted to be left alone to focus on his cooking. So that's what Carl did.

As soon as he was by himself again, Omar couldn't help but dwell on Carl's comment about him missing his calling. Lately, he'd been thinking a whole lot about what else he could do with his life. While he mashed the fried plantains and mixed in the other ingredients and seasonings, he pondered whether there *was* some other calling for him. Being a mailman had been fun at first. The benefits were good too. If he was being completely honest with himself, though, it was the people and their pets that he really enjoyed, not the job itself. He didn't find much joy in delivering bills and catalogs and the occasional package. It wasn't like the days when people actually wrote each other letters and postcards. Most of that old-fashioned charm was gone.

So what else could he do with his life?

Carl kept pressuring him about going to culinary school. But the more Omar considered it, the more he decided it was a terrible idea. He loved cooking for his friends and family too much. If he had to do it for a paycheck, he worried that all his joy would turn into frustration and stress. Plus, culinary school was expensive.

*Beeeeeep!* Their obnoxious buzzer rang.

"I got it!" yelled Carl from the living room.

Omar placed the mashed plantain mixture into the cup molds so he could tip them over for serving. Then he wiped the sweat off his forehead and washed his hands before leaving the kitchen to greet his guest. When he entered the living room, Núria was already there. She was a vision with a mane of thick, bouncy curls, barely there makeup, and a dress that accentuated her figure in just the right way.

"Núria! It's so nice to see you somewhere besides the street," said Omar.

She smiled and handed him a bottle of wine. "Thanks for having me. I hope a sparkling white is okay?"

"Sparkling is perfect. It's been hotter than Hades's butt crack these last few days. Let me put it in the fridge so we can have it after dinner and sangria."

She giggled at the butt crack comment. "Do you need any help in the kitchen?"

Omar furrowed his brow and waved her off. "No. You're our guest. Carl will bring you out to the terrace to our outdoor dining area. The food will be out in a sec."

Off he went to the kitchen to finish plating the mofongo. As if he were a professional server, he walked to the terrace with three dinner plates in his arms, situating them on the small table they'd set up outside, which was surrounded by a variety of potted plants and small trees. Then he went back to the kitchen and made a couple more trips to bring the pot of habichuelas, a bowl of rice, and a gravy boat with the piping-hot mushroom gravy.

"I love your setup out here. It kind of feels like we're in the Hamptons, if you ignore the street noise," said Núria.

"Well, that is all Carl's doing. If it weren't for him, this place would look like a college dorm," said Omar.

Carl chuckled. "Amen! Ain't that the truth."

Omar rolled his eyes. "C'mon. Let's eat before it gets cold."

Núria pulled her phone out of her pocket, angling it over the food to take a photo. "For my mom," she said, cringing.

Omar got off his chair and kneeled beside her plate. "We can do better than that. Give her something to *really* look at." He leaned closer and smiled with all his teeth.

She took a couple of shots before putting her phone away. "Thank you. You're seriously a lifesaver."

Carl poured them each a glass of ice-cold sangria from a pitcher. "So, does this mother of yours *actually* approve of Omar? I'm dying to know," he said.

"Well, to be honest, she's the kind of woman who has something bad to say about everyone. But she approves that he exists," said Núria with a weak smile.

Carl frowned. "Oof. Well, that's rough. And here I thought that women had it easy. Date, find a good match, get engaged, then get married and move to the suburbs to pop out a couple of rug rats."

"Oh God, no. There will be no popping out of anything in my future. Though I could easily be talked into getting another cat or two."

"Same diff." Omar served himself some rice, beans, and gravy. "Pets are children, too . . . but don't tell those Park Slope moms with their thousand-dollar strollers that I said so," he said, covering his mouth so he could laugh.

"For real! They're always getting pissed at me for feeding the cats," said Núria.

Omar swept the air. "Just brush it off and ignore them, hon. You're doing good work out there."

"Thank you."

He shoved the bowls of food closer to Núria and Carl. "Are y'all going to eat or what?"

Núria blushed. "Yes. Of course. I'm actually starving. It's just that I don't have many conversations these days. My best friend, Rocky, says talking to cats doesn't count."

"Nonsense," said Omar.

Finally, she helped herself to some beans and rice, then took a big bite of the mofongo. Her eyes widened. "Shit. This is amazing. You could open up a restaurant or something."

Carl poked Omar. "See! I told you! If you'd only give culinary school a chance. Then you could open up your own restaurant, which I would *of course* decorate. It would be absolutely perfect! We could be like one of those Brooklyn power couples. . . ."

Omar opened his mouth as if to say something. He paused and glanced at Núria, then at Carl, then at the plate of food in front of him. What he wanted was to blurt out some sort of jab at Carl's ridiculous fantasy. But they had company. He wasn't about to ruin the good vibes by picking a fight. So, after hesitating for a couple of beats, he reached out and placed his hand on Carl's. "Well, you'll be happy to know that I'm thinking about making an appointment to check out the Brooklyn School of Culinary Arts."

Carl's blue eyes sparkled. "Oh, I *am* happy to hear that. I just *know* that you're going to love it."

"Hold on. Don't get too excited, now. I only said I was thinking about it," said Omar, his Adam's apple bobbing as if he'd just swallowed something. "Because deep down inside, I still kinda feel like cooking is my passion, *not* my career."

Núria got up off her seat abruptly. "Let's toast to that." She raised her glass of sangria. "To passion and not knowing what the fuck to do with our lives!"

They clinked glasses. Except Carl didn't sip from his glass after the fact. Instead, he leaned back and sighed for what seemed like forever.

Omar tried not to notice, focusing his attention on Núria. "So, you too, huh?"

"Me too, what?" she said, furrowing her brows.

"What you said. About not knowing what to do with our lives . . ."

Núria relaxed her face and slumped back in her chair. "Oh. *That*. Well, I suppose I'm just channeling what my mom always likes to tell me. She doesn't think being a barista is much of a career, even though I've been doing it for practically forever."

"*Do* tell. How long *is* 'practically forever'?" piped in Carl.

Before responding, she picked her glass up and took a big glug of sangria. "Let's just say that I've been working as a barista for longer than most marriages last."

Carl stared at her. "Ten years?"

Núria squinted.

"Fifteen?"

She covered her face with her hands.

"Twenty?"

She exhaled. "*Almost*."

"Oh, quit harassing her, Carl," said Omar, swatting him across the table with a napkin.

Núria smiled. "It's okay. Seriously. I don't mind."

Omar scooped a heaping spoonful of rice and beans into his mouth, staring into the air thoughtfully as he swallowed. "Is there something else you'd like to do with your life?" he said, relieved for the spotlight to be on someone other than him.

"Honestly, I think coffee and cats are it for me . . . Though when I first started out, I used to daydream about opening my own café. You know, with a couple of rescue cats to hang out with the customers . . . But it's stupid. I don't have the money for any of that," she said, her cheeks turning dark pink.

Omar reached out and squeezed her forearm. "It's not stupid. Who knows? It *could* happen. Maybe you'll win the lotto or something."

Núria chuckled. "Except I don't play."

"Well, whatever. Something miraculous could happen. This is New York City, after all, where your wildest dreams could come true!"

For a moment, the three of them sat there, entangled in their own thoughts. Omar clenched his jaw. He felt shitty about the white lie he'd spewed out to appease Carl. He glanced over at Núria, wondering if she'd bought his whole spiel about miracles and dreams. She was staring at her plate of food, her eyes watering as if she was remembering a sad, distant memory.

"Hey, what's the matter?" Omar asked.

She blinked and snapped out of it. "It's nothing. I'm okay . . . I was just thinking of my dad. . . . When I was young, we used to spend hours daydreaming out loud together. We'd just blurt out the most fantastical scenarios, you know. Most of them were pretty silly. But the one idea he'd always go back to was that one day, he wanted to retire from being a cop and open a bed-and-breakfast with rescued cats for the guests to hang out with. . . . Sort of like a smaller-scale version of The Hemingway Home and Museum in Key West."

"*And?* Did he ever get to open that bed-and-breakfast?" said Omar.

Núria shrugged. "I-I don't know. He left me and my mom when I was a kid. I haven't seen or heard from him since."

"Oh, sweetie. I'm so sorry." Omar leaned in and hugged her from the side.

"I guess I just haven't daydreamed too much since then," she said, dabbing her eyes with her napkin.

Carl reached for the pitcher of sangria and refilled all their glasses.

"Hon. We're going to have to change that," he said, lifting his glass. "Let's toast to dreams, and to making the most of the years we have left on this fucking planet!"

Once again, they all clinked their glasses. And they kept on clinking into the wee hours of the morning.

# THIRTY-SIX

## Cat

*Bang! Bang!*

Cat stuck his head out of his cardboard house. It was still dark outside, at least a couple of hours before daybreak. So what could that racket possibly be? It sounded like a bunch of rats scavenging in the garbage cans. If it *was* a bunch of rats, maybe he should investigate and have a little fun. It had been a while since he'd played toss-the-rat-in-the-air.

He skulked out of his house, making sure to stay close to the ground in case there was danger. His gaze shot over to the garbage bins. Nothing seemed out of order. Maybe there weren't any rats out there after all. How disappointing.

*Bang!*

The noise was coming from the sidewalk. He glanced over to the left and saw someone leaning on the alleyway gate. From the long curly hair and the dress, he guessed that it was a woman. Cat pointed his nose in the air and sniffed. *Strange.* She smelled an awful lot like Rainbow Lady—the aroma of cat fur, the smoky richness of coffee grounds, and the scent of her shampoo, which smelled like the summer herbs people grew in pots on their stoops. But there was also another smell, like rotten fruit or something. From behind, it didn't look like her at all. And she certainly wasn't acting like herself. The way she was moving was like the people he saw stumbling down the street as if they had zero control over their bodies. Sometimes he actually witnessed them puking into trash cans, or on the sidewalk, or even all over themselves.

The woman moved again, rifling through her purse until stuff began to fall out onto the ground. Then she pulled out a crumpled piece of paper and a pen and scribbled something on the paper, which lay on her wobbly palm. Clearly, she was a mess, whoever she was.

Cat quietly snuck over to the side of the gate where the hedge cast its shadow. She wouldn't be able to see him there even if he was only a couple of feet away. Suddenly, the woman pushed herself off the gate again. This time, she was able to stand without falling back. For a moment, she turned her face, and he was able to get a good look at her. It *was* Rainbow Lady!

He watched as she staggered over to his neighbor's pot of flowers and plucked a stone from it. Then she backtracked toward the hedge, placing a piece of paper on the sidewalk with the stone on top. After a couple of minutes, she headed off down the street, slowly, like one of those injured cockroaches that Cat messed with on occasion.

As Cat watched her get farther and farther, he couldn't help but worry about her. She was obviously in a vulnerable state. He needed to make sure she was okay. So he decided to follow her, at least until the corner where the bodega was. After that, she would cross the street toward her apartment. Cat made sure to stay away from cars. He'd seen way too many creatures get run over through the years—other stray cats, rats, pigeons, cockroaches, and once even a squirrel that had somehow wandered away from the park.

He took off through the hedges, staying close to the buildings to take advantage of the shadows. He didn't want her to see him. All he wanted was for her to get back to the safety of her own home so she could go to sleep and wake up herself again. Rainbow Lady was a good fifteen feet ahead of him. It was better that way. From that distance, he could keep an eye on her without being detected. The way she walked was worrying, swerving left and right, stumbling and nearly tripping over her feet. There was hardly anyone on the sidewalk, but at one point a delivery guy approached her and said something. Maybe he wanted to make sure she was okay too. But she mumbled something and brushed him off. The guy shrugged and went back to minding his own business.

By the time they reached the bodega, she still wasn't acting anywhere near normal. Rainbow Lady stood on the corner, confused, looking one way and then the other way, as if she'd forgotten how to cross the street. He jumped onto the bench. After what seemed like forever, she finally stepped onto the road, wobbling a bit before catching herself. Cat's eyes went wide, and his heart thumped inside his chest. When she reached the middle of the road, she stopped, almost dropping her purse. A cab swerved around her, honking its horn obnoxiously. She didn't even notice it. Three, four more steps and she was almost on the other side. A delivery truck appeared, speeding toward her. At the last minute it halted, brakes shrieking as she took the last step.

"Watch it, lady!" the angry driver screamed.

Her foot landed on the curb. *Phew.* She was safe again. Except she still wasn't paying much attention. She walked over a ventilation grate, the heel of her shoe getting stuck in one of the openings. Immediately, she lost her balance, falling forward with her arms raised. *Splat!* Rainbow Lady face-planted. Unfortunately, there was nothing Cat could do to help her. Was she okay? Was she injured?

Cat had never felt so helpless. All he could do was watch over her and hope someone would come to her rescue. *Oh, wait!* There was a guy approaching her. He was wearing one of those black hoodies and jeans that some of the younger guys in the neighborhood sported. When he reached the spot where her feet were, he gazed right and then left, and then behind him, looking like one of those suspicious crows in the park that were up to no good. Cat jumped off the bench and hurried over to the curb just as the man bent down and placed his hand on her naked thigh where her dress had hiked up.

*No! No! No!*

This guy, this man, this miscreant wasn't there to help her. He was going to hurt her, take advantage of her. Cat couldn't let that happen. Not to *his* Rainbow Lady. His beloved person. His paws trembled as he stepped off the curb, looking both ways. There weren't any cars. *Go, Cat! Go!* he cheered himself on, leaping onto the road like a jaguar chasing its prey. He ran and ran and ran; everything to either side of him was a blur. His heart was racing so fast that it felt as if it might explode out of his chest.

*Beeeeeep!*

A car screeched to a halt a mere foot or two away from him. Instinctively, he bolted to the side and tumbled.

*Beeeeeep!* The car honked again.

Cat scrambled to his feet, his paws slipping for a couple of seconds until he gained enough momentum to run again. *Hurry, Cat!* It wasn't just about saving Rainbow Lady anymore. It was also about saving his own life. *Run. Run. Run.* The curb on the other side was near; he could almost touch it. Just a few more steps and he leaped, giving it all he had as a bicycle whizzed by, grazing the tip of his tail. Finally, he landed on the sidewalk.

As much as he wanted to stop and rest after his traumatic ordeal, Rainbow Lady was in trouble. The man's hand was even farther up her leg.

*It's now or never . . .*

Cat growled and hissed with all his might before charging toward the man with his back arched, fangs exposed, claws extended, and fur standing on end as he readied himself for a fight. The man pulled his hand away from Rainbow Lady and whipped his head around just as Cat pounced on him, scratching the side of his face.

"What the fuck!" The man poked his arm out defensively, pushing Cat to the side.

But Cat had too much adrenaline coursing through his little body. He pounced on the man again, hissing even louder as he aimed for the man's wrist, biting him until he could taste blood.

"Fuck!" the man screamed again, his other hand grabbing Cat by the neck and squeezing hard.

As much as Cat wanted to keep his fangs locked into this bad man's flesh, he could feel his eyes bulging, his breath running out. He loosened his jaw and let go. *Thud.* The man dropped him on the hard concrete. Cat was too dizzy to run away, which he needed to do as fast as possible, because from his blurred peripheral vision, he could see a red-and-white sneaker about to stomp on him.

"Stop! Right now! I'm calling the cops!" a woman's voice screamed.

The guy pulled his leg back and looked over his shoulder at the girl who was standing there with her cellphone to her ear.

"Help! There's an assault happening on St. Marks Avenue near Neptune Diner. . . . Come quick!" she said loudly into her phone.

The man ran off without saying a word.

Cat pushed himself off the sidewalk with wobbly limbs, his vision focusing again. The young woman with the cellphone took a couple of steps forward, hyperventilating. Then she spun around, as if she was searching for help. Nobody else was there, though. It was just her, Rainbow Lady, and Cat. She glanced over at Rainbow Lady, and then at Cat. Even in the darkness he could see that her eyes were blue, he could tell they were scared, he could glimpse kindness in them. This girl, this young woman, was going to help Rainbow Lady.

Cat had had enough with the heroics. All he wanted was to run across the street and back to his house, where he would hide until the sun went up. He glanced over at Rainbow Lady one more time before escaping to the curb.

"Wait! Are you all right?" the young woman shouted after him.

But he wasn't in the mood for conversation, even with a nice girl like her. He looked both ways again, this time making sure there weren't *any* cars or trucks or bicycles, before darting back to the safety of his street.

## THIRTY-SEVEN

*Lily*

On nights when Lily couldn't sleep, she would go out for a walk. She knew it wasn't necessarily the best idea, since it was New York City and there were probably muggers and rapists and kidnappers on every corner. She tried not to think about it. Instead, she would imagine she was back home, taking a stroll in her small town, bathed by the moonlight as she listened to the swishing of the fragrant magnolia trees. As happy as she was to be living somewhere else, part of her missed her old life—the comfort, the familiarity, the security. Most of all, she missed her dad. Meeting Bong at the cemetery had made her realize just how much she longed for a father figure. She needed someone to lean on, someone to give her advice, someone who would listen without judgment.

The last thing she'd expected was to stumble upon a crime-in-progress during one of her impromptu middle-of-the-night strolls. But there she was, shocked out of her wits, as she stared at a woman face down on a subway grate. A man was beside her with blood dripping down his face. And a black cat was cowering below him.

Without even thinking she shouted, "Stop! Right now! I'm calling the cops!"

Then everything sort of became a blur. Her hands were shaky, too shaky to dial 911, but she had to do something. "Help! There's an assault happening on St. Marks Avenue near Neptune Diner. . . . Come quick!" she said loudly into her phone, bluffing.

The man took off sprinting down the street. *Thank God.* The woman moved a bit. She was still alive. The cat pushed itself off the sidewalk. It stared at her, and she stared back at it. Before she could do or say anything, it scrambled for the curb to make its escape.

"Wait! Are you all right?" Lily blurted out.

The cat didn't respond. Of course it didn't. It was a cat.

Lily watched as it ran across the street, disappearing from her sight halfway down the block. Clearly, the cat was all right. She caught her breath, her shoulders relaxing. Her heart was still beating too fast, and the tips of her fingers were numb from squeezing her phone too hard. In all of the time she'd been living in Brooklyn, nothing remotely close to this had ever happened. Of course, she'd been well aware it *could* happen, but nothing had prepared her for this moment. For a second she felt kind of faint. There was the woman, though. She had to make sure she was okay.

"Uh, miss. Are-Are you hurt?" she said.

The woman groaned.

"Should I call 911? Do you need an ambulance?"

The woman shifted and groaned again.

Lily turned around, searching for someone else to help. There was no one. She kneeled on the sidewalk and reached out to touch the woman's shoulder.

"I-I think I'm fine. . . . I'm okay. . . . I just need some help getting up," the woman said, turning toward her with another groan.

Lily gasped because the woman wasn't some random stranger. It was her sister, Núria! A moment passed as she recuperated from the shock.

"Are you sure you're all right? The man . . . did he hurt you?"

Núria winced, and even in the shadows, Lily could tell her cheeks were bright red. "Not really. But I'm glad you came along and scared him off."

"Well, to be honest, I don't think it was really me who saved the day. . . . There was a cat. The man's face and arm were all scratched up—"

Núria pushed her chest up clumsily. "A cat? What cat? Where?"

"It was a black cat. It ran across the street. Don't worry, I don't think it was injured."

"Are you sure?"

Lily nodded. "I'm pretty sure."

Núria exhaled. "I can't believe it. . . ."

"C'mon. I'll help you up." Lily took hold of Núria's armpits. "At the count of three. Okay? One. Two. Three." Lily tightened her core, tensed her legs, and lifted as hard as she could. She may have been on the petite side, but she was surprisingly strong. The years of cheerleading had given her the core strength of an elite athlete. With Lily's support, Núria slowly got up off the ground.

"Th-Thank you . . . my shoe got stuck on the grate . . . and. Um. I've had a little too much to drink," admitted Núria, her face flushed and sweaty.

Lily held on to her forearm in case she toppled over again. "It's okay, we've all been there."

Except that was a lie. Much to the chagrin of her roommates, Lily wasn't a drinker. At high school parties, she'd sipped soda or water from her plastic cup, pretending to drink like everyone else. Truth be told, she didn't want to consume even a drop of alcohol. Ever since she could remember, her mother had been a high-functioning alcoholic, and Lily didn't want to risk becoming anything like her.

"Well, I guess I'd better get home now and sleep it off," said Núria with a sheepish smile.

"Wait. I don't think it's a good idea to walk home alone." Lily peered at her face. "Besides, I think you're bleeding," she said, pointing at Núria's forehead.

Núria reached up and touched her forehead with her fingers, wincing on contact. "Ugh. Great."

"I think I should keep you company until you're safe."

"It's fine. Really. I can manage."

"No. I insist."

Núria relaxed, allowing Lily to support her. "Okay. Thanks. I guess I'm just not used to the kindness of strangers," she said.

Lily flinched. She so badly wanted to tell Núria that she wasn't a stranger. That she was her younger sister. But she couldn't. Not yet.

"Hey. Don't I know you?" Núria stared at Lily with squinty eyes.

It was so quiet. Lily feared that Núria would hear how fast her heart was beating. "Yes. I-I work at the Foodtown. I think I've checked you out a couple of times," she mumbled. "You're the one with all the cat food, right?"

"Yup. That's me."

"Small world," said Lily.

Indeed, it *was* a small world. What were the chances that Lily would be on that street at that exact moment to help her? Was it the universe's way of bringing them together? Or was it just a weird co-incidence?

They walked slowly down the street. Every couple of steps, Núria wobbled a bit. After ten minutes of walking and stopping and walking and stopping, they halted in front of a four-story walk-up.

"Is this your place?" Lily asked.

"Yeah. I'm on the second floor."

Lily peeked through the glass entrance. "Is there an elevator?"

"No. But it's all right. I can get up on my own. I've inconvenienced you enough," said Núria.

"It's fine. Really. I don't mind." Lily stuck her hand out. "Hand over the keys."

Núria reached into her purse and retrieved her keys—a jingly cluster held together with a keychain of a cat that looked like a loaf of bread. Lily unlocked the door and led them through it. The stairway was almost too narrow for two people side by side, but they managed to hobble up with Núria holding on to the railing with her right hand and tightly grasping Lily's forearm with her left.

"This is me," said Núria, gesturing at a cobalt-blue door.

Lily unlocked it and pushed it open. Immediately, she was accosted by three giant cats. "Oh. Hello," she said as they rubbed and jumped on her legs. "Are they always this friendly?"

"Pretty much. Anyone who walks in is fair game. Delivery people. Building maintenance. Census officials. Jehovah's Witness recruiters. Robbers. Murderers . . . you name it," said Núria.

Lily could tell that she was more alert, less wobbly. However, she didn't want to leave her yet. She wanted to see what was inside the apartment to learn more about her sister. "C'mon. Let me take a look at your forehead. I took a first aid course in high school," she said.

"Oh gosh. My apartment is a mess. And I've bothered you enough for one night," said Núria.

"Seriously. It's all good. This is the most fun I've had since moving here." Lily pressed the light switch by the door and then led them inside as if she lived there.

It didn't take long for them to pass through the tiny entryway that led to the compact studio apartment. For a moment, they sort of lingered by the refrigerator while Lily took the room in.

"I warned you," said Núria with a sheepish grin.

"No. It's cool. I love your bedspread. And your windows. You must get a lot of light." Lily pointed at the two-seater sofa. "Go sit. I'll get some first aid supplies in the bathroom."

Núria limped to the sofa, the three cats crowding around her legs like hungry piranhas. She plopped down with a groan. "There should be some peroxide, cotton pads, and Band-Aids under the sink," she said.

But Lily was already in the bathroom grabbing said items. When she stood back up, she couldn't help but look around a bit. There were bottles of rosemary-scented shampoo and conditioner in the shower caddy, as well as an old, rusty razor and a bar of soap. At the sink there was a bottle of Castile liquid hand soap, a wooden toothbrush, and a tube of coconut oil toothpaste. She opened the mirrored cabinet, expecting to see a bunch of medications, but there was only some floss, a bottle of melatonin, and some essential oils.

"Did you find the stuff?" said Núria from the other room.

"Yeah! I'm just using the bathroom." Lily flushed the toilet even though she hadn't used it. Then she went back to the living area, holding the stuff in her arms. Unfortunately, the cats had taken over the small sofa. She stood there awkwardly while Núria wrangled them onto the floor.

"Sorry. This is clearly *their* apartment. Not mine," said Núria.

Lily sat. "No worries. I get it. My dad loved cats. But my mom was allergic, so we never had any at home. But once in a while, he'd bring me to a cat café in the city."

Núria frowned. *Shit.* Had she said too much? Lily hadn't meant to bring up her dad. *Their* dad. It had slipped out of her mouth like a rogue spaghetti noodle.

Without saying anything more, she put some peroxide onto one of the cotton pads and proceeded to dab Núria's forehead with it. Lily glanced at her sister's arms and legs to see if there were any other cuts or scrapes. "Your knee," she said, pointing at Núria's left knee.

Núria looked down and gasped at the scrape that was oozing there. She scooched closer to the edge of the sofa so Lily could reach better and watched as she gently dabbed on the peroxide. "You're good at this. You should be a nurse."

Lily shrugged. "I'm not very good at school." She placed the cotton pads aside and proceeded to apply the Band-Aids where they were needed. "There. You should be good now, though you'll probably be sore in the morning. If you've got an ice pack, you might want to use it," she said, standing and then heading over to the kitchen sink so she could wash her hands.

Núria smiled. "Thank you—" She paused, trying to remember if Lily had said her name.

"Lily."

"Thank you, Lily. I'm Núria."

Except, of course, Lily already knew her sister's name.

# THIRTY-EIGHT

# Bong

It was nearly ten A.M. Bong was in front of the bodega, waiting. He hadn't known exactly how to dress for this mysterious mission to help Omar, so he'd gone with something practical— a lightweight blue collared T-shirt, cargo shorts, and his trusty walking shoes. Additionally, he had a baseball cap tucked in his pocket in case they'd be out in the sun.

Bong gazed down the street on one side, then the other. Still, there was no sight of Omar. Had he gotten the day and time mixed up? Conchita had always been the one to keep track of his appointments. He was forgetful, which had been problematic before. These days, though, he rarely had anything to do other than work, church, and visiting the cemetery. He hadn't really felt the need to come up with some sort of calendar system. Sighing, he wiped the sweat off his forehead with a handkerchief. One more time, he checked his watch. It was five after ten. Five more minutes and he would give up waiting.

*Beep! Beep!*

An old green Volvo station wagon pulled up. The passenger window rolled down, revealing a fresh-faced Omar. "Good morning, Bong. Sorry to keep you waiting," he said.

"It's okay," said Bong. He opened the door of the back seat and got inside.

Omar reached to shake his hand. "Thanks for coming. I *really* appreciate it," he said with a warm smile.

"No worries. Happy to help."

Omar placed his hand on the driver's shoulder. "This is Carl, my partner. He's our driver for the day."

Carl rolled his eyes at him before looking over his shoulder at Bong. "Don't mind him. I just came for the—"

"Shhhh!" Omar swatted his leg. "Not a word until we get there."

Bong frowned. He was even more confused than he'd been before. If they were going to move some furniture or deliver something or do some other menial task that required three people, why all the secrecy? But as confused and unsure as he was, there was a little part of him that was enjoying it. This was the first time in a long time that Bong had felt needed. When his daughters had lived nearby, he would often go to their homes and help them with odd jobs—fixing leaky pipes, spraying WD-40 on a creaky door or window, repainting a wall here and there. He'd felt useful. Not anymore, though.

"So, Bong, let me ask you a question. Are you a man of adventure? Perhaps a thrill-seeker?" Carl blurted out.

Bong had been looking out the window. As soon as Carl said that, Bong shifted his gaze to the front of the car, catching Omar giving Carl a dirty look.

"Well, not so much anymore. But in my younger days, I used to hike up mountains and go fishing in my province. I even had a Honda motorcycle that I used to ride around Manila to avoid traffic. My wife, Conchita, hated it," he said with a chuckle.

"Well, you're a better man than I am. The most adventure I've ever had was flea-marketing in Paris for a client. It was *exhausting*," said Carl dramatically.

Omar peeked over the seat so he could face Bong. "Carl is an assistant to one of the top interior decorators in the city. His idea of adventure is haggling, even though his clients live in million-dollar homes," he said with an eye roll.

"What? Is there something wrong with that?" said Carl in a huff. "Just because you're rich doesn't mean you should get ripped off."

The last thing Bong wanted was to get in the middle of an argument. For the rest of the car ride, he leaned back and watched the scenery go by. He was more than content to listen to Omar and Carl bicker. The bickering wasn't hostile by any means. It was the sort of back and forth that Bong and Conchita used to do all the time—challenging each other, bettering each other, teaching each other. Besides, their fights, if you could call them that, always ended in a hug and a kiss. It was healthy, something all couples did once in a while.

"Keep your eye out for a spot!" said Carl as he maneuvered the station wagon through traffic.

Bong gazed out the window, but instead of a parking spot, he noticed a Ferris wheel peeking through the buildings. Another block and he saw an old wooden roller coaster. He sat up straight. "Is that Coney Island?" he asked.

"It sure is," said Omar.

Bong couldn't stop staring at all the rides and the colorful signs, and at the beach and blue sea beyond. "Huh. All the years I've lived in Brooklyn, and I've never had the time to see this place. We always wanted to bring our daughters when they were younger, but somehow, it just never happened," he said.

"Well, today is your lucky day!" exclaimed Carl, pulling into a tight spot.

Omar sighed. "Way to spoil the surprise, Carl."

"Surprise? You mean, that's where we're going?" Bong asked.

Omar got out of the car, then opened the back door for Bong. "Yes. I'm sorry that I wasn't more forthcoming. But I wasn't sure you'd come if I told you the truth," he said.

Bong slid off the back seat. "But I'm confused. You said you needed help."

"That part wasn't a lie. I *do* need help. It's just not the kind of help you might expect. You see, Carl"—he gestured at Carl, who was brushing the wrinkles out of his orange-and-blue striped shirt—

"refuses to go on any rides with me. And it's really no fun to go on them alone. So I figured you might be able to help me out with that."

Carl shot Omar a dirty look. "I only come here for the cotton candy and the guys in muscle tees."

"See what I have to deal with?" said Omar with a chuckle. "But seriously, I hope you're not mad, Bong."

"No, of course I'm not mad. Maybe a bit surprised. But not mad." Bong gazed off into the distance and stared at the roller coaster as it slowly made its ascent, higher and higher and higher, until *whoosh*, it dropped fast. The people on it screamed and shrieked and threw their arms into the air.

After a couple of minutes, he turned and met Omar's gaze. "Is it okay if we . . . I mean, can we go on the roller coaster first?" he said with the grin of an excited nine-year-old boy.

# THIRTY-NINE

# Collin

Collin hadn't slept a wink. He'd tossed and turned all night long, unable to shut down the thoughts running in circles in his mind. Eventually, just as the early morning light peeked through his window blinds, he'd fallen asleep from sheer exhaustion. It was past ten when he finally managed to drag himself out of bed to brew a large pot of coffee, which he would need to get through the day.

As he poured himself an obscenely large cup, thoughts from the night before rushed back into his head, giving him a sudden whopper of a headache. He couldn't stop thinking about what had happened at the liquor store. Núria had recognized him among the hundreds of customers she had at the café. In fact, she'd even flirted a bit. Or had she? He shook his head, confused.

One thing was certain, though. He'd acted like a complete and utter fool.

Nevertheless, what did it all mean? Surely her striking up a conversation was a good sign, right?

Except there was one tiny thing nagging him. Well, maybe not so tiny. Why had she been so dressed up? Had she been on her way to a date? With the mailman perhaps?

Collin poured some coconut-almond creamer into his coffee and sat by the kitchen table. He stared at the brown liquid in his cup, as if he was willing the foam latte hearts to appear. He needed a sign. Any sign. Except nothing was going to happen if he kept his sorry ass at home all the time.

He suddenly stood, nearly spilling the coffee all over the table. Maybe he should go see if she was at the café. Maybe seeing her would give him some clarity. If she treated him like any other customer, then he would know she wasn't interested in the slightest. But if she smiled like she'd smiled at him at the liquor store, maybe he still had a chance. Maybe it would be worth it to put himself out there and risk a broken heart. *Yup*. That was what he would have to do. He hurried into the hallway, stomping up the stairs, so he could change.

And if she *was* there, he would play it cool as a cucumber. He would order a drink, maybe a pastry too, and sit in front of his laptop and pretend to write. Collin most definitely would *not* sit there and ogle at her like a lovestruck teenager.

When he was dressed, he grabbed all of his stuff and hurried out of his house as if he were late for an appointment. He unlatched his front gate and then turned left, taking extra-long steps so he could get to the café faster. Except there was something by the hedges that caught his eye. He halted abruptly. A note! She'd left him another note! He scrambled toward the semi-crumpled piece of paper and snatched it off the sidewalk as if it were a one-hundred-dollar bill. He read it. Or rather, he *tried* to read it. The words were crooked and jagged and smeared. But years of deciphering his father's illegible doctor's writing had given him the superhero ability to read almost any kind of penmanship.

*Do YOU miss me when I'm not around?*

Collin grinned. Unbeknownst to Núria, he actually *did* miss seeing her when she wasn't there. This was it. The sign he needed. Today was *the* day. If Núria was at the café, he would come clean. He would tell her that he'd been the one writing to her.

❦ ❦ ❦ ❦ ❦

Despite it being a weekend, the café was surprisingly not crowded. Maybe its regular patrons had decided to sleep in to nurse their hangovers, or maybe they'd all gone to brunch at one of Brooklyn's hippest new eateries.

Collin pushed the glass door open and went inside, nearly tripping on the uneven wooden flooring. "Crap," he mumbled to himself, glancing down at his feet and cringing when he noticed he'd put on mismatched shoes. On his left foot was a checkered Van, and on his right, a leather moccasin. He halted for a split second, wondering if he should go back home and remedy the situation. But he forged ahead, confident that Núria wouldn't care one bit about his mismatched footwear. What mattered more was finally getting his secret off his chest. It was the only way to move forward.

"Good morning. Can I get you something?" said the guy who usually manned the register.

Collin glanced to his right, eyeing the espresso machine. Núria wasn't there. Instead, a tall, skinny dude with a man-bun was crafting the beverages.

"Um. Uh. Well . . ." He glanced up at the menu, then over at the espresso machine again while the cashier grinned at him, his pierced eyebrow raised as if he knew a secret that Collin didn't. "The woman . . . the one who usually works here," he managed to mumble, even though his cheeks were hot and his hands were like bricks hanging by his hips.

"Oh, you mean Núria?" said the cashier, this time raising his second eyebrow.

Collin forced a smile. "Yes. She knows what I usually order."

The cashier chuckled, looking somewhat amused by Collin, which made him even more anxious. "It's her day off. But I can call her," he said, reaching for the phone near the register.

Collin practically leaped over the counter to snatch his hand away from the phone. "No! It's okay. I-I only meant that she usually knows what I want. Admittedly, I'm pretty indecisive," he said, trying to play it cool, even though he was sure his cheeks were the same color as the container of beet hummus in his fridge.

"It's all good. I'm sure Chuck over there is happy to read your mind and whip you up the beverage of your dreams. Right, Chuck?" said the cashier, glancing over at the man-bun dude.

Man-bun dude whipped his head around, making his bun bob from side to side. "Huh?" he said with a frown.

The cashier smiled. "One mystery drink and a triple-chocolate brownie for this guy," he said, gesturing at Collin. "No offense, but you look like you could use the sugar. That'll be eight dollars and seventy-five cents, please."

Collin reached for his wallet and handed him a ten-dollar bill. Then he pulled out a five-dollar bill and stuffed it into the tip jar, hoping that the tip would erase any trace of this memory from their minds.

*Ahem.* The customer behind him cleared their throat. Collin hopped to the side to wait for his mystery beverage. After a minute or two of nervous shuffling, of stuffing and unstuffing his hands in his pockets, of glancing over his shoulder, half expecting Núria to waltz into the café even though it was her day off, his order was finally ready.

"Enjoy!" said the man-bun dude, handing him what looked to be a coffee milkshake with whipped cream and cookie crumbs on top. "It's my very own creation. A salted caramel frappé with Biscoff cookies! It pairs really well with chocolate," he said.

For a moment, all Collin could do was stare at the monstrosity of a beverage. Did grown men really order drinks like these? It reminded him of his childhood, when his mother would bring him to Serendipity for a frozen hot chocolate as a special treat for getting straight A's on his report card.

"Uh. Thanks. It looks great," was all he could say.

"You're welcome!" said the man-bun dude with a friendly wave.

Collin turned to leave so he could wallow in his own humiliation at a table far, far away. He hadn't even walked three steps when he heard the man-bun dude's voice call after him.

"Ooooh! Love your shoes . . . very on trend, my man!"

It was at that moment that Collin lost the last bit of pride he had left.

He sighed and wandered over to a small table in the corner that had just freed up. Núria wasn't around. He wouldn't get a chance to confess to her. But maybe he could salvage the morning by getting some actual work done. He pulled out his laptop and situated it on the table next to his coffee-slash-milkshake and triple-chocolate brownie, which actually looked pretty good. Just as he was about to open his still-untitled manuscript, his phone vibrated in his pocket. He fished it out and squinted at the text.

COLLIN. I NEED A FAVOR. ALESHA IS OUT OF TOWN AND MY SITTER CAME DOWN WITH A COLD. I HAVE A WORK DINNER IN THE CITY. A REALLY IMPORTANT ONE. I KNOW IT'S LAST MINUTE, BUT CAN YOU PLEASE WATCH BERNIE? PLEASE? ALL I NEED IS TWO HOURS TOPS. I CAN DROP HER OFF AT SIX. I'LL OWE YOU ONE.

He grinned. His sister, Caroline, had a ridiculous habit of texting in all caps whenever she had an emergency. She and Alesha had a seven-year-old daughter, Bernie, named after Senator Bernie Sanders, for whom they'd ferociously campaigned in 2016. His sister was always having emergencies when it came to childcare. Caroline was a director of housing development, so there was always some dinner or fundraiser or meeting that she urgently had to attend. Alesha was a celebrity stylist, flying here and there to style singers and actresses for magazine shoots and events.

Whenever Caroline messaged for him to babysit, he would pretend that it was a massive inconvenience, even though he secretly enjoyed Bernie's company. Though he wasn't generally a huge fan of children, he basked in the role of weird and sometimes grumpy Uncle Collin.

Collin texted her back, sensing that time was of the essence.

Sure. No problem. But don't you already owe me like twelve? Or is it thirteen? I've lost count. See you at six, big sis. P.S. Has Bernie grown out of her white food phase yet?

His phone vibrated almost immediately.

> Thank you. I promise I'll make it up to you. Bernie says
> she'd like a pepperoni pizza, but only the kind with the
> crispy, burned crusts. I trust you know what she means.
> See you at six!

Suddenly, it didn't matter that he hadn't seen Núria, that his coffee craving had been ruined by man-bun dude's mystery beverage, and that he still only had four measly words written in his manuscript. He hurriedly put his laptop away and crammed half of the brownie into his mouth.

A visit from Bernie might just be the perfect distraction to get his mind off of Núria and his sudden desire to unmask his mystery persona. He and Bernie would draw, tell stories, watch some cartoons, and eat a gloriously greasy pepperoni pizza with burned, blistered crusts.

But first, he would write Núria another note. Maybe she would drop by the feeding spot later on. If that was the case, he didn't want to miss an opportunity to communicate with her.

Collin reached for the pad of Post-its he kept in his bag and stared at the top sheet. Had Post-its always been this small? How could he possibly say everything he needed to say with so little room? He frowned. No, this wouldn't do at all. He rifled inside his laptop bag, hoping that there was something else in there he could use. One, two, three pens in different colors. A yellow highlighter. A travel-size pack of tissues for when his allergies acted up. His phone and laptop chargers. A spray bottle of screen cleaner. Just when he was about to give up, he gripped something that felt like a notepad at the very bottom of one of the side pockets. He pulled it out and grinned. It wasn't exactly a notepad, but rather a wad of hotel stationery he must have shoved into his bag the last time he'd stayed at the Four Seasons in Chicago. Perfect. He plucked his favorite black pen from the table and furrowed his brows. The pen hovered for a good minute. Then another minute. Then another. For someone who supposedly had so much to say, he was finding himself somewhat speechless. Had his writer's block seeped from his creative life into his everyday life? He sighed and gazed out the window. For a moment, he imagined Núria was walking past the café, the way the warm light hit her auburn curls making her look like some sort of modern-day goddess. His hand twitched. He was light-headed for a brief instant. And then, *whoosh*—a flurry of words whirled out of him onto the page.

*Have you always loved cats more than people? I mean, I get it. People can be awful—so awful that most days I'd rather stay at home by myself. But I'll admit that when I see you with the cat—as cheesy as it sounds—I get a warm and fuzzy feeling. Even from afar, I can see the adoration that exudes from your eyes. It makes me a bit envious of your furry friend. I'll confess that there's only one person whose eyes light up like that whenever they see me. She's seven. And she's my niece. I know, I know. It's kind of pathetic. In fact, she's coming over tonight for pizza and cartoons. That there is as exciting as my weekends ever get. Don't get me wrong, I enjoy her company. But if I'm being completely honest, it can get lonely. I'm not really a fan of bars and nightlife. And online dating, God . . . Just the thought of it makes me break out in hives. Nope. Definitely not for me. If I'm ever going to meet someone, it'll have to be the old-fashioned way. Maybe that's why I like writing notes so much. Because that's what people did way back, when the internet and cellphones didn't exist. There's just something more intimate about it. You know what I mean? Not to mention that, well, it makes it easier for me to open up. As a matter of fact, I find it quite challenging to talk to people most of the time. It's hard for me to figure them out. But I see you out on the street and you make me want to know more about you. You make me want to get out of my comfort zone. To take risks. I just hope that I can find the courage to meet you one day. Until then, I look forward to exchanging many more words, as awkward as it may be. Take care. P.S. Is it silly for me to admit that I do miss seeing you when you're not around?*

Collin read the letter once and then twice, and then a third time for good measure before folding it in thirds. Writing to her in such a personal manner was a bold move. "Collin" and "bold" were rarely spoken in the same sentence. But for a reason he couldn't quite put his finger on, he felt rather bold at that moment.

He only hoped it would pay off.

Otherwise, he might never leave his house ever again.

# FORTY

# Omar

Omar couldn't believe what he was seeing. Bong was a new man. His back was straighter, shoulders snapped back. His eyes sparkled. His smile was as contagious as a daycare measles outbreak. Omar couldn't help but smile too. He'd thought it would be harder to bring Bong out of his funk. Who knew that all it would take was an amusement park, the sound of squealing children, and the scent of corn dogs and cotton candy?

"Carl. Are you sure you don't want to come with us?" said Bong, placing his hand on Carl's shoulder.

Carl scrunched his freckled nose. "Nah. You boys go ahead. I'll just be over there, watching the lifeguards oil themselves," he said, gesturing at the boardwalk.

Bong grinned. "Well, enjoy the view!"

"Don't egg him on, Bong. You might regret it," said Omar.

"Toodle-oo!" They watched Carl march toward the beach. Every so often he would halt and fan the heat off his face.

Omar shook his head. "Please excuse Carl. He can be kind of dramatic."

"No. No. Don't apologize. I can tell that he is a good man. The two of you seem perfect for each other," said Bong.

As soon as Bong said that, Omar could feel the guilt niggling away at his gut. Ever since the dinner at his place with Núria, he'd tried hard to brush off the little white lie he'd told Carl about booking a school tour. He couldn't, though. The guilt was eating him alive. But today wasn't about him and his emotions. It was about making Bong feel better. So he would do his best to ignore the guilt.

They shuffled forward in line, chitchatting about this and that. Omar was careful not to mention Bong's wife. The purpose of this outing was to give the old man some respite from his grief. The last thing Omar wanted was for him to get all weepy and sad when they were supposed to be having fun.

"Hey, so I noticed you don't have anyone else working at the store these days. You thinking of hiring? I can ask around. I might have some cousins or nephews looking for part-time work," said Omar.

Bong blinked. For a second, Omar was worried that Bong was thinking about his wife again. Was he reminiscing about the days when she used to work with him in the store? Was he going to break down right there in the middle of the crowded amusement park? But Bong raised his eyebrows and opened his mouth into a circle, as if he had just come up with a brilliant idea.

"*Actually,* now that you mention it, I think I might be hiring someone part time. I could use an extra set of hands. It's not good for business to be closing up the store every time I have to do something."

Omar grinned. "That's great, Bong! I'm so happy to hear that. So does that mean I've got an amusement park buddy now? Because I was thinking of driving out to Splish Splash in Long Island before the summer ends. As you can guess, Carl doesn't approve of water parks, either."

"What do you mean? He must enjoy seeing all the men in swim trunks," said Bong.

Omar guffawed. "Well, unfortunately for Carl, it's mostly dad bods at Splish Splash. Not enough eye candy to keep him amused."

Bong stuck out his gut on purpose, making himself look as if he were eight months pregnant. "Does this qualify as a dad bod?"

"I'm afraid so, my friend," said Omar.

Bong shrugged. "I'm guessing with my bald head *and* my gut I've probably graduated to grandpa bod by now."

"Nah. You look good for your age. Nothing wrong with a little paunch and thinning hair. It makes us more human. You know?"

At long last, they reached the entrance to the Cyclone. They handed their tickets to the attendant, then situated themselves in the frontmost seats, since nobody had taken them yet. As they began to move forward, they grasped the bar up front. The wooden slats below them creaked as the bright-red roller coaster clanged on its tracks. Slowly, they went higher and higher, and when they were almost at the very top of the highest point, they glanced at each other, eyes wide, jaws clenched, knuckles turning white as they tightened their grips.

And then, *whooossshhh!* The roller coaster dropped. Fast. Omar could feel his stomach almost leave his body through his throat and mouth. His fear turned to laughter. When he looked over at Bong, he saw something he hadn't expected to see. Bong's hands were no longer holding on to the bar; they were up high, waving around like one of those inflatable air dancers in front of car dealerships.

"Ahhhh!" Bong shouted and squealed. "Woohoo!" The expression on his face was one of complete and utter joy, making him look ten or fifteen years younger. Maybe it was the gravity pulling up his lines and wrinkles. Maybe the wind was making it look as if he had more hair. Maybe the sunlight was making his skin glow.

*Whooossshhh!*

The roller coaster hit the bottom and then turned sharply and went up again with so much force that both of their heads pulled back. Up they went, higher and higher, and when they were at the top again, Bong tapped Omar's arm, pointing toward the ocean. "Look! Isn't that Carl over there?"

Omar squinted at the dot of a human with a striped T-shirt and crisp white shorts. "It *is* Carl!"

They both laughed like a couple of hyenas, waving their arms in the air and shouting, "Carl! Carl! Carl!" as if he could have possibly heard them from all the way on the boardwalk.

*Whooossshhh!*

They dropped again, this time even faster. As Omar's body slammed into Bong's, he suddenly felt this intense desire to leave a part of himself behind, just as he hoped that Bong might leave some of his grief behind too. Except Omar wasn't quite sure what part of himself he wanted to lose. But he knew that something had to change.

Bong *had* to heal from his grief and move on with his life.

And Omar *had* to figure out where his life was supposed to take him next.

*Whooossshhh!*

One last drop and then the roller coaster slowed to a stop. The two men were still laughing, their flushed faces moist with sweat. They high-fived and clapped each other's backs when they got off. As they passed the line of people waiting to get on the roller coaster, Bong halted and said, "Thanks, Omar. I really needed that."

Omar chuckled and grinned. "You wanna go again?"

"Yes. Yes, I do."

# FORTY-ONE

*Núria*

Núria's head was pounding. She could even hear her own heart beating in her ears as she stared at her cut and bruised face in the mirror. *Great. Just great.* She'd been too reckless. Not only had she hurt herself, but she'd nearly been assaulted on the street. Had it not been for Cat and Lily, who knew what might have happened to her.

All of a sudden, her stomach dropped. What if Cat was hurt? If something happened to him, she would never forgive herself. She pushed the thought aside and bent over to splash some cold water on her face. Her head felt as if it had been filled with cement. In fact, her entire body was heavy and sluggish and sore.

*Twinkle-twinkle . . . Twinkle . . . Twinkle-twinkle . . .*

She hurried out of her bathroom and frantically searched for her phone. *Twinkle-twinkle . . . Twinkle . . .*

*Ah!* She found it under Miel's furry belly. "Um. Hello?" she said without checking who was calling.

"Nú . . ." It was Anh from work.

She plopped onto the sofa. Miel gave her a look of death for making the sofa cushions bounce. "Oh. Hey. What's up?"

She could hear the phone shifting in Anh's hand and the chaotic sounds of the café in the background. "You'll *never* guess what happened!" he said, sort of whispering and screaming at the same time.

"Harry Styles came in again?"

Anh laughed. "Well, it's not *that* good. Not even remotely *that* good. But you're kind of, sort of close."

"Uhhh . . . the health inspector came in while rats were scurrying across the counters?" said Núria, trying not to laugh because her ribs hurt.

Anh sighed like he did whenever he was losing patience. "C'mon, mate. You're not even trying." The phone shifted in his grasp again. "Fine. I'll tell you. You ready?"

Núria nodded. "I guess?"

He took a deep, dramatic breath before blurting out, "Collin Thackeray just came in looking for you!"

There was a moment of silence. Núria could hear milk gurgling and the clinking of ceramic coffee cups. "Who?" she finally said, breaking the pause.

Anh sighed again. "Collin Thackeray? The cute bestselling author guy? The one you were flirting with?"

Núria choked on her own saliva, coughing for a good minute as she tried to absorb what Anh had said. "Me? Flirting? What are you talking about?"

"It's okay, Nú. You're allowed to flirt, ya know. Nobody's gonna judge," said Anh.

"No. For real. I wasn't flirting with that guy! He just needs a bit of encouragement when it comes to ordering. You know how those indecisive people are. Annoying. Right?"

She could almost hear Anh rolling his eyes. "Okay. Fine. Deny it if you like. Anyhoo. I just wanted to let you know. But I guess it doesn't even matter since he's just another one of those annoying customers. Ta, babes! See you tomorrow." He hung up.

Núria sat there with her phone still pressed to her ear. She blinked. And then blinked again. What she hadn't fully absorbed while arguing with Anh about how she'd most definitely *not* flirted with the guy was the fact that this man—Collin Thackeray—had actually gone to the café looking for her. Why? She'd only just seen him the night before in the liquor store. She thought about it. How she'd watched him enter the store; how she'd observed what he was wearing; how she'd said hi to him, even though he'd barely spoken to her; how she'd stared at him long enough to notice something that maybe resembled a cat hair on his shirt.

*Was* she flirting after all?

*Shit.*

Never mind. She had more important matters to take care of. As much as she wanted to hole up in her apartment for the next twenty-four hours in denial, she *had* to make sure that Cat was okay.

# FORTY-TWO

## *Cat*

C at hadn't left his cardboard house except to do his business in the hedges and drink an occasional sip of water from his bowl. He was still traumatized by what had happened the night before. It was almost as if the fear and adrenaline had weakened him. The energy had been zapped from his body and all he wanted to do was sleep. Yet sleep had also been somewhat of a challenge. Every time he closed his eyes, he saw the speeding car that nearly hit him, the man who almost hurt Rainbow Lady, the girl who shouted for him as he made his escape. Just thinking about it made his heart pound inside his furry chest. His appetite was gone. Cat should have been starving. But the hunger pangs stayed away, as if they too were scared to come out. It didn't really matter, anyways. Rainbow Lady was a no-show, Awkward Neighbor Guy had rushed out of the house, and it was Cheery Mailman's day off. Nobody had been there to feed him.

Instead of roaming around trying to find something to snack on, Cat stayed put. The sounds of stroller after stroller passed by—too many to count. There were also skateboards, bouncing basketballs, squeaky sneakers, and the *tap tap tap* of high-heeled shoes. Finally, he heard familiar shuffling footsteps. Awkward Neighbor Guy was back. As much as Cat wanted to stay cooped up inside his house, he yearned for the comfort of a familiar face. He peeked through the little doorway and then sauntered over to the iron gate.

"Hey. Oh my God. Shit. You haven't been fed yet, have you?" said Awkward Neighbor Guy, slapping his hand over his mouth as soon as he spotted Cat.

If Cat could speak, he would have told him not to sweat it, since he didn't have much of an appetite anyways. Instead, he tried his hardest to make his face look contented, eyes bright, whiskers straight, ears perky as he meowed politely. Now, one may wonder what a polite meow sounds like. Anyone who has had a cat or two knows. Meows come in all shapes and sizes—screeching meows, barely there meows, short and sweet meows, hungry meows, so on and so forth. It was obvious, though, that Awkward Neighbor Guy didn't know the difference.

He hurried off toward the front door, mumbling, "I'm sorry. I'm sorry. Hold on. Don't go anywhere. . . ." before disappearing through the door, reappearing a few moments later in the side alley, his messy hair plastered to the sweat on his face.

"You want some salmon?" he said, popping open a can of food and kneeling to scoop it into his dish.

Cat sniffed the air, smelling the fishy aroma. *Nope.* Still not hungry.

"There you go. Eat up," said Awkward Neighbor Guy.

Cat meowed appreciatively and sauntered over to the food dish. He would force himself to eat so Awkward Neighbor Guy would cheer up. It was the least he could do after the guy had made such an effort to make his new digs and all. Cat owed him that much.

*Nom. Nom. Nom.* Cat gobbled the food, grumbling and groaning in between bites to show appreciation. About halfway through his meal, Awkward Neighbor Guy pulled something out of his pocket— a piece of folded-up white paper. He sighed and glanced through the gate longingly. Then he stared down at the paper again.

Cat was confused. Why was Awkward Neighbor Guy so nervous?

"Fuck it," Awkward Neighbor Guy blurted out. He stomped over to the gate, pulling it open with so much force that it almost hit the side of his house. The stomping continued all the way to the potted plants by the front steps. His hand reached for a stone, and then he backtracked over to the hedges and stood there for a good minute with a pained expression on his face. "Here goes nothing," he mumbled, bending down and placing the paper on the pavement before laying the stone on top.

Awkward Neighbor Guy wandered to his back door. Something about him looked dazed, confused, even panicked. Maybe he was sick or something. Maybe he just had to throw up and he would feel better. That's how Cat usually acted when he had a hairball lodged in his throat. A bit of hacking and then puking it up made it all better somehow. The door opened and closed. Cat was alone again.

The little bit of food he'd eaten had had a beneficial effect. He was somewhat revived. So instead of retreating back to his cardboard box, he stayed put by the gate—the inner, safer side—and continued licking his paws. He hadn't done any grooming since the previous night, and he had a lot to catch up on. He tended to lose track of time when he groomed, almost as if the licking was meditative. What felt like just a minute or two sometimes turned out to be fifteen or twenty or even thirty minutes.

*Pssspssspssspss! Pssspssspssspss! Pssspssspssspss!*

Cat halted the licking and widened his green eyes. Was that Rainbow Lady?

He poked his head in between the metal bars and stretched his neck as far as it would go. Past the hedge, he spotted the glint of a gold sandal. It *was* her! And she was okay, very much alive by the looks of it.

Excitedly, he hopped through the gate and pranced over to the hedge with his tail twitching. *Meow! Meeeooow!*

"You're here! You're okay! Thank goodness!" said Rainbow Lady at the sight of him. "I was so worried!" She kneeled on the sidewalk, trying to get a good look at Cat as he walked circles around her. When she was satisfied with what she saw, she pushed herself back up, but not before Cat unexpectedly bopped her knee with his head.

"Oh. I'm happy to see you too!" she said with a chuckle.

Cat stepped back, almost surprised by his own actions. He wasn't one to touch or be touched. But he'd been so overjoyed at seeing his person in one piece that he'd momentarily forgotten himself.

*Meow.* He went back to his usual, more bashful ways, circling her from a safe distance.

Rainbow Lady smiled at him. "You know, you didn't have to do what you did. . . . But I'm grateful. I heard you did a number on that guy. Serves him right," she said, pulling her backpack over to her chest. "I brought you some extra food and some treats. You deserve it, my little hero."

As much as Cat wanted to take advantage of the extra treats, he'd just eaten *and* groomed himself. Plus, in the back of his mind, the image of Awkward Neighbor Guy's worried frown, trembling hands, and hunched frame as he walked back into his house nagged him.

*Meeeooow!* Cat gazed up at Rainbow Lady and twitched his tail again as he trotted over to the spot where she usually fed him. She followed him with a can of cat food in her grasp, ready to serve him. But instead of meowing up a storm, begging for food like he usually did, he went over to the folded-up piece of paper with the stone on it and proceeded to swat the stone with his paw, as if it were one of those fallen acorns he liked to play with. Except the stone was a lot heavier, so he had to swat with all his might.

Rainbow Lady stared at the white piece of paper with surprised eyes. Then she looked over her shoulder before bending down and picking it up. For a second it looked as if she might open it and read it. She didn't. Instead, she stuffed it into the front pocket of her bag. Like usual, she scooped his canned food onto a paper plate, but rather than the half-can portion, she scooped out the entire can. Not only that, but she also squirted a couple of sachets of creamy treats beside the pile of food, like some sort of dessert.

"There you go, little buddy. Eat up and enjoy," she said before walking off to let him enjoy his feast in peace.

That's not what Cat did, though. The feast remained untouched. What he did was watch her leave until she was out of sight, wondering what the heck was written on that damned note.

~

# FORTY-THREE

## Lily

Lily was outside Bong's bodega, staring at the metal gate. She'd been there for a good thirty, maybe forty minutes, waiting.

Why was it closed? Weren't bodegas supposed to be open, like, all the time?

Her shoulders slumped as she exhaled. After what had happened with Núria the night before, Lily was desperate to talk to someone. Talking to her roommates was pointless. They didn't give a shit about her or her problems. The only person she could really, truly confide in was her dad. But he was gone.

Lily was alone.

There were eight million people living in New York City, yet somehow she found herself waiting for an old man who owned a bodega—someone she'd met only once. That's how sad her life had become. No friends. No family. No career.

She glanced at her watch again. *Sigh.* Maybe she should give up and try again tomorrow. But if she didn't talk to someone, the lumps in her throat, in her chest, in her stomach would niggle at her all night and she wouldn't be able to sleep. When she didn't sleep, she got dark, puffy circles under her eyes.

Lily looked at her watch again. She would give it ten more minutes. Except her feet were killing her, so she went over to the storefront bench and sat, trying not to look as pathetic as she felt. Every time a passerby would pass her by, she'd check her watch—a kid skateboarding, *check*—an old lady with her granny cart, *check*—a frazzled mom with two little girls dripping ice cream on the sidewalk, *check*.

"Lily!"

She looked up right into Bong's warm brown eyes. Except he wasn't the same old Asian man that she'd met at the cemetery. This time he looked almost clownish, as if he'd just come from a kid's birthday party. On his head he had a sort of rainbow balloon crown, and someone had painted his face to look like a jolly tiger's. Under his right arm he held a giant pink unicorn stuffed toy. And his T-shirt was stained with what looked like ketchup, mustard, and God knows what else.

Lily's face must have been contorted in shock, because Bong glanced at himself, as if he'd forgotten how ridiculous he looked, and chuckled. "I just got back from Coney Island," he explained. He hurried over to the bench and sat down next to her. "Have you been?"

She shook her head.

"It was my very first time, if you can believe it. All these years living in New York City, and Conchita and I never had much time for anything besides work, church, and taking care of our children. Such a shame. I really think Conchita would have loved it," he said.

Lily smiled and peeked at Bong shyly. "M-Maybe we could, I dunno, like, maybe we could go sometime?"

Bong patted her back. "Of course! We should go before the summer ends. Maybe your sister can tag along. What do you think?"

At the mention of Núria, her body tensed. The thought of telling Núria her secret made her want to hurl into the rusty trash can on the corner. "Well, that's kind of why I'm here," she said softly, avoiding Bong's eyes.

"Oh. Did something happen?"

Lily stared at her hands, focusing on the chipped nail polish, which she hadn't had time to fix yet. "I bumped into her last night . . . and we talked."

Bong grinned. "That's great! How did it go? What was her reaction when you told her?"

Silence.

A kid passed by, dribbling a basketball as he walked. *Thump. Thump. Thump.*

The beat was almost in sync with her heart. She could feel it thumping inside her chest. Sweat dribbled down her temples and neck. She felt so stupid. So useless.

Lily glanced up at Bong. "I-I didn't tell her. I just couldn't, you know. She was drunk, in trouble. She'd fallen on the sidewalk. So I helped her back to her apartment. It just . . . it just didn't seem like the right time," she said, cringing so hard that her eyes closed into slits.

"Don't be so hard on yourself, Lily." Bong rubbed her sweaty back with his hand, just like her dad had done whenever she was upset. "Be patient. You'll find the right time. I promise, things have a way of falling into place when you least expect it. I mean, look. We were both at the cemetery at the same time, and now we're friends. Right?"

She nodded, and the up-and-down movement forced the tears to drip from her eyes to her cheeks. "We're friends?" she asked.

Bong took his hand off Lily's back and squeezed her shoulder. "Of course we're friends. Would a stranger give this glorious unicorn to someone they weren't friends with?" he said, placing the giant stuffed toy on her lap.

She wiped the tears off her cheeks and smiled. The gesture had brought her right back to her childhood, when her dad would bring her a cute stuffed toy he'd seen somewhere. As the years had gone by, her bedroom filled with teddy bears and cats of all sizes and colors, along with giraffes and monkeys and elephants and even unusual animals like armadillos and sloths and such. In fact, they were all still in her bedroom back home, collecting dust. Well, except for Ellie the elephant—her favorite—which she'd crammed into her backpack when she moved to the city.

"Really? Are you sure? Don't you have some grandkid you'd rather give this to?" she said to Bong.

He shook his head. "Nah. I think this unicorn would very much like to go home with you."

Lily wrapped her arms around the unicorn and squeezed it. "Thanks." Miraculously, she did feel a bit better, as if the pink and sparkles had seeped into her pores and cheered her up.

"Oh, and one more thing. I have a proposition for you. But feel free to say no. It's just an idea, and it would really help me out," said Bong with a toothy grin.

She frowned, because the word "proposition" sounded so official.

"I'm looking to hire someone to work here part-time. And I was wondering if you'd be interested? I could sure use the extra help," he said.

Lily almost dropped the unicorn in shock. She'd only just met this man, and here he was, offering her a job.

"You want *me* to work here?" she said, placing her hand on her chest.

For a second Bong looked kind of embarrassed, his normally brown cheeks tinged with pink. "I know it isn't much, but as far as bodegas go, it's pretty special. The place is clean and organized and we have the best selection. Oh, and I'm a pretty good boss if I say so myself," he said with a sheepish grin.

"Oh, no. No. That's not what I meant. I'm just surprised that you're offering me a job. That's all. I practically had to beg the manager at the Foodtown to hire me," she explained.

"Well, the job is yours if you want it."

Lily looked at Bong and then at the entrance of the bodega. She really did need the extra cash. Otherwise, her roommates were going to kick her out at the end of the month. For weeks, they'd been threatening to activate the Craigslist ad if she didn't come up with the rent on time. All of a sudden, a job had fallen on her lap like magic. She gazed up at the sky and wondered if this was her dad's way of looking out for her. It had to be. There was no other reasonable explanation.

"All right. When do you want me to start?" she said.

Bong's eyes crinkled at the corners. "Tomorrow. Come by tomorrow at eight."

# FORTY-FOUR

# *Núria*

Núria managed to make it to the entrance of her building before her curiosity got the best of her. It was almost as if she could feel a radiating sort of warmth every time her bag bounced against her back. She unzipped the front pocket of her backpack and retrieved the note. Right then and there, standing in front of her building with the blur of passersby coming and going, she unfolded the white piece of stationery and stared at it.

The first thing she noticed was the logo of a tree at the very top, with *The Four Seasons Hotel, Chicago* written underneath. *Huh.* Was that some sort of clue? Or were they simply too frugal to buy their own stationery?

She frowned and then proceeded to read what was written, her eyes lingering on every single word so she could grasp their full meaning. Her head was still heavy, her thoughts foggy. So she took her time, trying to understand, to absorb, to process.

*Have you always loved cats more than people? I mean, I get it. People can be awful—so awful that most days I'd rather stay at home by myself. But I'll admit that when I see you with the cat—as cheesy as it sounds—I get a warm and fuzzy feeling. Even from afar, I can see the adoration that exudes from your eyes. It makes me a bit envious of your furry friend.*

Reading all those words, some of them so intimate, so sweet, made emotions whirl inside of her. For so long, she'd scoffed at the idea of falling in love. It was something that existed only in the rom-coms she watched. Love like that didn't actually exist in real life, did it? In real life it was about practicality. People wanted to settle down, get married, and have kids. To achieve those goals they had to find the most suitable mate. And to make themselves feel better about it, they would fool each other into thinking it was love. Núria was sure that's how it worked. After all, she'd never witnessed it in real life— not between her parents, not among anyone else in her family, not among her friends and acquaintances.

Yet, in spite of all the negative thoughts filling her already-heavy head, she found herself wanting to know more about the person who was capable of writing such words. They were words that nobody had ever uttered to her, words that really did make her wonder if love was somehow possible in the cold and cruel world she lived in.

She folded the letter and reached for her keys. Her hand trembled as she unlocked the door.

What would she say?

How would she make herself sound eloquent when she could barely write a grocery list?

As intimidated as she was, though, she was desperate to get to her apartment upstairs so she could find a half-decent piece of paper and a pen that wasn't running out of ink.

Somehow, she would have to find the right words.

# FORTY-FIVE

# Cat

Cat was tired. For some reason, saliva kept leaking out of his mouth in thin, slimy strings as he licked his fur. Now that he knew Rainbow Lady was okay, all he wanted was to curl up in his cat bed and take a nap. Strangely, he was wired, though, as if the adrenaline from the night before was still in his body. He was uneasy. Fidgety. His fur was ruffled even after his grooming.

He decided that doing a little people-watching was the perfect way to kill some time. Maybe, after an hour of observing the humans passing by, he would feel sleepy enough to turn in. Unfortunately, it was hot. Like, hot, hot. So hot that the pavement burned the delicate pads on his paws. There was a small patch of shade next to the hedge, so he planted himself there, waiting for some action.

A woman with hair the color of day-old pizza sauce walked by, pushing a stroller with one of those annoying little humans in it. The little human, who also had a head full of pizza-sauce-colored curls, pointed right at him and said, "Mom! Mom! Kitty!"

The woman halted for a moment and glanced over at Cat. "No, sweetie. That cat is dirty. Tomorrow we can visit Auntie Alice and you can play with Dorito. Okay?"

The little human squealed, chanting, "Dorito! Dorito!" as they sped off. *Humph. Who names a cat Dorito, anyways?* If Cat were given one of those green, crinkly dollars every time a person called him dirty or diseased, he would be able to buy himself hundreds, maybe even thousands of cans of salmon pâté.

He stretched his neck out and gazed down the street. Skateboarder. Kid. Another kid. A delivery guy. No, two delivery guys. Nothing all that interesting, really. Just when Cat was about to give up and slink through the gate, he saw something bright pink and sparkly headed his way. *Well, lookee here.* Finally, something worth his attention. The closer the bright-pink person got, the more fascinated he was. There was something familiar about this human. A warm breeze blew by. He stuck his nose up and took a big whiff. They even smelled kind of familiar. *Hmmm . . . Interesting.* Still, it was a big mystery, because the person's face was completely obscured by the bright-pink thing they were holding.

Who the heck was this person coming his way?

Cat was awfully confused. Were his senses failing him in his old age?

The bright-pink person was only a few feet away. He whiffed the air again. Was it Rainbow Lady? Was she already back? If it *was* her, she would surely stop and look for him. Except this person almost didn't stop. Cat meowed, but it came out sounding more like a raspy croak. The bright-pink person halted. The pink fluffy thing was lowered so Cat could finally see the person's face.

"Oh. Hello! It's you!" said the person who was most definitely not Rainbow Lady.

He squinted. There was something so familiar about her. The scent of her skin, the way she moved. Suddenly, it dawned on him. It was the girl who had helped Rainbow Lady. The girl who had shouted after him when he'd run off across the street. His heart quickened. He cowered as he considered running away to hide.

"Wait! Don't go!" The Bright-Pink Person smiled and took a step back. "I was worried about you when you ran off. . . . Are you okay? Are you hurt?"

Cat untensed his body, relaxing his guard. She seemed harmless enough. Even nice. He gazed up at her, all of a sudden curious instead of scared. She definitely was the same lady from last night, with the same kind blue eyes. But there was something else there. Something even more familiar. Something about her reminded him of Rainbow Lady. How was that possible? *Huh.* Bright-Pink Person had the same nose as Rainbow Lady. And the same lips too. Their scents were somewhat alike, except not 100 percent. The scent of rosemary and coconut was missing; instead there was a hint of apple and mint. That was it, though. Everything else was different. Bright-Pink Person turned, and for a moment, Cat thought she was going to leave. Instead, she kneeled down, reaching out to pet him. On instinct, Cat stepped back, not knowing if he could trust her. Normally, he wouldn't let anyone touch him, not even Rainbow Lady. There was something in this woman's eyes that transfixed him, though. She seemed sad and lonely and lost. Something within Cat stirred. Because he too often felt that way.

For the first time in his life, he willingly allowed a stranger to pet him. Really quick, her hand grazed his head, his neck, and then he backed off a couple of feet. The spot where her hand had touched him was warm and tingly.

"Can I tell you a secret?" said Bright-Pink Person.

Cat stared into her eyes and waited.

She smiled. Then she leaned forward just a little, puckering her lips before whispering, "Núria is my sister."

# FORTY-SIX

# *Collin*

*Ding-dong.*

Collin rushed to open his front door, not wanting to make his sister and niece wait any longer than they should. As soon as the door opened, Bernie launched herself forward, wrapping her tiny arms around Collin's leg. "Uncle Collin!"

Collin grinned. "Hello, Bernie. It's nice to see you too."

She let go of his leg and gazed up at him, her brand-new eyeglasses a bright emerald green. "Did you get the right pepperoni pizza?"

"I sure hope so," he said.

Caroline stepped forward, handing him a tiny backpack covered in multicolored sequins. "She's got a change of clothes and some books in here. I appreciate this, Collin. I *really* owe you this time."

"It's fine. Really," he said, taking the backpack.

Caroline exhaled. As usual, she was dressed simply, in a burgundy shift dress and the same pair of practical flats that she always had on. Her dark hair was pulled back in a neat ponytail, and the only jewelry she wore other than her wedding band were tiny, understated diamond studs. If he didn't know her, he would have never believed that she was married to one of the top celebrity stylists in the country.

"Hey, and thanks again for the other day. I really needed to vent. Alesha wasn't around . . . and even if she had been, well, you know. She doesn't really get the whole Mom thing," she said, pressing her lips together like she did whenever she was talking about something unpleasant.

He nodded. "I know. I know. I don't think anyone *really* gets the Mom thing, except for you, me, and maybe Dad. She's so goddamned pleasant and polite to everyone else."

Caroline rolled her eyes. "Tell me about it."

He reached out and squeezed her shoulder. "You want to come in for a minute?" he asked.

"No, I have to run. But seriously, thanks. I promise I'll be back to pick her up at eight."

"Okay. No rush. I'll see you later," he said.

Bernie looked up at her mom with wide eyes made wider by the thickness of her glasses. "Go kick some butt, Mom. Don't pick me up until you get those old people's money," she said before waltzing past Collin and into the house.

Caroline chuckled, then skipped down the stairs toward the Uber that was waiting for her.

"C'mon, Uncle Collin. Quit wasting time. I'm hungry," shouted Bernie from the kitchen.

Collin closed the door. "Hold your horses. I'm coming!"

When he reached the kitchen, he found Bernie already seated at the kitchen table, staring at the box of pizza. "I *sure* hope you got the right one. Mom told you, right?"

Collin grabbed two plates and some napkins and placed them on the table. "Yes, she did. I'm pretty sure you're going to be one satisfied customer," he said, opening the pizza box. "Well, what do you think?"

Bernie leaned in to analyze the pizza, her gaze traveling from the oozing cheese to the glistening pieces of pepperoni to the red streaks of tomato sauce until finally it landed on the perfectly blistered crust. "I approve," she said, nodding so her chin-length curls bounced. Instead of grabbing a piece like any other seven-year-old would, she pulled out a notebook that she'd been holding under her arm and proceeded to sketch the pizza, scribbling notes all over the page as if she was trying to document the moment.

"Are you going to sketch or eat?" Collin asked.

She glanced up at him for a brief moment. "I'm sorry, Uncle Collin. I just need to add a couple of notes." She glanced at the page of her notebook again, writing a couple of letters and numbers before putting it away.

Collin placed two slices of pizza on her plate. "So, what's with the notebook? Is it a diary?"

"A diary?" Bernie said, scrunching her nose. "It's not a diary. It's a journal. A research journal. I make drawings of all the interesting things I see and take notes. Lots of notes."

"That's very scientific of you, Bernie. I'm sure your moms are quite proud," he said, taking a bite of his pizza.

She frowned. "Mommy Caroline says that I need to be more selective with my observations. But I think she's just tired of buying me notebooks. This one"—she tapped the notebook on the table with the tip of her finger—"is my fifth notebook in three months."

"Well, at least now I know what to get you for Christmas," said Collin.

Bernie grinned with all of her teeth. "That would be excellent! And I like markers too. The dual-tip ones."

"Noted." Collin stuffed the last bit of crust into his mouth and picked up another slice.

In between bites of her own pizza, Bernie stared at Collin, her eyes squinting and widening as if she was trying to come to some sort of conclusion. When she had only a solitary piece of crust left, she pointed the charred tip at Collin and said, "So, are you done with your midwife crisis yet?"

Collin almost choked. "What do you mean?"

She wiped her hands with her napkin and then proceeded to flip through her notebook until she found a specific page. "Mommy Caroline and Mama Alesha were talking the other day, and I took lots of notes. I even drew a picture of you. What do you think?" she said, pointing at a doodle of a man with shaggy hair and legs that were ten times too long.

He went closer and studied the page. On the opposite corner there were more doodles that appeared to be of women running away. In between, Bernie had written copious notes in her crude, blocky hand-writing. *Midwife crises. Hermet. Lonly. Girlfriens? Maybee he needs a dog? Will he ever finis his nest book?* And at the very bottom, Bernie had written *CONCLUESON* in all caps, followed by *Uncel Collin need a waife, a dog, and to finis his nest book.*

Collin blinked. "Those are very comprehensive notes."

"Thank you. I thought so too," said Bernie, beaming at his praise.

He cleared his throat and said in a calm, not-at-all-confrontational voice, "You should know that I've had a couple of life changes, so you might want to update that journal of yours."

"Really?" Bernie stopped chewing, her lower lip dropping in an-ticipation.

"Uh-huh. You'll be pleased to know that I do in fact have a pet now. Sort of. *And* there's a woman that I like. Her name is Núria. Oh, and I've started my next book and it's going quite well!" he said with a nervous cough. That last bit was a bit of an exaggeration, but what the hell, he might as well make the story as good as possible.

Bernie frowned, her thick eyebrows knitting together into one suspicious caterpillar. "*You* have a pet?" she said, glancing around the room like any good detective would. "And what kind of name is Núria?"

"It's Spanish. Specifically, Catalan," he said defensively.

How had it come to this? He was sitting in his own kitchen, eat-ing lukewarm pepperoni pizza while trying to defend himself to his niece, who might as well have been the reincarnation of Ruth Bader Ginsburg.

Instead of replying, she opened her journal to a fresh page and furiously scribbled a slew of words, none of which he could read up-side down. She paused and stared at him with her chestnut-brown eyes. "And where exactly is this pet of yours, Uncle Collin?"

Collin wiped his hands with a napkin, then stood. "C'mon. I'll show you."

# FORTY-SEVEN

# Cat

It wasn't even dark, but Cat was already in his little house, resting. He was exhausted. Worrying about Rainbow Lady and interacting with that Bright-Pink Person had zapped all the energy out of him. Slowly, his eyelids dropped; they were too heavy. So were his limbs, which ached and felt as if they'd been encased in cement.

*Shuffle-shuffle.*

Were those footsteps? He forced his eyelids back up and peeked out of the nearest window. There were legs. More specifically, Awkward Neighbor Guy's legs, which were covered in denim rather than the usual plaid fabric of his pajamas. *Wait. Hold on.* Cat stretched his neck farther so he could get a better look. Was that a little human? What was a little human doing here in *his* alley? Were they coming to see him?

Cat had never been overly fond of little humans. But he was curious. He decided to crawl out of his house to see what was up.

"See? I told you," said Awkward Neighbor Guy, gesturing at Cat with his hand.

The little human's eyes studied him from the tips of his ears to the tip of his tail. After she got a good look at him, her gaze jumped over to his house, then to his food and water bowls. "Did you make that house, Uncle Collin?" she finally asked in a clear, high-pitched voice that reminded Cat of birds trilling in the morning.

Awkward Neighbor Guy nodded. "I sure did. What do you think?"

"I like it! But it could be more colorful. I think it needs to be cheerier, you know what I mean? I could ask Mama Alesha to bedazzle it for you if you like," she said, gazing up at him.

*Bedazzle? What does that even mean?* Whatever it was, it sounded kind of fancy.

"I think he is quite happy with the way it is," Awkward Neighbor Guy said.

Cat gazed over at his house. He couldn't agree more. The house suited him just fine.

The little human's face scrunched up like a raisin. "But Uncle Collin. How come he doesn't live inside with *you*? Don't you think he's lonely out here by himself?"

As much as Cat wasn't all that fond of little humans, he had to admit that it was pretty sweet of her to care. Perhaps not all little humans were annoying and loud and uncontrollable. This one certainly seemed quite tolerable.

Cat blinked at her as a show of appreciation.

"Well, I think he likes it out here. Plus, he's got friends who visit him. The mailman and the . . . woman, the one I was telling you about," said Awkward Neighbor Guy, his cheeks suddenly turning pink. He glanced over at the gate as if he was looking for a certain someone, most likely Rainbow Lady. His eyes widened. "Hang on. I'll be back in a minute," he said, wandering over to the gate and unlatching it.

Both Cat and the little human followed him with their gazes. When he reached the other side, he bent over and picked up a bright-yellow piece of paper that had been folded in half. He unfolded it and grinned, quickly folding it again and making his way back to the alley.

"How about I go inside and put the leftover pizza away? Then I'll make us some popcorn for the movie. You can hang out here with the cat for a bit if you like," he said.

The little human stood silent for a moment, considering what he'd said. After a couple of seconds, she pulled out a notebook from under her arm and gazed at Awkward Neighbor Guy with a grin that showcased a missing front tooth. "Is it okay if I draw him, Uncle Collin? Do you think he'd mind?"

Awkward Neighbor Guy smiled back. "Of course. I'm sure he won't mind one bit. Just make sure to give him his space. He's not used to strangers. . . . I'll call you when the popcorn is ready. Okay?"

She plopped herself on the ground and crossed her legs, placing the notebook on her lap. "Yes. And don't forget the butter on the popcorn, please. *Lots* of butter."

"You got it." Awkward Neighbor Guy hurried back inside. Only a couple seconds passed before Cat could see him watching them from the kitchen window as he tidied up.

Cat had never experienced someone drawing him before. He was quite flattered, actually. So he sat *really* still and pulled his neck out in an attempt to look as regal as possible. His eyes remained wide open to showcase their green color.

The little human sketched in silence, her marker making scratchy sounds against the paper. Once in a while, she would glance at him, as if she was staring through his soul, which frankly made Cat a bit nervous. Not once, though, did he feel scared.

A couple of minutes passed before the little human looked up with a satisfied smile. She turned the notebook around so it was facing him and said, "What do you think? It's you, me, Mommy Caroline, Mama Alesha, and Uncle Collin at Thanksgiving. You see that turkey? Mama Alesha makes the best turkey in the world. I promise you can have all you want."

Cat stared at the drawing in front of him. There was a long table, and seated around it were two women and a tall man he recognized as Awkward Neighbor Guy. At the head of the table, Cat sat at his own seat, looking as regal as he'd ever imagined. He even had his own place setting. And beside him was the little human with a fork in her hand, reaching over and dropping what looked like a big slice of meat on his plate.

At first, he didn't really know what to think. The idea of him sharing a meal with this little human and her family was quite absurd. Despite that, though, he found himself swallowing a lump that had somehow formed in his throat. He was touched by this little human's fantasy.

Was it really *so* absurd? He was pretty sure there were loads of inside cats that shared meals with their people. Yet somehow, he'd never pictured himself one of them. Not until today.

"You wanna know something?" said the little human, leaning in closer to him with an impish look about her.

Cat perked his ears up and puffed his chest out, waiting for her to spill the beans.

"*You* and *me*, we're going to be besties," she finally revealed.

"Bernie! Popcorn is ready!" he heard Awkward Neighbor Guy shout from inside the kitchen.

Before he even knew what was happening, the little human wrapped her arms around him and hugged him. Cat stiffened. But the stiffness lasted only a split second. Suddenly, his insides were warm, quickly radiating to his outsides until he felt gooey, like that melted half-eaten chocolate bar he'd once found on the sidewalk.

The little human pulled away. She bounced off the ground and waved at him before skipping toward the back door and disappearing. She was gone. Something inside Cat stirred.

Strangely, he found himself wondering when he would be seeing her again.

# Collin

Popcorn kernels, oil, butter . . . Collin fumbled with the ingredients, almost knocking the open bag of kernels all over the counter. He glanced out the kitchen window to make sure that Bernie was okay, then glanced down at the folded piece of yellow paper on the table. It wasn't a sheet of paper from a notepad, but rather a lost cat poster that Núria had recycled by writing on its unprinted back. The last thing he needed was for Bernie to draw another journal entry that featured him with bright-pink cheeks and hearts floating out of his eyeballs, so he'd decided to read it inside the house, where he could savor Núria's words without fear of embarrassment.

*Hey there. I'll be honest. I haven't quite decided if you're a creep yet. I mean, can you blame me? This city is full of creeps. In fact, just last night a creep nearly—never mind. I won't go into the gory details. But I'll say this. That black cat I feed is a fucking hero. And that there is why my eyes light up for cats in a way that they will never light up for a fellow human being. Cats are 100 percent honest about who they are. If they want to love you, they'll love you. If they want to be alone, they'll be alone. If they want to bite your foot, they will surely bite your foot. There are no mind games with cats. People, on the other hand . . .*

*POP! POP! POP-POP-POP!*

Collin glanced at the popcorn maker to make sure nothing was burning. Then he went back to reading Núria's words.

*Don't get me wrong. I know there are good people out there. Of course there are. It just seems like too much work to weed out the gems from the big pile of rocks that is life. You know what I mean?*

*POP-POP-POP-POP-POP-POP-POP-POP!*

He had to hurry. The popcorn was almost done.

*One thing is for sure, though. The qualities I value most in people are loyalty, honesty, kindness, and authenticity. If those are things that you possess, then maybe you're a person worth my time. . . . Now, I have to ask, because, well, I guess I'm curious. What exactly is it about a cat-passionate, coffee-loving, not-so-put-together almost-forty-year-old woman that you find so attractive? I'm dying to know. Seriously.*

*POPPPP!*

Collin flinched and jumped out of his chair so he could turn off the popcorn maker before the extra-buttery popcorn burned. His heart was beating so fast that he had to put his hand on his chest to calm himself. Reading her words made him light-headed, dizzy. If he could barely keep it together after reading a letter from her, how on earth was he ever going to meet her without passing out?

*God. I'm so fucking hopeless.*

But he couldn't worry about all that now. He dumped the popcorn into the giant bowl he'd purchased for such occasions, then went over to the window and shouted, "Bernie! Popcorn is ready!"

Later, he would figure out what to write back.

# FORTY-NINE

# *Omar*

It was Monday. Normally, Omar would have a spring in his step after the weekend, as if he were walking to one of his favorite merengue songs. Not today. Carl had had to practically drag him out of bed. Then they'd had another discussion about why Omar *should* or *shouldn't* quit his job immediately, so he could already enroll in culinary school. Even though it had been the perfect opportunity to 'fess up about his little white lie regarding the supposed school tour, Omar had found himself unable to. Exhaustion and frustration had caused the truth to become lodged inside his throat, as if he'd swallowed a large bitter pill without any water. Carl had slammed the door on him when he left for work, which made Omar want to crawl back into bed to sulk. Even after two coffees, he was still moving like a sloth, which wasn't all that great for a New York City mailman. Still, he had his usual visit with Mrs. Lewis to look forward to.

Before Omar knocked on her door, he heard Sinatra yapping inside. Sinatra may have been the size of a rotisserie chicken, but he sure could make a racket.

"Omar! My dear boy. I was expecting you half an hour ago," said Mrs. Lewis as soon as she opened the door. She looked more frazzled than usual. Her silver hair, which was typically braided or in an elegant chignon or in a turban, was in a loose bun with feathery strands escaping around her face.

Omar grinned. "I know. I got a slow start today. Will you forgive me?"

"Of course. Come in. I've got some tea and spiced cookies," she said, opening the door for him. Almost immediately, Sinatra hopped around like a kangaroo.

"Hey, Sinatra! You want a treat?" Omar scooped him up and hand-fed him a couple of pieces.

As per usual, she'd set up the table with his favorite tea set. From the aroma, the tea was something spicier than the usual Earl Grey. In the middle of the table was a small platter of cookies and a couple of crustless egg salad sandwiches. He sat, petting the overly excited Sinatra as Mrs. Lewis poured the tea.

"So, my dear boy. What brings you here thirty minutes late? Did you have another disagreement with Carl? Was the train behind schedule?" she asked, nibbling on a cookie as her tea cooled.

Omar shrugged and gazed down at the top of Sinatra's head. "Yeah . . . Carl is still trying to sell me the whole culinary school idea. *And* to make matters even worse, I feel like someone stuffed my pockets with a couple of fifty-pound barbells. It's just one of those mornings."

"I get it." Mrs. Lewis nodded. "But you know, my dear boy, I am quite certain that Carl means well. He clearly cares a lot about you. I think the two of you need to have a serious conversation. But before that happens, *you* need to a do a bit of soul-searching. You need to figure out exactly what it is you want in life so you can make a case for yourself."

Omar looked up and met her gaze. She was right. Of course she was right. As annoying as Carl could be sometimes, he was only trying to encourage Omar. He wanted him to be happy.

"Thanks for the advice, Mrs. Lewis. As usual, you are one hundred percent correct in your assessment of the situation. I think you may have been an advice columnist or maybe even a psychic in a previous life," said Omar with a chuckle.

Mrs. Lewis's eyebrows bobbed up and down as if she was insinuating something. "You know, a fortune teller in Poland once told me that she could see several of my past lives! Apparently, I may have been a Celtic witch at some point."

"I knew it! I always thought you had a little brujería in you, Mrs. Lewis," said Omar.

Mrs. Lewis winked playfully.

There was a moment of silence as she served him a cookie and one of the sandwiches. Omar's gaze traveled around the room, searching for his favorite antique pieces. Instead, he noticed boxes scattered around and rolls of bubble wrap and tape. "Wait. Are you getting ready to sell some stuff?" he asked.

She didn't answer right away, instead reaching out and placing her liver-spotted hand on his. "I meant to tell you the last time you visited. But it escaped my mind."

Omar tensed his jaw. Whatever it was, it sounded like bad news, and the last thing he needed was bad news to ruin his already-shitty day. "Are you all right?" he said.

Mrs. Lewis smiled and squeezed his hand. "Oh! It's nothing like that, my dear boy. Well, it is a *bit* sad. But I'm not dying anytime soon. At least, not that I know of."

"Then what? What's going on?"

Mrs. Lewis exhaled. "My daughter . . . She's finally convinced me to move to Boston to live with her. There's more than enough room for me in her brownstone. But there isn't enough room for everything in this house. So I'm packing whatever I'm keeping and the rest will be sold in an estate sale."

Omar was relieved. Still, the news made his heart squeeze in his chest. Over the years, he'd grown extremely fond of Mrs. Lewis, as if she were his own grandmother. He blinked and held back tears. "When?" he said, his voice cracking.

"Next week. I've hired a firm to take care of the estate sale. I'm flying to Boston with Sinatra so they can appraise and tag everything properly. It's going to be a mess in here," she explained.

He didn't know what to say. Instead of speaking, he reached for his tea and took a small sip. Sinatra burrowed into his lap, whining softly, as if he knew exactly what they were talking about. Omar petted him until he stopped whining, then one tear and then another dropped on Sinatra's cream-colored fur. "My route isn't going to be the same without you and Sinatra," he said.

"I know, my dear boy. I know. We're going to miss you too. You've been like the son I've never had." She squeezed his hand again. "But please come visit me in Boston with Carl. You know an old lady like me loves visitors!"

As much as Omar wanted to envision fun-filled long weekend visits to Boston to eat chowder and lobster, he couldn't help but feel a void in his gut. A void that no amount of tea and spiced cookies could fill. He looked around the room, thinking of all the times he'd sat there with Mrs. Lewis, and Mr. Lewis when he'd still been around. Then there was Sinatra, the costar of his enemies-to-friends story, his favorite dog on his route, the reason he began making homemade dog treats to begin with.

Omar sighed and lifted Sinatra to his chest, hugging him and kissing him on the top of his furry head. Had he attempted this when they'd first met, Sinatra would have bitten his face off. Now all he did was wiggle his butt and whine excitedly.

Unfortunately for Omar, his shitty day really *had* become shittier.

All he could do was wipe the tears from his cheeks, take a deep breath, and think about Mrs. Lewis being able to spend all her remaining days with those beautiful grandkids of hers. It was the kind of retirement she deserved. He couldn't help feeling guilty. Selfishness was an uncommon emotion for Omar. But losing another grandmother figure was going to be tough on him.

"I'm *really* going to miss you both," he finally said.

Mrs. Lewis leaned over and hugged him. "I'm going to miss you too, Omar. More than you'll ever know."

They remained embracing for a good minute. There were tears all around; even Sinatra belted out a couple of sad howls. After the moment passed, they parted, wiping their tears with napkin squares.

Mrs. Lewis tried to smile, but her efforts failed miserably. "Until then, we're going to have ourselves the best teas and most delicious treats every day. I want to leave you with a little bit more meat on those bones," she said.

Omar chuckled. "I don't think Carl will approve."

"Oh, you tell Carl that a soft teddy bear of a man is far superior to any chiseled, six-pack-wielding hunk. Trust me on that!"

"I will. I will." Omar stood. "I'd love to stay here discussing the pros and cons of abs, but I have a cartful of mail to deliver. I'll see you tomorrow?"

Mrs. Lewis placed a dozen or so cookies in a box and handed them to him. "It's a date, my dear boy."

Omar placed Sinatra down on the chair and left, closing the door behind him. For a moment, he stood on Mrs. Lewis's stoop, breathing the warm, humid air, taking in the view of the street where he'd delivered the mail for so many years. It wasn't just the fact that she was leaving that was making him sad. Something about the news felt like closing a favorite book for the very last time.

# FIFTY

# Collin

"Don't go to the café. Don't go to the café. Don't go to the café," chanted Collin as he sat at his desk, trying and failing to write. He was sure that the cashier guy had called Núria the minute he'd left with his revolting frappé. They probably thought he was a weirdo or a stalker or both, and if he went in there today, it would reinforce that idea.

"No. I'm *not* going to the café," he said to himself, this time with more conviction.

But he had only decaf left. If he was going to get any words written, he *needed* caffeinated coffee, something with a real kick. He could go to the bodega. Surely they had coffee there, right? Would they have the kind that Núria made, though? With frothy almond milk and perfectly roasted arabica beans and a crispy cookie to go with it? No, he was certain that bodega coffee would disappoint.

What if he went in there really quick, without saying a word other than ordering? He wouldn't even make eye contact. He wouldn't linger by the counter. It would be an in-and-out situation. That wouldn't be so bad. People needed coffee. And Núria worked in one of the best cafés in his neighborhood. It wasn't his fault that *she* made the coffee he liked best. It was harmless for him to pop in. Totally harmless.

Collin shut his laptop, ignoring the fact that he hadn't written one word. Instead, he'd spent *way* too long writing another letter to Núria after Caroline picked Bernie up. He'd dillydallied for almost an hour deciding on what stationery to use. The Four Seasons stationery had been a mistake; it made it seem like he was an elitist snob. This time, he'd used something more unassuming, yet fun—a notecard from a Museum of Natural History stationery set his sister had gifted him. After that, he dillydallied for another hour, feeling indecisive about what to say. It had been late at night when he finally shuffled outside and situated the note at their usual spot. At the time, he'd been satisfied with what he'd written. But as the hours dragged by, he'd had second thoughts and been tempted to get out of bed and retrieve the letter so he could rewrite it.

*Sigh.* He was exhausted. That coffee was really more of a necessity at this point. He would go get the coffee and be back home in thirty minutes, and then he would figure out what to write to get Quentin off his back.

He grabbed his wallet and trudged down the stairs, making it outside his front door before realizing he hadn't even considered what he looked like. He stood there on his stoop and glanced down at his outfit and shoes—khaki shorts with frayed edges, a faded Depeche Mode T-shirt with a couple of old stains, and his house slippers. If he changed into something snazzier, he might seem like he was trying too hard, so he just darted back inside, swapped the slippers for a pair of flip-flops, and ran his fingers through his unruly hair before heading out again.

Would he really be wearing an old, stained T-shirt if he was going there to see the woman he was interested in? Of course not. Clearly, Núria and this cashier guy would see his scruffy, just-got-out-of-bed look and realize he was just there for the coffee. Right?

When he reached the hedges, he glanced over for a split second. The envelope was still there under the stone. For a moment he felt his stomach drop, disappointed that Núria hadn't found it yet.

Part of him was tempted to snatch the letter back and retreat into his house where it was safe, where nobody would look at him, or judge him, or expect anything from him. But the other part, the part that so yearned to get to know Núria, forced him to leave the note where it was and trudge on.

Collin walked fast, so fast that it only took him a mere five or so minutes to reach the café. He didn't go in right away. Instead, he lingered outside, peeking through the storefront window until he spotted Núria, her eyes down as she worked.

*You can do this, Collin,* he said to himself, except in his head, the voice sounded exactly like his mom's every time she pestered him about something.

*You can sleep without the lights on, Collin.*

*You can make the lacrosse team, Collin.*

*You can get into Yale, Collin.*

*You can find the right girl and get married if you really put your mind to it, Collin.*

He opened the café door and tried his best to ignore his mother's voice. The place wasn't too crowded; there were even a couple of tables available. He approached the counter casually, standing at the end of the line, which had three people on it. From the corner of his eye, he could see Núria, ducking here and there as she crafted the beverages. He forced himself not to stare, instead looking straight ahead at the cashier guy, who now had lavender hair as opposed to the bleach blond he'd had the day before. So he wouldn't lose his nerve, he counted the piercings on the cashier's face until, finally, it was his turn to order.

"Oh, hello again. What can I get you today?" said the cashier guy with a smile that Collin could best describe as "loaded." Loaded with what, though? Slyness? Curiosity? Sarcasm?

Never mind. He was only here for coffee.

Collin smiled back. "I'll have my usual. Thanks."

The cashier guy snickered, before facing Núria and hollering, "Hey Nú, give this guy his usual!" Then he winked and tapped on the cash register with a satisfied look on his face. "That'll be four dollars and ninety-five cents."

"Uh, thanks." Collin handed him a ten-dollar bill. "And that'll be to go, please."

The cashier guy took his money and faced Núria again. "That's to go, hon!"

When Núria finally glanced over at him, she raised her eyebrows at the sight of him, the movement highlighting a greenish-yellowish black eye and a Hello Kitty Band-Aid on her face. Collin frowned, but immediately smoothed his forehead, hoping she hadn't caught his initial reaction.

*What the fuck happened to her? Is that what she meant in her letter about a creep she'd encountered?* He tightened his fists against his hips and moved over so the person behind him could order. As much as he wanted to pour his heart out to her and then ask about her cuts and bruises, he resisted. The moment just wasn't right. Instead, he faced the street, counting the passersby to distract himself. In the background, he could hear the hum of the espresso machine as it dripped coffee into the cup, the milk steamer as it frothed the almond milk, the thump of Núria's shoes as they landed on the rubber floormat, and her shallow breaths as she worked.

Collin was so angry, but there was nothing he could do but stand there like a useless oaf. Because if he said something, if he even looked at her the wrong way, his cover would be blown. And if that happened, God only knew what the consequences would be. What if she flat-out rejected him? What if she just laughed in his face? What if she was so shocked and horrified that she threw the entire latte at him, milk foam hearts and all?

"Excuse me. Here you go," he heard her say from behind. Something about her voice was forcefully chipper.

He turned around and quickly glanced at her face. It looked even worse up close; her cheek was also bruised, and she had a nasty scrape on her chin. In his mind he kept on playing out various scenarios— Núria getting mugged on the street, Núria walking face-first into a door, Núria slipping and falling in the shower . . . He tried not to dwell on that one because he didn't want to imagine her naked, except he already had. Collin's face radiated heat.

"Did you want something else?" she said, still holding his drink out to him.

Collin flinched. "Um. No. Thanks. Thanks so much," he mumbled, grabbing the paper cup before hightailing it out of there.

Outside, he inhaled deeply, which wasn't an altogether good idea because there was a garbage truck driving by at that exact moment. He gagged and coughed, almost dropping his precious coffee cup. As much as he wanted to turn back and catch another peek of Núria, he resisted. Something about the heat on the back of his head made him think that the cashier guy and Núria were already talking about him. They were probably laughing at his awkwardness, gossiping about his lack of a social life, making fun of the way he looked.

He hurried home, hoping that by the time he reached his front door, he would have calmed down enough to actually write something. Walking fast, he stared at the sidewalk and at the various kinds of footwear of the people around him. Leather clogs. Gold sandals. Neon-green Nike sneakers. More Chuck Taylors than he could count. Five minutes passed. Flip-flops. Another pair of flip-flops. Then, finally, he approached his stoop. Black leather work shoes were coming his way. Collin gazed up at the shiny brown legs, the blue shorts, the blue button-down shirt, and the USPS bucket hat that his mailman was wearing.

"Good morning, Mr. Thackeray," the mailman greeted him.

Collin halted. Suddenly, an image of Núria on a date with the mailman flashed in his mind. Had the mailman made inappropriate advances? Had Núria turned him away? Had the mailman gotten violent with her? Was *he* the creep she'd been referring to?

A surge of adrenaline coursed through his body. His face was even hotter than before, the scorching sunlight making it even worse. Collin blinked. What he really wanted to do was accost the man, shove him against the iron gate and tell him that if he ever hurt Núria again, he would beat him to a pulp. But he didn't have it in him. Collin was a pacifist, the kind of man who coaxed spiders into a cup so he could release them outside. He wasn't about to get into a fight with a dude just because he was pissed off.

"Did-Did you hurt her?" he finally said through his clenched teeth.

The mailman's smile vanished. Instead, he frowned, as if he was confused. "Excuse me?" he replied.

Collin took one step forward. "Did. You. Hurt. Her . . ."

The mailman was sweating profusely, so much so that rivulets of sweat were dropping on his shirt collar. "Hurt who? I don't know what you're talking about," he said, raising his hands as if to surrender.

"Núria. The woman who feeds the cats. Did you hurt her?" said Collin.

The look of confusion on the mailman's face disappeared, replaced with a look of concern. He dropped his hands and relaxed his shoulders. "Did something happen to her? Is she all right?"

It was only at that moment that Collin realized he'd made a mistake. Being an author made him quite observant. He silently watched people all the time, studying facial expressions and complex emotions so he could use them in his writing. The mailman was obviously innocent.

Collin backed up and unclenched his jaw. "I-I'm sorry. I didn't mean to accuse you like that," he mumbled.

The mailman still looked concerned. He wiped the sweat off his face and sat down on Collin's front steps. "Please. Tell me what's going on. Is Núria hurt? I wanted to put her in a cab the other night, but she insisted on taking the subway. She was supposed to message me when she got home, but she never did."

Collin exhaled and sat down next to the mailman. His legs were weak from the confrontation. "I just saw her at the café, and her face is bruised. She has a black eye and some cuts on her face. I just thought . . . I'm sorry," he said, looking down at his feet.

The mailman's frown was so deep that droplets of sweat were trapped in the folds of his skin. He wiped his face again, then turned to face Collin. "Wait. I'm confused. How do you know Núria? How did you even know she was out with me?"

There was an awkward silence. All Collin wanted to do was shrink and disappear into a sidewalk crack, but if there was one good thing his father had taught him, it was to own up to his actions. To be direct and honest. He sat up as straight as he could and gazed into the mailman's brown eyes.

"I saw you and her talking, flirting, taking selfies. I saw you exchanging numbers. The other night, I ran into her at the liquor store. She looked different, dressed up. I put two and two together that she was going on a date with you."

"A date with *me*?" The mailman laughed. Like, really, really laughed. Collin could even see his tonsils. "I'm gay, Mr. Thackeray. I have a live-in partner named Carl. She came over to have dinner with me and Carl, nothing more. I mean, clearly, she did have *way* too much wine and sangria. She was drunk. We all were. . . . Maybe on her way home, she stumbled and fell?"

Actually, the mailman's theory seemed quite possible. Now Collin felt even more humiliated. He'd acted like one of those dude-bro jackasses. It definitely hadn't been his finest moment. "I'm sorry—" He looked up at the mailman, trying to recall if he knew his name.

"Omar. My name is Omar," said the mailman, reaching out to shake his hand. "Are we good?"

Collin shook his hand. "Yes, we're good. I'm sorry if I delayed your route."

Omar went over to his mail cart, reaching in and handing Collin several envelopes and a couple of magazines. "It's okay, I was already running late."

Collin took his mail and pushed himself off the steps. He exhaled, relieved. "Thanks for understanding," he said, turning around so he could slink away to the confines of his house and bury his face in some leftover pizza.

"Wait."

Collin paused and looked at Omar from over his shoulder.

"So I take it you're into Núria, huh?" said Omar with a big, stupid grin.

# FIFTY-ONE

# Cat

All Cat wanted was to nap in his cardboard box house and daydream about the roasted turkey that Little Human had promised him. That morning, though, Cat heard a commotion in front of Awkward Neighbor Guy's house. Was it Rainbow Lady? Was Little Human back? No. There were men talking, and the tones of their voices seemed agitated, even raised at times. Cat mustered up the energy to uncurl his body so he could check out the situation.

What he saw was an odd interaction between Awkward Neighbor Guy and Cheery Mailman. Odd, because he'd never seen them speak to each other. What were they talking about? From where he was sitting, Cat watched their faces go from angry to confused to amused. At the end of the whole scene, they parted ways, Cheery Mailman chuckling as he walked off and Awkward Neighbor Guy shaking his head as he went up his front steps. Cat was tempted to follow Cheery Mailman to get the scoop. But the hot pavement and his lack of energy made him turn back around and go back into his little house.

He'd almost dozed off again when he heard the side door squeak open. Awkward Neighbor Guy's slippers shuffled toward him. Curious, Cat crawled through the entrance of his box and peeked outside.

"Hey, little buddy. Sorry if I disturbed you," he said.

Cat meowed softly. He tried to shake off the sleepiness, wondering what Awkward Neighbor Guy was going to say and do. For a second, it seemed as if he was going to turn around and go back inside the house. Then he changed his mind, instead hunching over and folding his long limbs until he was seated on the ground with his knees pressed against his chest. He looked like one of those sulky little kids Cat saw in the playground at the park. Not at all like Little Human, who exuded determination and confidence.

"So what am I supposed to do now?" asked Awkward Neighbor Guy.

Cat waited for him to say something else. *What is he supposed to do about what?* Cat needed more context. Though clearly it had something to do with Awkward Neighbor Guy's conversation with the mailman.

Then he sighed for so long that Cat wondered if he would ever run out of breath. When he finally inhaled, he placed both of his hands on the sides of his head and said, "Don't ever fall in love. Nothing good can come out of it."

*Love?* Cat knew that love was something people were obsessed with, especially on that one day every year when they walked home from work with bouquets of flowers and boxes of chocolate. He'd even witnessed marriage proposals, usually men getting down on one knee with panic stamped all over their faces. Though one time, he'd also seen a woman with long curly hair and a tuxedo propose to another woman in the middle of the street while cars honked and passersby cheered. Cat wasn't so sure he understood love.

Awkward Neighbor Guy sighed again. "Do you think it's humanly possible for Núria to be interested in me? I mean, you know her pretty well, right?"

*Núria?* Wasn't that Rainbow Lady's real name? Was that what this was all about? Awkward Neighbor Guy was in love with Rainbow Lady? For real?

"What am I supposed to do? She probably thinks I'm some sort of weirdo stalker, and now Omar is probably going to tell her. . . . I wouldn't be surprised if she gets a restraining order or something. God, even I would place a restraining order on myself. *Gahhh!*"

Now it all made sense. All those notes, all those excursions to the café, all the angst that Cat constantly saw on Awkward Neighbor Guy's face. He was in love, and he wasn't sure if Núria loved him back. In fact, Cat was certain that she had no idea who'd been writing the notes to her or why. No wonder humans were so obsessed with this love business. It was clearly a complicated matter.

"If only you could speak." Awkward Neighbor Guy slumped his shoulders in defeat.

What he didn't know, though, was that Cat *did* have his own way of speaking. He had an idea. Cat meowed, the kind of meow that begged for attention. He stood up off his haunches and walked with purpose, pausing at the gate so he could find Awkward Neighbor Guy's gaze. Their eyes locked. Awkward Neighbor Guy followed as Cat shimmied through the metal bars. He unlatched the gate and joined Cat on the other side. "What is it?" he asked.

In spite of the hot pavement, Cat went over to the exact spot where Rainbow Lady usually fed him. It was also the same exact spot where Awkward Neighbor Guy left her those notes. The last letter he'd written her was still there with the white stone on top. Cat tapped his front paw on the envelope, then swatted the stone to the side so it rolled several inches down the pavement. Awkward Neighbor Guy frowned and scratched his head. "I don't get it," he said, staring into Cat's green eyes.

*Oh dear. For a grown man, he sure is a bit slow on the uptake.* So instead, he trotted over to a nearby tree and picked up a fallen acorn with his mouth. When he got back to the envelope, he dropped it on top, then glared at Awkward Neighbor Guy, trying his best to telepathically send him a message.

Awkward Neighbor Guy's frown deepened. But after a couple of seconds his eyes widened, as if Cat's telepathy had finally infiltrated his thick skull. "Is that a gift? For me? A gift . . . You think I should leave her a gift? Is that what you're trying to tell me?" he said, eyebrows raised. A second or two of silence passed. Then he chuckled and shook his head. "*This* is what my life has come to. . . . Me talking to a cat about my love life . . ." He chuckled again, then looked at Cat straight in the eye. "I'm pretty sure you really have no idea what I'm whining on and on about, but thank you for the acorn. You've inspired me!"

Frankly, if Cat hadn't been so excited about the fact that Awkward Neighbor Guy had actually understood him, he would have been somewhat insulted by the insinuation that just because he was a cat, he couldn't understand. But whatever. He would have to set his feelings aside to help the guy out.

*Meow.*

*C'mon, dude. Get on with it already. Go inside your house and find something beautiful to give her. Chop, chop. We don't have all day here.*

For a moment, Awkward Neighbor Guy looked as if he was deep in thought as he rubbed the stubble on his chin. Several seconds passed, then he leaped in place and ran back into his house.

Cat waited, even though the pads of his feet were uncomfortably warm. One minute. Two minutes. Three minutes. Four. Then Awkward Neighbor Guy burst out of the front door and ran down the steps. He waved what looked to be another stone in his hand and plonked it down on top of the envelope.

Cat examined the object, which, in fact, was not a stone at all. It was a heart-shaped piece of smooth glass with a shocking swirl of colors inside. It was perfect.

"It's a Murano glass paperweight . . . I bought it for my mom in Italy, but she refused it, saying the colors would give her a headache. Now that I think about it, it was probably meant for the woman I hadn't met yet. Doesn't it remind you of Núria?" he said with a huge grin.

Awkward Neighbor Guy was actually onto something. Cat followed the bright swirls of color with his gaze, picturing Rainbow Lady in each and every swirl. There was a reason, after all, that he'd nicknamed her "Rainbow Lady."

For a second, Awkward Neighbor Guy reached out as if to pet him. But he changed his mind, instead kneeling down and staring into Cat's eyes with a gaze so warm it reminded Cat of how much he loved to soak up the morning sunlight. "Thank you for listening," he said.

Cat meowed his *you're welcome.* Then he planted himself on a shady spot so he could keep watch over the precious gift, to make sure nobody stole it. They *did* live in New York City, after all.

# FIFTY-TWO

# *Núria*

As soon as Núria got off work, she hurried to meet Rocky for an emergency friend-meet, something they did once in a while when one or the other was in crisis mode. Rocky wanted to meet at one of her favorite dive bars, but Núria wasn't in the mood for sticky floors littered with peanut shells and drunk guys telling her she'd be prettier if she smiled more. Instead, she suggested her favorite vegan bakery.

Even though she was already five minutes late, she decided to drop by to check on Cat. She was still feeling extremely guilty for putting his life at risk because of her impaired judgment. In her pocket, she had a can of his favorite salmon pâté, a plastic spoon, and a small paper plate she'd snagged from work.

As she made her approach, she made her usual *pssspssspssspss* sound. The bush didn't stir, though. She didn't hear his familiar meow.

*Pssspssspssspss! Pssspssspssspss! Pssspssspssspss!*

She shook the bushes, but still nothing.

Where was he?

Just when she was about to give up, she heard a faint meow on the other side of the bush. Cat was there, sitting primly, as if he was wondering what all the hubbub was about.

"There you are!" said Núria, relieved.

*Meow!*

She was reaching for the can in her pocket when suddenly, from the corner of her eye, she spotted a small envelope with a beautiful heart made of glass on top, its corner tucked under Cat's front paw. He didn't stir. He didn't even meow at the sight of the can of salmon pâté. All he did was sit there and stare at her as if he was trying to tell her something with his eyes. Núria tucked the can back into her pocket and picked up the heart, which was smooth and warm. She held it against the sunlight and studied the spectrum of colors inside it. It was probably one of the most beautiful things she'd ever seen. Was it for her? Had her secret admirer left her a gift? She glanced at the envelope still on the pavement. The glass heart warmed against her palm. She squeezed it and then slipped it into her pocket.

"Fuck it," she mumbled under her breath before snatching the envelope off the ground. She tore it open, carefully. Inside was a notecard from the Museum of Natural History with a kaleidoscope image of pink flamingos. She gasped. How did they know she was from Florida? She glanced over her shoulder to see if anyone was watching her. But the only one minding her was Cat, still sitting on the same spot.

"Do you know who this person is?" she asked him.

He blinked once.

She sighed. Of course he did. If only cats could talk so she could grill him. There was no point in fantasizing about the impossible. Instead, she opened the notecard to see what this mysterious person had to say.

*Are you okay? I saw the bruises on your face and the cut on your chin, and I couldn't help imagining all the bad things that could have happened to you. And then you mentioned the creep, and that made me worry even more. I really hope nobody hurt you. I know, it's strange to worry about someone you don't even know. In some ways, though, I kind of feel like I do know you. Plus, I'm just a natural worrier. My frown lines will attest to that. As much as I worry about myself, and others, and the world, though, sometimes I find it hard to do something about it, to reach out, to help others. Truth be told, I'm just too terrified to put*

*myself out there, to stray outside the comfortable little universe with the*
*great big walls I've built around myself. From your letter, I know that*
*you value authenticity. So this is me baring my real self to you. The*
*reason I've found it hard to go up to you and strike up a real conversa-*
*tion is because I'm afraid. I'm afraid of rejection. I'm afraid of letting*
*people get too close, only to lose them. I'm afraid that nobody will ever*
*truly like the real me. You asked the reason why I'm so drawn to you?*
*Well, I've given it some thought. I think it's because you are precisely*
*the kind of woman my mother would be horrified by. Try not to be in-*
*sulted. I mean it as the highest compliment. I've grown to love and ap-*
*preciate my mother, but if I'm to be completely honest, she is cold,*
*unkind, selfish, and only cares about herself, even though I've tried to*
*be a good son. For the longest time, that is the kind of woman I sur-*
*rounded myself with. But you are nothing like that. And it is those*
*characteristics—your selflessness, your generosity, your warmth, and the*
*colors you surround yourself with—that also scare the shit out of me.*
*You asked for honesty, so here it is. I hope that one day, when I'm feel-*
*ing somewhat braver, we can meet in person. Until then, please try to be*
*patient with me. I just need a little bit of time.*

She blinked. Then read the note a second and third time. So the
person *was* a guy. He sounded kind and polite. And he had pretty
much poured his heart out on the page, something she had never
experienced from a man before. *Huh.* Now she was even more intrigued.

"Do you know where he lives?" she asked Cat.

Cat was still staring at her with amused, upturned eyes.

Núria sighed. She folded the note and then slipped it into her
pocket next to the glass heart. She was late. Like, *really* late. Another
minute wouldn't really matter, though. She searched her other pocket
for a piece of paper. *Aha!* She found an old receipt. For now, it would
do. She fished for the USPS pen in her bag, then scribbled the guy a
quick note back.

*Twinkle-twinkle . . . Twinkle . . . Twinkle-twinkle . . .*

Crap. It was her phone. As usual, Rocky was probably pissed off
that she was late. She placed the receipt under a white stone that she

found nearby and hurried off down the street to avoid being murdered by her best friend.

"*Finally,*" said Rocky from the two-seater table closest to the door.

Núria jogged over, mumbling, "Sorry. Please don't kill me."

"Girl. If I was going to kill you for being late, I would have done it a long time ago. Besides, by the bruises on your face, it looks like someone beat me to it. Now sit your late ass down and tell me what in the hell happened to you," said Rocky.

The waiter, a blue-haired Peter Pan–type boy with a septum piercing, approached them. "Halloo! I'm Sage, he/them/they. What can I get you today?"

Rocky glanced over her shoulder at the pastry display. "I'll take the biggest cinnamon roll you got and a café latte with an extra shot, please."

Núria didn't even need to peruse the display. She knew exactly what she wanted. "I'll take a crème brûlée cupcake, a double-fudge brownie, and an iced oat milk latte, please."

"You want coconut whipped cream on your iced latte?" said Sage.

Núria nodded. "Yes, please."

He dashed off behind the counter, leaving Rocky and Núria alone. The bakery was tiny, with only six pistachio-green tables and pink walls with touches of gold. It reminded Núria of an ornate, pastel-hued Fabergé egg inside and out.

"So, are you going to fill me in or what?" said Rocky.

Núria inhaled, then exhaled, allowing a good minute or two to pass, as she tried to figure out where the heck she should start. "Do you *really* wanna know? Because it's honestly pretty embarrassing and kind of scary, and I really don't want to worry you unnecessarily," she finally said.

"I'm your friend. Your *best* friend. You know I'm here for the good, the bad, and the ugly," said Rocky, tilting her head, something she did whenever she was being sincere.

Núria furrowed her brows. "God, I don't know if I'm ready to be judged and lectured yet. Can we have this conversation *after* some sugar and caffeine?"

"C'mon, now. Get it over with, already. I promise, I'll try not to be too judgy. Okay?" said Rocky, pursing her lips after speaking.

Thank goodness for Sage, who came back just in time, with a tray of goodies and their drinks. He arranged everything on the table, buying Núria another quick moment to find her words.

"Enjoy!" he said as he skip-walked back to wherever he'd come from.

Núria bit into her gooey, custardy, burnt-sugary cupcake and swallowed before saying, "I got drunk. *Really* drunk. Then I face-planted on a subway grate, and some creep tried to feel me up while I was out of it."

"What? For real? Why the hell didn't you call me? Did you report it to the police?" said Rocky with a deep frown.

Núria lifted her drink, trying to hide behind it. "No. Nothing really happened. I mean, not nothing. One of the cats I feed scratched his face off and this girl who works at the supermarket helped me back to my apartment. But seriously. I'm fine."

"I mean, obviously you're fine. Look at you, you're practically in-haling that muffin," she said. "But next time your drunk ass is in trouble, please call me so I can come pick you up. Okay?"

"*Oh*-kay. But just so you know, this is a cupcake, not a muffin."

Rocky held her hands out as if to strangle her. "Argh! Same diff!"

Núria laughed, because as much as Rocky frustrated her, she also loved her to pieces. "Anyways, you'll be glad to know that I *also* have a man-related crisis—"

"Oh my God. Tell me already!" Rocky pushed her cinnamon roll aside so she could slam her hands on the table.

Núria took another bite of her cupcake, delaying her news to tor-ture Rocky just a little bit, because in true Rocky fashion, she was practically foaming at the mouth. After swallowing and taking a long sip of her oat milk latte, she finally came out with it.

"There's this guy. This new customer at the café who's been com-ing in. He's kind of weird. Not bad weird. Just kind of awkward. He doesn't talk much, but yesterday he came in and asked for me. My coworker, Anh, seems to think he's got a crush on me, but to be honest, I'm not really sure. The guy is kind of hard to read."

"What does he look like? What does he do? Give me *all* the deets," Rocky replied.

Núria stared off into the space above the top of Rocky's head, thinking. "Hmmm. I guess he's cute, in that bumbling, awkward professor kind of way. According to Anh, he's some sort of bestselling author. But who knows?"

"Ohhh. An author? Quick. What's his name?" said Rocky as she yanked her phone out of her purse.

"Collin Thackeray."

Rocky tapped her screen to google the hell out of him. After a minute, which felt like an hour, she gazed up at Núria with a look that could be best described as "dreamy." "Holy shit. He's hot! Like super hot! And he *is* a *New York Times* bestselling author. He's legit, Núria. If you don't date him, I will."

"But there's more. . . . Check this out." Núria pulled out the flamingo notecard and the glass heart from her pocket and placed them on the table.

Rocky picked up the note and read it. With each line, her eyebrows rose higher and higher. "Wait. Is this the secret admirer?"

"Yeah. I mean, I guess."

"And you've been writing back to him?" she asked.

Núria cringed and squeaked out, "Yes? In fact, I just left him a note before meeting you."

"And what *exactly* did you say?"

Núria covered her face for a couple of seconds. When she uncovered herself, her cheeks were splotchy and flushed. "I might have told him that I would *really* like to meet him . . . and that he shouldn't be afraid and to . . . like . . . come into the café. And if he wants me to know who he is, he should order a Guillermo."

"But what if someone else comes in and orders a Guillermo?" said Rocky.

Núria waved in the air between them. "I'm pretty sure nobody around here knows what a Guillermo is. It's like a super-secret cult coffee drink."

For a moment, Rocky didn't say anything. Her lips were pursed and twisted to the side as she tapped her fingers on the table. Then, all of a sudden, *wham!* She slammed the table again with so much force that some of her drink spilled onto the table. "Hold on, sweet honey child. How far exactly is the café from this note-swapping spot of yours?"

"Three blocks," said Núria.

"Oh shit!" Rocky held her hands up like she was summoning the heavens. "I mean, hello, it's obvious the man can write . . . My dearest Núria, has it crossed your mind that this secret admirer of yours and that *New York Times* bestselling author, Collin what's his name, might actually be the same person?"

# FIFTY-THREE

# Bong

Bong whistled as he restocked the soda cooler. Every once in a while, he looked over his shoulder at Lily. It was only her first day, but she had been quick to learn the ins and outs of the bodega. He'd forgotten how pleasant it was having someone else to work with, someone he could tell his corny jokes to, someone to pick up the slack when he wanted to take a break.

"You doing okay there?" he asked once the store was free of customers.

Lily smiled. "Yeah, I'm good. This register is actually easier to use than the one at the supermarket. And I like how fast all the transactions are. Gosh, you should see how slow some people are to unload their groceries. Not to mention the super-chatty customers who want to give you their life story. I really like it here, Bong."

He nodded. "Good. I'm glad. I like having you here, Lily."

The door opened and in walked one of his regulars—Freckles, the one who always asked for paper plates. She breezed past the register, down one aisle, and then down another, until she was standing right next to him. Something about her looked frazzled. Maybe it was because her hair wasn't in its usual bun; instead it was loose and wild and frizzy from the humidity.

"Excuse me," she said to him.

"Oh, hello. How can I help you?" said Bong.

From up close, she looked paler, so pale that her freckles stood out even more. Not only that—she had a yellowish-green bruise around her left eye, some cuts, and a scrape on her chin.

"Do you have anything for headaches?" she said with a frown.

"Of course. Let me show you." He gestured for her to follow him to the register. He reached for the Tylenol, Advil, and Aleve on the glass-covered shelf and placed them on the counter. "Which of these do you prefer?"

She glared at all three. "I don't know. I don't usually take these kinds of meds."

"I'm partial to Advil," said Lily, reaching for the bottle and handing it to her.

For a split second, they stared at each other. Bong glanced at Lily, then at Freckles, then back at Lily. There was something in the air between them, but he wasn't quite sure what.

"Oh, I didn't know you worked here," said Freckles.

Lily smiled. "It's my first day."

Freckles smiled back, her cheeks reddening. "Cool. I'm here all the time."

Bong watched her hand Lily a ten-dollar bill. Lily fumbled with the bill, almost dropping it. She was avoiding the customer's gaze, suddenly confused by the coins in the register. When she handed her the change, her hand trembled a bit.

"Thanks. I'll see you around," said Freckles.

As soon as she was out the door, Bong glanced over at Lily, who looked as if she might throw up. In his mind, he pictured the two women staring at each other; he imagined Lily's face and Freckles's face. Their noses, their chins, their lips. And then something hit him. He placed his hand on Lily's shoulder and said, "Was that your sister?"

Lily's eyes widened. "Y-Yes . . . that's her. That's Núria," she whispered.

# FIFTY-FOUR

# Núria

"Nú! Someone is here to see you," shouted Anh.

Núria's heart skipped a beat. Was it him? Was it Collin? She shoved the carton of oat milk back into the fridge and then went over to the register. Standing on the other side of the register was none other than Omar, dressed in his USPS uniform. Instead of his usual grin, his mouth was in a straight line.

Her stomach dropped. The sudden feeling of guilt over not replying to Omar's concerned texts made her temples start to throb again.

"Omar! What a surprise," she said with a weak smile.

Omar exhaled. "Well, I'm relieved to see that you're alive and well."

"I'm sorry. . . . I hope you're not too mad at me for avoiding your texts. . . . The last couple of days have been *a lot*," said Núria, scrunching her face in shame.

"I'm just glad you're okay. Apology accepted . . . Are you free for a quick chat and a coffee?" he said, gesturing at an unoccupied table nearby.

Núria shrugged. "Sure. I can take a break. What would you like? My treat."

His lips curled slightly at the corners, and his shoulders relaxed. "Great. I'll have a café cortado, please."

"Sure thing. Go ahead and sit, and I'll be there in a minute."

Núria made his coffee and then joined him at a two-seater by the window. "I *really* am sorry I worried you, Omar. That was really shitty of me."

"Well, I'm not gonna lie. I *was* worried, and rightfully so. Your face . . . does it hurt?" said Omar, glancing at her fading bruises and crusty wounds.

She touched the scab on her chin with her finger, as if she'd completely forgotten it was there. "No. I'm good. If anything, it's my ego that's taken the worst hit. I feel so stupid. I mean, my mom is always harping on me for not being a responsible adult. Maybe she's right."

"Oh, c'mon. Don't be so hard on yourself, Núria. Even adults can have lapses in judgment."

Núria sighed. "I don't know. You seem like a responsible adult to me. I'm pretty sure you wouldn't get drunk and face-plant on a subway grate."

"Ha!" Omar shook his head and then took a sip of his café cortado. "Actually, that's kind of why I'm here. I mean, don't get me wrong, I did want to check up on you and taste your delicious coffee. But I have a bit of a dilemma. I could really use some advice from a neutral party."

"Of course. What happened?"

Omar took a deep breath, then leaned back with his shoulders slumped. "You probably recall Carl badgering me about culinary school when you were over at our place for dinner, and me telling him that I was thinking about doing a school tour? Well, it was sort of a bit of a white lie. I-I just wanted to get him off my back, you know. . . . But the truth is that I have no intention of doing the tour. I feel really bad about lying to him. . . . I don't like to lie, Núria. It's not something I make a habit of doing."

Núria reached out and squeezed his hand. "You're human, Omar. We're all human. And humans make mistakes sometimes . . . I mean, shit. I make them all the time."

"I know. I know. But what am I supposed to do now? How am I supposed to tell Carl that I lied to his face?"

For a moment, it was silent at their table. Omar's face looked somewhat pale and splotchy as if he was already dreading having to confess to Carl. Núria, on the other hand, was slightly panicked; she wasn't exactly the best person to dole out advice. But there she was, scrambling for tidbits of wisdom to make Omar feel better. In her friendship with Rocky, it was always Rocky giving Núria much-needed advice. Now it was her turn, and she didn't want to fuck it up.

"Well . . . I'm not exactly the wisest person on the block. I mean, my own mother still tells me I act like a teenager. But I will say this. You can never go wrong with being honest about your feelings. If Carl gets mad, let him get mad. As much as you're entitled to your feelings, he is entitled to his. At the end of the day, it's your life, and you get to decide what to do with it. Carl has to either accept that or move on."

Omar stared at his hands on his lap, his forehead creased as if he was slowly absorbing what she'd said. A couple of seconds passed before he looked up with eyes on the verge of tearing up. "You're right. I guess I just need to be brutally honest with Carl *and* myself. For so long I've shrugged off his career advice with jokes. We've never really sat down and had a serious conversation about our future. I suppose now is as good a time as ever," he said.

"Hey, Nú! The espresso machine's a callin'!" yelled Anh from the register.

Núria glanced over at the small line of customers that had formed. "I've got to go." Before leaving, she stood and leaned over for a quick hug. "Good luck, Omar. Let me know how it goes. Okay?"

"I will. Thanks, Núria."

And then off she went to whip up a slew of coffee orders with a sunshiny grin. Because suddenly she felt awfully proud of herself. For the first time in her life, she'd been a good friend. She'd given rather than taken. It was an unexpected twist, but a good one nonetheless.

# FIFTY-FIVE

# *Collin*

It was a scorcher of an afternoon. Even though it was approaching five, the sun was still radiating an unbearable heat outside. Collin was in his air-conditioned study, staring at his laptop screen with a vengeance. Why wouldn't the words come to him? He had this sudden urge to pick up his beloved MacBook Air and throw it out of the second-floor window. Except he wasn't one to do anything thoughtlessly. In fact, he tended to go toward the complete opposite, overthinking everything until his head hurt.

"Ack!" He closed his laptop and got up. Maybe he just needed to stretch his legs and have an ice-cold beverage.

He headed downstairs to the kitchen and opened the fridge, allowing the cold air to envelop him as he perused the shelves. He grabbed a bottle of ginger beer and popped it open, chugging about half of its contents in one go. *Ahhh. Better.* His throat burned from the pungent ginger, but it was a good kind of burn. One that made him feel reinvigorated.

The sunlight outside suddenly shifted, pushing through his window blinds, illuminating his stainless-steel sink. If it was hot inside, he couldn't imagine how it would feel being outside, breathing the sticky, humid air. Was the cat okay? Maybe he should bring him some fresh water and check up on him. He filled a bottle with ice cubes and water and went off to the alleyway.

Just as he'd suspected, it was sweltering outside. The pavement was hot through his slippers, and there wasn't a breeze to be felt. "Hey, little buddy. You there?" he said softly as he approached the cardboard house.

Through the cut-out window, he spotted a black furry head and a pair of green eyes.

*Meow.* It was a hushed meow. Barely there. But he seemed okay.

Collin poured out the old water, which was warm, and refilled the bowl with the ice water. "You want to cool off? Come, have some cold water," he said, squatting so he could peer into the box more easily. Except the cat wouldn't budge. Instead, his green eyes watched Collin curiously.

Maybe he'd come out if Collin backed off a little. He retreated, step by step, until his back hit the gate separating the alleyway from the street. "C'mon, little buddy. Drink up. It's too hot to stay cooped up in there," said Collin.

Still, nothing happened. Maybe the cat just wasn't all that thirsty. *Oh well.*

From the corner of his eye, Collin spotted something white on the other side of the gate. Then he remembered the notecard and gift he'd left for Núria. He unlatched the gate and then hurried over to retrieve the paper with a stone on top of it. It was an old receipt. On the other side, though, she'd written her response.

> *As much as I would LOVE to be patient—patience has never been one of my virtues. I would really like to meet you in person. If you can find the courage, come by Brooklyn Brew when I'm working and order a Guillermo. I hope to see you soon! P.S. Thanks for the gift. It really, truly is one of the most beautiful things anyone has ever given me.*

What in God's name was a "Guillermo"? Collin's heart was beating so fast that it was almost worrying. His legs were suddenly weak and he felt as if he might faint. He stuffed the note into his pocket and hurried back inside, not only because he didn't want to pass out in the middle of the sidewalk, but because he was eager to Google the shit out of "Guillermo."

Collin ran upstairs to his study and opened his laptop. Once he had the Google browser open, he typed in "Guillermo coffee." Almost immediately, he found websites for coffee shops with Guillermo in their names and bloggers named Guillermo who were coffee connoisseurs. Close to the bottom, though, he spotted an article entitled "Coffee and Lime Is Quite Sublime." Collin clicked on it, and as he read, he quickly learned that a Guillermo was a shot of espresso poured over a few slices of fresh lime. *Huh.* Simple, yet unique. He laughed even though he didn't quite know why.

"Espresso with lime?" he said out loud to absolutely no one. He laughed again.

It was almost like a secret password of a beverage, something only a secret agent would use. His chest felt warm as he thought about sharing a secret with Núria.

But as much as he liked the idea, it did not change the fact that he was way too chicken to attempt such a stunt. He leaned back in his chair and tried to visualize himself marching into Brooklyn Brew and boldly ordering a Guillermo. In his mind, he was confident and witty and somewhat debonair. In real life, Collin was none of those things.

*Wait. Hold on.*

Collin almost bolted off his seat with excitement. Tweed. Coffee. A debonair secret agent. A mission. Time travel. Portals situated in coffee shops around the world. Magical cats. And a damsel in distress.

Quickly, he opened his untitled document and typed at warp speed. His creative juices were suddenly flowing and fizzing and popping like a bottle of soda that had been shaken and then opened. It had been so long since an idea had fully formed in his head. Adrenaline was coursing through his body, his heart thumped inside his chest, and his fingers stabbed the keyboard as if his and the entire universe's lives were on the line.

## FIFTY-SIX

# Omar

"What do you mean you didn't schedule the school tour?" Carl demanded, his blue eyes bulging from their sockets.

Omar, who was seated on the sofa, hung his head low, as if he was trying to curl into himself and hide. "I'm sorry, Carl. I know you're disappointed. But I *did* say I was just thinking about it. I never made any promises."

"Oh, c'mon! Be honest with me. Were you ever *really* thinking about it? Or were you just trying to get me off your back?" Carl leaned on the windowsill with his arms crossed against his chest. "Because I'm starting to think it was all a lie. And you *know* I don't like lies, Omar."

"Okay. Fine. I lied. Is that what you want to hear? But you didn't exactly give me much choice, Carl. . . . You don't listen. Culinary school isn't for me. Starting a restaurant is your fantasy, not mine. But every time I say that, you just shrug and dismiss me," said Omar, rubbing his temples. His head was starting to throb.

Carl exhaled and stared at the floor. "This is meant to be a partnership. We're supposed to grow together. But how can we grow together when you can't even decide on a more meaningful career? Can you really see yourself delivering mail in your fifties or sixties? Is that what you're envisioning for the rest of your life? For the rest of *our* lives?"

"Would that be so bad? Or is it not part of your plan to turn us into the ultimate Brooklyn power couple? Is that what this is, Carl? I'm not fitting into your Pinterest board?" said Omar, snapping his back straight and glaring at him.

Carl touched his cheek as if he'd been slapped. "That hurts, Omar. Is that what you really think of me? That I'm some vapid social climber? Do you really think I would have *ever* gone out with you if that had been the case?"

Omar flinched. There it was. The truth bomb. Carl was embarrassed to have a mailman for a partner.

The room was dead quiet, like they'd both spewed out so many words that they'd run out. Minutes passed before they finally found each other's eyes across the room. They'd been together long enough to know that for the moment, there was nothing more to say. Omar could not change Carl's mind. And Carl could not change Omar's mind. They were at an impasse.

"I need time to think. I'm going to go stay with my brother for a while. We can talk in a couple of weeks." Carl uncrossed his arms and headed to the bedroom to presumably pack a duffel bag full of his stuff.

Omar stood and opened his mouth, but nothing came out. He wanted to protest, to stop Carl from leaving. But he also knew that they both needed some space to re-evaluate their relationship and decide if they really, truly had a future together. All he had left in him was to go to the kitchen and pour himself a shot of bourbon. He kept on pouring, tears streaming down his cheeks, mixing with the bourbon as he swallowed.

The sound of the front door opening and then closing echoed from the other room. Carl had left without saying a peep. Not a *goodbye*. Not a *see you later*. Not even a *take care* from the one person who was supposed to love him.

How had his life taken such a shitty turn?

One day they were joking around and flirting over coconut shrimp and margaritas, and the next, they were fighting. Now Carl was gone.

Omar was alone in their one-bedroom apartment, listening to the refrigerator hum while he drowned his sorrows.

As the bourbon burned his throat, he closed his eyes and tried to envision himself in a restaurant kitchen, wearing a white chef's coat, steam billowing around him, the sounds of frying in the background, line cooks shouting at one another as plate after plate of food was handed over to runners. Even though it was merely a vision in his mind, he could feel the stress and anxiety coming on. He could feel his shoulders tense, his hands curl into fists, his jaw clench on reflex.

He poured himself another shot and chugged it in one go.

No. The restaurant life wasn't for him. It just wasn't. Mrs. Lewis was right. So was Núria. It was his life, after all.

Sure, he wanted a change in career. Sure, he wanted to find something more meaningful, more gratifying. Sure, he wanted to be more successful, and make a better income. There was something else out there for him. With time, he knew he would find it.

He just hoped that Carl would still be there for him when he figured out what it was.

# FIFTY-SEVEN

# *Lily*

Lily had just finished stocking the chip section when Bong walked in holding a bunch of shopping bags. "Good afternoon, Lily." He looked at his watch and then at Lily. "Oh, well, it's almost six, so I guess it's more like good evening."

She wiped the sweat off her forehead, then exhaled. "Hey, Bong. Are you sure there isn't anything wrong with the air-conditioning? I swear, I think I've lost a couple of pounds since my shift started. . . . I had no idea it could get this hot up north."

"Ha! You haven't experienced heat until you've lived through a Philippine summer. This is nothing."

Lily raised her eyebrows. "Uh. I think I'll take a pass on that."

Bong went over to the register and pulled out a clipboard and some envelopes from a drawer. "Why don't you take off a bit early and get yourself a frozen treat? There's a wonderful ice cream parlor just around the corner."

"Oh. I can't afford any fancy ice cream right now," she said with a frown.

He grinned and handed her one of the envelopes from the counter. "Sure you can. Go on, live a little."

The envelope was plain and all-white except for her name, which was written on it in cursive. "What is it?" she asked.

"It's an advance on your salary. I figured you would need it to pay your rent on time," said Bong.

Lily's eyes widened. *"Really?"*

He shrugged. "Sure. I know it's hard to imagine, but I was young once. I remember what it's like to struggle from paycheck to paycheck."

"Thank you, Bong. You're a lifesaver. For real." She reached out and took the envelope from him. "Are you sure you don't need me to stay and help out?"

"I can handle the rest. Don't worry. Besides, I'm closing up early today," he said.

Lily retrieved her purse from behind the counter. "I'll see you to-morrow, then. Have a good night, Bong." She waved, then hurried through the door. Her mind was whirling at the fact that she would *finally* be able to pay her rent on time. What a relief! It really did feel as if she'd lost some weight; her shoulders were lighter, and suddenly, she had a spring in her step.

*Ooofff.* Except she crashed face-first into someone. She'd been so ecstatic that she hadn't seen the customer coming inside at the same time as she'd been exiting.

"Oh. Hi, Lily! I was just coming in to buy a popsicle. Maybe a whole box, if this heat doesn't let up," said Núria.

Lily could feel her heartbeat quickening. The lightness she'd felt moments ago was gone. "Uh. Yeah. I know. Tell me about it. I-I was just going to get some ice cream. You know, to cool off," she blabbered.

"You want some company? I could go for some vegan chocolate-peanut-butter-cup ice cream and a freshly made waffle cone dipped in dark chocolate and sprinkles. There's a place nearby that has it," said Núria.

"Sure. That-that would be nice," replied Lily.

So off they went down the street, strolling side by side.

Hopefully, Núria hadn't noticed her hands shaking. She was nervous. Because it was the very first time that she and her sister would be going out together on purpose. Like a date. A sister-date.

The *Ice Cream, You Scream* server, who resembled a tattooed Dr. Seuss character, held out Núria's giant waffle cone with three scoops of ice cream. "Here's your vegan chocolate-peanut-butter-cup ice cream with chopped pecans, and of course, our house-made vegan chocolate sauce, *and* vegan whip on a waffle cone. Enjoy!" he said, handing it to her.

Núria grabbed it, immediately sticking her tongue out to taste a dollop of the chocolate-sauce-drizzled whipped cream. "Yummm."

"What can I get for you?" he said to Lily.

"I'll have the vanilla soft serve with sprinkles, please," she said, pulling her wallet out.

Núria pushed her wallet away. "No. The ice cream is on me, as a thank you for helping me out the other day."

"No. I got it. Bong just gave me my first paycheck, so I'm not feeling *quite* as poor," said Lily with a chuckle.

"All right, all right. But come by Brooklyn Brew for a coffee on me anytime. Okay? I seriously still owe you for helping me peel my face off the subway grate."

Lily nodded. "It's a deal." She opened her wallet and reached inside for a twenty-dollar bill.

Unbeknownst to her, Núria was peering over her shoulder as she licked away at her cone, which was already starting to melt. "Wait. Is that you?" she said, peering even closer at the old photo that was inside Lily's wallet. The photo was of a little girl with pigtails next to an older man.

Lily flinched and fumbled to hide the photo. It was too late, though. Núria had already gotten a good look. "Y-Yes . . . that's me . . . and . . . and . . . my dad."

It was quiet. Too quiet. Lily could hear Núria's shallow breaths behind her as she stared at the photo, which Lily was no longer hiding.

"Here's your vanilla soft serve with the *best* sprinkles in town." The server handed Lily her ice cream with a smile.

She took it and gave him the money in return. "Thanks, keep the change."

That's when Lily turned around to face her sister.

Núria's hazel eyes darkened, her jaw tensed, the waffle cone in her hand was completely forgotten. She parted her lips and whispered, "Your dad . . . He looks an awful lot like *my* dad."

"Let's go to the bench outside." Lily led the way. Her heart was beating fast and hard; she could practically feel her chest contracting to the beat.

Thankfully, the bench outside was empty. They sat beside each other, leaving a noticeable gap between them. For a good minute, neither of them said anything. Lily cleared her throat, finally finding the courage to explain herself.

"I don't really know what to say . . . where to start," she mumbled, staring at her uneaten ice cream cone to avoid Núria's gaze.

Núria leaned forward, seemingly desperate to look straight into Lily's eyes. "Start at the beginning. *Please*."

"I'm sorry, Núria. I'm so sorry. I-I should have told you. I just didn't know how and when." Lily opened her wallet and held it out so Núria could see the photo more clearly.

"Your father . . . he met my mom in Florida. And then she became pregnant with his baby, but she ended up having a miscarriage. The doctors said she might not ever get pregnant again. I think your dad . . . *our* dad felt sorry for her. He just couldn't leave her after that. . . . They moved to Georgia for a fresh start. And then, many years later, by some miracle, I was born. I'm so sorry, Núria. I only found out about you when he died last year. I stumbled on a photo of you and him and your mom when I was looking through his stuff. I know I should have told you sooner. But I was just waiting for the right time."

Núria sat there silently, the chocolate-peanut-butter-cup ice cream dripping from her fingers to her hand to her wrist. Except she didn't even seem to notice, because she was staring at the photo so hard that she wasn't even blinking. "He died?" she uttered softly.

"Yes. Over a year ago. In a car accident. I'm sorry you didn't know," said Lily.

Tears began falling down Núria's cheeks as she processed everything that Lily had just told her. "All these years, I didn't know why he left, where he was. In my mind he was already dead," she whispered. "He was alive the whole time?"

"I-I'm sorry." Lily heaved, trying to get a breath. They were outside, yet it felt as if there was no oxygen in the air around them. "I'm sorry, Núria. I'm sorry that you had to find out this way. I can't change what happened. I wish I could . . ."

"Stop saying you're sorry!" Núria shouted and then stood, her brow furrowed, skin splotched with red. "All along, I thought you were kind for helping me . . . a supposed stranger. But I was wrong. *So* wrong. You've been watching me this whole time, haven't you? Like a sicko stalker. Were you ever going to tell me the truth? What the fuck, Lily!" She tossed her ice cream cone in the trash. "I can't look at you right now. I can't. I just can't. I-I need to think. This is all too much." Then she took off, running down the street without looking back.

Lily was left behind, speechless.

# FIFTY-EIGHT

# Núria

Núria was face down on her pillow in an attempt to muffle her crying. On either side of the pillow were Gazpacho and Miel. Churro was trying but failing to burrow into her armpit.

*Meeeow!*

Churro dug into the sheet underneath her arm, trying to make space for his furry body to crawl through. She sniffled and then lifted her arm, allowing him to nestle in beside her. "I wish I were a cat. Life would be so much simpler," she said, hugging him as she wiped the tears and snot off her face.

Churro gazed at her with his orange-yellow eyes and then licked her shoulder as if to comfort her. It worked. Núria scooched up onto the pillow, taking a deep breath to calm herself.

Except she couldn't stop picturing the photo from Lily's wallet. Her father, a version of him she'd never seen before—older and with a mustache. His arm had been around Lily's shoulders. Núria couldn't help but feel a pang of jealousy. Had he just replaced her with another daughter? Had he been that unhappy?

Oh, how she wished she could ask him all these questions. Her entire life she'd wanted answers, but she'd never gotten any. Now it was too late. He was gone.

Lily was lucky. She'd had him in her life for seventeen or eighteen years. Her memories were plentiful and vivid, unlike Núria's, which were mostly faded, only resurfacing on special days like her birthday or Christmas or Halloween to cause her pain all over again.

She was mad and sad and jealous. But was there also a part of her that was happy? Or at least hopeful? Never in a billion years had she expected a long-lost sister to turn up in her life. When she was a teenager, the thought had crossed her mind; she had often imagined that her father had another family that he had created somewhere far, far away. But she'd convinced herself that if that were true, he would have found a way to let her know that he hadn't forgotten her. Maybe he'd been whisked away into the witness protection program. For Núria, that had been easier to think about than accepting that her father had just walked out of her life without ever looking back.

And then, *bam*! Lily had appeared. A sister. She could hardly believe it. All these years she had lived as an only child, and Lily had been somewhere out there. She might have lost her father, but she'd gained a sibling—one who'd presumably traveled all the way to New York City to find her.

When it rained, it sure did pour.

Núria's once-simple and relatively uncomplicated life had been turned upside down.

She glanced at her phone on the bedside table and furrowed her brows. A minute passed. Then she reached for it, swiping it so the wallpaper photo of the ingrates lit up. Another minute passed. Was she going to regret this? Perhaps. But she had so many questions . . . *Fuck it.* She opened her contacts and tapped her finger on the screen before she could change her mind. Only a second had gone by—she hadn't even had enough time to put the phone to her ear—when her mom's voice, shrill and loud, said, "Oye, qué pasó? Are you hurt? Are you in the hospital? Do I need to get on a plane to New York?"

"Mom, I'm fine. Well, sort of . . ." said Núria with a long exhale.

There was a whole bunch of shifting and footsteps and doors opening and closing on the other end before her mother replied, "*Sort of? Qué significa eso?* I don't understand, mija. You're either fine or not fine."

It was silent. Núria blinked, staring into the air as she pictured the photo of Lily and her dad. "Did you know?" she whispered.

"Núria, what do you mean? Did I know what? Dígame!" exclaimed her mom.

"Did you know about Dad . . . and-and . . . his other family?"

She heard her mom gasp. The phone must have slipped from her mother's hand, because she heard a long sliding sound and then a thud. "Mom! Mamá!" she shouted, hoping she hadn't fainted and hit her head. "Mamá!"

"Estoy bien. I'm here," her mom finally replied after picking up the phone. "How-How did you find out?"

"So you *knew*?" asked Núria.

Silence.

Then her mom breathed in, wheezing as if she was about to cry. "For years I didn't. . . . In fact, well, I knew nothing about what became of him and *that* woman, and I made sure he couldn't find us. That's why we moved. And I never filed for a change of address. Our phone number wasn't listed, either. I didn't want to have anything to do with your father. I needed to forget him. It was just too painful, mija. . . . But then, after you left college and moved to New York, I ran into Sandra, you remember, she used to work with your dad . . . She told me—she told me they'd gone to Atlanta to visit family, and by chance, they ran into your father, and-and his new wife. They had a baby. A baby girl . . ."

Núria clenched her jaw. "Why didn't you tell me?"

"You were all grown up, mija. You had moved on. You had your own life. I wanted to protect you. I didn't want you to get hurt all over again. I'm sorry. . . . Maybe I *should* have told you. But-But I just did what I thought was best for you. . . . You always loved your father so, so much. I didn't want your heart to break all over again. I'm sorry." Her mother sniffled and wheezed. It was obvious she was crying and having a hard time catching her breath.

Núria didn't respond right away. She didn't know what to say. She didn't even know what to think. Had her mom done the right thing? Would it have been better to know? To have been able to keep in contact with her dad?

"Te amo, mija. I only did what I did because I love you. . . . Please don't hate me," her mom said softly.

"I don't hate you, Mom." Núria sighed. "I'm angry and disappointed and confused. . . . Lily . . . my sister. She came to New York to find me. I met her. She had a photo of her and Dad. . . . Did-Did you know he died?"

"No! Of course not."

Núria wiped the tears that suddenly dribbled down her cheeks. "I just don't know what to do."

"He's gone, mija. There's nothing you can do to change that. . . . But I guess you have a sister now. If there is one good thing to come out of what your father did to us, maybe this is it. Do what's right for you, mija. If you want to get to know her, to have a relationship with her, then don't let me stop you. You're an adult now. Make your own decisions, whether good or bad. And I'll be here anytime you need to talk. Okay?"

"Okay. I guess I have a lot to think about," Núria said.

"I love you, mija."

Núria's chest tightened. Her stomach was queasy. Her head hurt. "I have to go, Mamá. I need to lie down."

"I'm here if you need anything. I'll call you tomorrow," her mom said.

Núria hung up, feeling scared, relieved, sad, happy, and excited all at once. It was overwhelming.

*Meeeow!*

Churro gently pawed at her face. On either side of her head, Miel and Gazpacho were curled up sleeping. She inhaled and exhaled and tried her best to be in the moment. It was quiet. Her cats were snuggled nearby. The bedsheets were freshly laundered.

*Breathe in. Breathe out. Relax, Núria.*

Núria plopped down on her pillow and scooched to the left so she could bury her cheek in Miel's fur, which smelled curiously of coffee.

She smiled and relaxed, feeling herself being pulled into a dark, velvety slumber.

Later, she would figure out how to make sense of the chaos around her. First, she would rest.

# FIFTY-NINE

# Bong

It was Conchita's birthday. Bong had expected to feel all kinds of sad, but surprisingly, he'd woken up that day feeling joyful. Birthdays had always been celebrated simply in their household, with good food, cake, and small, meaningful gifts. Conchita hadn't been one for excess; she'd scoffed at fancy parties and luxury items, preferring intimate gatherings and tokens of love.

Good thing he had Lily to work at the bodega now, because it had given him some time and freedom earlier in the day to go shopping for his beloved. He'd known exactly what to buy to commemorate her sixty-eighth birthday, and he'd known exactly what she would have wanted to eat too. He'd spent the afternoon taking the subway into Manhattan to visit one of her favorite stores, and when he'd finished with that, he'd taken another subway to Queens to pick up some Filipino takeout from Renee's. When he'd returned to the bodega, he'd been in such a good mood, he'd insisted Lily take off early, even if it meant he'd have to do all the restocking and cleaning all by his lonesome self. No matter. There was still plenty of time to do everything he needed to do, before closing up early so he could celebrate his beloved, Conchita.

After he finished closing up with the register and locking the doors, he went to the back of the store and climbed the stairs to his apartment. When he reached Conchita's altar, the first thing he did was light the candle and kiss her portrait. "Happy birthday, mahal!" he said with a smile, knowing that somehow she would hear him. Then he placed a blue shopping bag on the table and opened it, bringing out the box that was inside. Thankfully, there was an empty spot next to the crystal lovebird figurines. Bong lifted the lid of the box, then picked up the blue velvet pouch so he could take out what was inside it.

The Swarovski cat glittered under the light. Its stance was playful, swatting at a red crystal ball. He situated the cat beside the lovebirds. It was perfect. If Conchita had been with him, she would have cooed with joy.

"I know you always wanted to add a cat to your collection. Isn't he beautiful?" said Bong.

Of course, Conchita didn't reply. Yet he knew exactly what she would have said: "*Bong. Mahal. You shouldn't have!*" Except her eyes would have been saying something completely different; they would have sparkled as brightly as the crystal itself.

Bong pulled up a chair and opened up another bag. Inside was a container of Conchita's favorite pancit palabok and two other containers, one with lumpiang Shanghai and another with ube and pandan biko. While he ate, he told Conchita stories about Lily, Núria, Itim, Omar, and the various regular customers she was familiar with, basically everything that had happened and was happening. It had been their tradition to tell each other interesting tidbits of their days as they ate dinner. Bong didn't see any reason why the tradition should stop.

When it came time for dessert, he pulled out a single pink candle from his pocket and stuck it into one of the sticky rice desserts. He placed the container on her altar, then lit the candle so he could sing to her.

*Happy birthday to you! Happy birthday to you!*

If she'd been seated across from him, she would have covered her face in embarrassment, only to uncover it when it was time to blow.

"Make a wish!" he said before bending down to blow out the candle himself.

*Knock, knock, knock.*

Bong frowned. Who could be at the door? The only way to enter his unit was through the bodega, so whoever it was would need a key. Unless, of course, someone had broken in. But then, why would they knock?

"Who is it?" he shouted.

*Knock, knock, knock.*

Slowly, he approached the door. He didn't have a peephole, so instead, he secured the door chain, then opened the door a crack. It was Lily, standing there with red-rimmed eyes.

"Lily, what's the matter?" he asked as he unlocked the door and swung it wide open.

She didn't say anything. All she did was fall into Bong's chest and cry.

# SIXTY

# Omar

Omar wiped the sweat off his forehead before opening the gate to Mrs. Lewis's brownstone. He parked his cart by the stairway and climbed the six steps to her front door.

*Yap! Yap! Yap! Yap!*

Omar chuckled, even though he was still pretty down about Carl having temporarily moved out. If anyone could make him smile, it was Sinatra. The door opened and the dog ran out so fast that he was practically a blur.

"Good morning, Omar. As you can see, Sinatra has been waiting for you," said Mrs. Lewis with a smile.

"Good morning, Mrs. Lewis. And good morning to you too, Sinatra." Omar squatted close to the floor and gathered Sinatra into his arms so he could hug him. "I suppose you want some treats, huh?"

*Yap! Yap!*

Sinatra hopped up and down as Omar pulled out two dehydrated liver treats from his pouch. "Here you go, my man," he said, holding his palm out.

"I've got some rooibos tea and some cinnamon cookies for us today." Mrs. Lewis opened the door so Omar could go inside.

Omar followed her into the sitting room. The house was an even bigger mess than it had been the last time he'd been in there. Almost everything had been taken down and covered in bubble wrap or placed in boxes. Rugs had been rolled up and most of the furniture was wrapped in fabric, except for the table and chairs where Mrs. Lewis had set up their usual spread.

He didn't want to upset Mrs. Lewis, but seeing the contents of her home being prepared for moving and selling made him nauseated.

"Sit, my dear boy," she said.

Omar did as he was told, picking Sinatra up so he could place him on his lap. Mrs. Lewis poured the tea, then served Omar two cinnamon cookies on a plate.

"Thanks, Mrs. Lewis. It looks delish, as usual," said Omar, biting into one of the cookies. It was then that he noticed she had set up a different tea set than their usual. This one was a white bone china set with touches of gold around the bouquets of painted pink roses. "Oh, have you already packed the other tea set?" he asked.

Mrs. Lewis nodded. "This one is my backup set."

He tried not to look disappointed, but he couldn't help the lump that had formed in his throat.

"Omar. You're looking a bit down this morning. Is anything the matter?" Mrs. Lewis reached over and squeezed his hand.

Somehow, she'd read his mind yet again. *Brujería*, he thought to himself.

He sighed. "It's Carl. He's moved into his brother's place to give me some space. He thinks I need to be on my own for a while to think about my future. Our future."

Mrs. Lewis squeezed his hand again. "I'm going to dole out a bit of tough love, my dear boy. I think Carl is absolutely right! There is nothing wrong with a little time apart, especially if it'll help you clear your mind. Did I ever tell you that Stanley and I separated for two whole months, way back when he was just starting out his antiques business? Being apart not only gave him time to focus on work, but it also fortified our love for each other. Not one day went by when I didn't miss him. And when we did get back together, our relationship was stronger than ever. Take this time to work on yourself, Omar. You deserve to be just as happy and fulfilled with your career as Carl is."

Omar blinked and wiped the single tear that was threatening to come out of his left eye. "But what if we grow apart? What if I lose him?"

"That is, of course, a possibility, my dear boy. There are never any guarantees . . . but I have a feeling you'll both work it out. Just try to have faith in the process. Okay?" Mrs. Lewis squeezed his hand one more time and then let go.

"I'll try, Mrs. Lewis, I'll try," he said, focusing his gaze on his tea-cup so he wouldn't cry.

Mrs. Lewis scanned the messy room and exhaled. "Well, I'm afraid this might be our last tea party for a while. This place is such a ter-rible mess. My daughter got me a ticket to fly out to Boston tomor-row."

She reached over to the other side of the table and took hold of a brown box with a fragile sticker on it. "I want you to have this. It's just a little something to remember me by. I *sure* am going to miss our little chats. And I know Sinatra will miss them too. You are pretty much his favorite person. He might even like you more than he likes me!" she said with a chuckle.

Omar held his surprise in. "Thank you, Mrs. Lewis. This mail route isn't going to be the same without the two of you. I might really have to quit and find myself another job," he said.

Mrs. Lewis sipped her tea and nodded. "You *are* destined for greater things, my dearest Omar."

"I don't know, Mrs. Lewis. I just don't know. It's scary out there. This job, it pays pretty well, and the benefits are good. I'm not sure if I have it in me to start something else from scratch," he said.

"Of course you do. You're young! You have all the time in the world! I've had three careers in my lifetime. Trust me. It's never too late to find out where your true passions lie. You'll find your way soon enough."

Omar reached out and squeezed her hand. "Okay. If you say so, Mrs. Lewis."

"Now, take your gift and get going. You have an entire life ahead of you to plan out. But before you go, I want you to give this old lady a great big hug. One that's going to last me until the next time we see each other."

Omar only nodded. He was afraid that if he said anything, he would break down and cry.

Mrs. Lewis packed the rest of the cookies into a pastry box and placed it on top of the mysterious, fragile brown box. "Come on. I'll walk you out."

Mrs. Lewis linked her arm with his and they walked to the door together. "Thank you, Mrs. Lewis. Thank you for being my work grandma. I'm really going to miss you," he said, the tears finally gushing from his eyes.

"Oh, my dear boy. You take care of yourself, okay? And please, come visit me in Boston. I heard Thanksgiving is pretty nice up there," she said with a wink.

Omar grinned. "Thanksgiving in Boston. You got it, Mrs. Lewis."

"Now, give me that hug you promised me," she said, dabbing her eyes with the tips of her fingers.

Omar put the box down, then leaned in to wrap his arms around her narrow, bony shoulders. She wrapped her arms around his waist, resting her head right on his heart. "I fully expect you to call me once in a while. I want updates, *and* I want all the gossip from the block. Promise me."

He sniffled. "I promise."

*Yap! Yap!*

Sinatra bounced and hopped and ran around their legs as if he was feeling left out. Omar chuckled in spite of the heavy heart that sat in his chest. He pulled away from Mrs. Lewis and bent down to give Sinatra a proper goodbye. "Let's do one more for the 'gram, shall we?"

*Yap!*

Omar pulled out another liver treat. Sinatra stood on his hind legs just as Omar pulled his phone out for a selfie. "Say liver, Sinatra!"

All day, Omar had been eager to open the package Mrs. Lewis had given him. But he'd held out, until after work. For whatever reason, it had felt like something he should do in the privacy of his own home, in case he lost control of his emotions. So he'd been patient and waited.

Finally, he was alone in his tiny kitchen. The box was already on top of the two-seater table where he and Carl usually had breakfast. It had been there unopened for a good hour. Omar had been afraid to open it, as if opening it would finally make Mrs. Lewis's move feel real. There was a piece of her life in that box and discovering its contents would make it feel like she was really, truly gone.

But Omar knew that he couldn't leave it sealed forever. He had to grieve, to move on with his life. Carefully, he pierced a knife through the taped-up opening and dragged it to the other end. The top popped open, revealing a mountain of bubble wrap.

He breathed in and out and then pulled out one of the bubble-wrapped items, unwrapping the multiple layers until it revealed itself to be a teacup. Not just any teacup. It belonged to the green-and-gold porcelain Sèvres tea set that Mrs. Lewis had used for their tea and pastry get-togethers. That's when he lost it.

Tears gushed from his eyes. He put the precious cup down on the table so he could sit and have a good cry. His abuela had always said that crying was like detoxifying your soul. It was better to let all your sadness out than keep it bottled up inside.

Unlike his abuela, Mrs. Lewis was still alive and well, yet he mourned the loss of her. Boston may not have been all that far, but it just wouldn't be the same. He couldn't hug her, or hold her hand, or smell the sage-and-pear scent of her favorite perfume. Her stories and jokes and words of wisdom wouldn't fill his mornings any longer. He wouldn't be able to taste her aromatic tea blends or sample her delicious pastries, which were better than any he'd ever had.

Omar wiped his tears with a paper towel. Then he unpacked every piece of the tea set until it was displayed on the table in all its glory. He couldn't believe she'd given it to him. His eyes stung. He wanted to celebrate her gift. To celebrate and honor *her*. What better way was there to do that than to brew some tea?

In his cupboard there was a very special box of Silver Tips Imperial tea that Carl had brought back from a work trip to India. He searched for the green tin, then set some water to boil in his kettle. While the water heated up, he set all the bubble wrap and cardboard aside and arranged the teapot and one tea setting for himself. It was nothing fancy. There wasn't a bouquet of fresh flowers, or a delicate tablecloth, or a silver tray. But it would do.

The kettle whistled and he turned off the burner. So he measured out a scoop of the tea and lifted the teapot lid to sprinkle it inside. Just when he was about to tip the spoon, he noticed something inside the teapot. He put the spoon down and peered into the opening. There was a pale-pink envelope.

*Strange.*

Omar reached through the delicate opening with two of his fingers. Gripping the corner of the envelope, he was able to curl and fold it enough to squeeze it back out.

He grabbed the paring knife again and slid it through the top of the envelope. Inside was a matching page of pale-pink stationery. He pulled it out and opened it. A rectangular blue piece of paper fell to the floor. *Huh.* He picked it up and stared at it.

It was a check. With his name on it.

His gaze moved to the amount, and his knees nearly buckled. All those zeros blurred. Then he blinked, and they came into focus again. One hundred thousand dollars. That's what was written on the check in Mrs. Lewis's familiar handwriting.

For God knows how long, he stood there staring, blinking, counting each and every zero in disbelief. His knees were so weak and shaky that he had to sit. He opened the letter and read:

*My dearest Omar. The son that I've never had.*

*This isn't a goodbye. It's a see-you-later. Now, I know you're going to want to return this money. But this stubborn old lady won't take it back. It's yours now. I have more money than I know what to do with, anyways. I'm quite certain you will put it to good use, my dear boy. Thank you for always being there for me and Sinatra. You have a place to stay with us in Boston, so don't be a stranger. Think of me every time you have yourself a cup of tea.*

*Until the next time! Much love, Mrs. Lewis and Sinatra.*

# SIXTY-ONE

# Cat

It wasn't even noon yet, and Cat was already exhausted. He was thirsty too. His body ached and every time he tried to get up, his limbs wouldn't cooperate. All he wanted to do was curl up in his little house with his eyes closed. Except his eyelids seemed to hurt too. Something was clearly wrong, but he didn't know what. It wasn't like those times he'd eaten something from the dumpster and gotten sick. This was different. Even when he'd heard Rainbow Lady calling out for him, he'd stayed put in his bed, ignoring her *pspspsss* sounds until eventually, she'd gone away. When he'd heard the wheels of Cheery Mailman's cart, he'd ignored those too. Cat didn't know what to do. So he slept. As the minutes and hours passed his thirst worsened.

Finally, he heard Awkward Neighbor Guy's back door squeak open. He meowed softly, but it was barely a meow, more like a croak. Awkward Neighbor Guy's slippers shuffled closer until Cat could see his khaki linen pants through the window.

"Hey, buddy. Did you forget to eat your breakfast?" he asked.

Cat tried to meow again, but this time his throat wouldn't cooperate. As much as he wanted to crawl out of his house, he just couldn't. He was too weak. Instead, he waited, hoping that Awkward Neighbor Guy would figure out something was wrong. *Really* wrong.

After a couple of seconds, Awkward Neighbor Guy went over to his food and water bowls. He dumped the old water into the bushes and poured in some fresh water. When he was done with that, he carried the food bowl over to the entrance of his cardboard house, kneeling with his face low to the ground so he could peek inside. "Wakey, wakey, buddy. Here, eat up, otherwise it'll go bad," he said, nudging the bowl so it was halfway through the door.

Cat opened his eyes. His vision was kind of blurred, but he could see Awkward Neighbor Guy's eyes staring right at him. He tried to get up, but his body just flopped back onto the bed. It was as if his legs were made of those pillowy soft doughnuts he sometimes found in the trash. Except there was nothing sweet about the situation.

Awkward Neighbor Guy frowned. He stuck his arm inside and touched his dull, dry fur; it had been days since Cat had groomed himself. Ordinarily, Cat would have flinched whenever a person tried to touch him, but this time, he didn't react.

"What's the matter? Are you sick?" Awkward Neighbor Guy said, his voice shaky with concern.

Cat tried to meow again. He retched instead. There was no food and water inside his stomach, so all that came out were strings of slimy saliva. Awkward Neighbor Guy touched him again.

"Oh crap. I think you're really dehydrated, bud." Awkward Neighbor Guy poured some water into the palm of his hand and stuck it in front of Cat's face. "Drink," he commanded.

Cat turned his face away. Even though he was thirsty, the thought of water repulsed him.

"Shit. What am I supposed to do?" Awkward Neighbor Guy stood. Cat could hear him pacing while mumbling to himself. After a minute or two, he unlatched the gate and went to the sidewalk, as if he was looking for someone to help.

Then it was silent.

For a moment, Cat thought maybe he'd left. *Why? Why did you leave me, Awkward Neighbor Guy?* Cat buried his head deeper into the cushion of his cat bed. Saliva leaked from the corners of his mouth. Everything was spinning. Through the spinning, he caught flashes of Awkward Neighbor Guy moving. He reached into his cardboard house. "C'mon. We've got to go," he said, pulling the cat bed closer.

That's all Cat remembered before he blacked out.

# SIXTY-TWO

## Collin

Collin had no clue what to do with a sick cat. He didn't know of any vet clinics, and he was too panicked to go to his laptop and Google. All he knew was that the cat was very sick. Maybe he was even dying. Collin hadn't been taking care of him for long, but the thought that something might happen to him made his heart thump inside his chest. His hands shook as he scooped the cat's little body into his arms and ran down the street in his house slippers.

He ran past the dry cleaners. He ran past the liquor store. He ran past the bakery. Even though he was in his house clothes and slippers, carrying a cat against his chest, nobody gave him a second glance. It was Brooklyn and there were always plenty of weirdos on the street.

Except when he ran by the bodega, the old man who owned it was outside sweeping. As soon as he saw Collin with Cat in his arms, he frowned and called out, "Hey, what's going on? What are you doing with that cat?"

Collin didn't stop, though. He was afraid the cat would die in his arms. He kept on running, sweat falling into his eyes, blurring everything he was looking at. It was a miracle he didn't get hit by a car as he dashed across the road without looking at oncoming traffic.

"Watch where you're goin', asshole!" a truck driver shouted at him.

*Honk! Honk! Honk!*

Collin disregarded all the cars and kept on going, running and running until he reached his destination. Without even thinking, he opened the door and pushed his way through the throngs of people. "Excuse me. Sorry. I have to get through," he mumbled, elbowing his way past the bodies.

"Hey, there's a line, man," said an irate guy.

Collin didn't even bother looking at him, instead ignoring him and all the others who were giving him the stink eye. Finally, he spotted the cashier guy, who started to smile at Collin until he took in the state of him and the cat in his arms. Frowning, he backed away from the register. "Nú!" he shouted while glancing over at the espresso machine.

Núria was there. Thank God. She hurried over to the register and regarded Collin. There was a moment when she seemed to look right through him. But then she noticed the cat in his arms. Her eyes narrowed. She opened her mouth to speak, but nothing came out. The cashier guy nudged her with his elbow. "Nú?" he said again. Except Núria was just standing there with her mouth agape.

Collin stepped closer to the counter. "I-I need your help . . . with the cat," he said, his voice cracking. The customers behind Collin were getting antsy, pushing him as they grumbled about the holdup. "He's sick. I don't know what's wrong with him."

Núria flinched but didn't say anything.

Collin exhaled in frustration. His face was too hot, his legs wobbly. For a second, he thought he might pass out. All of a sudden, though, he knew *exactly* what he had to do. He took a deep breath and said in the loudest and clearest voice he could muster, "Guillermo! Guillermo! Guillermo!"

Núria gasped, her eyes finally coming into focus. "It-It's you," she said.

He nodded. "Yes. It's me."

The cashier guy sighed impatiently. "Okay. It's you and you. Now that we've got all that settled, can you please get this cat out of here?"

Without a word, Núria shimmied past the counter. She gently took the cat from his arms and said, "Hurry, there's a vet clinic nearby."

# SIXTY-THREE

# Bong

Bong watched the familiar-looking man sprint across the street carrying the black cat, almost getting hit by a newspaper delivery van. Part of him wanted to chase him and see what he was doing with Itim. But the man was tall and big and too fast for an old man like Bong.

Perhaps he should report it to the police. As he mulled it over, he decided that it was a terrible idea. His experience with the police wasn't altogether good. Over the years, he'd often felt dismissed by them. Was it because he was Filipino? Was it because he was an immigrant? Was it because he worked at a bodega? Was it all of the above? All he knew was that if he called the cops about a man possibly kidnapping a stray cat, they would think he was crazy for wasting their time.

Instead, he finished his sweeping, then went back inside to do some restocking. As soon as Lily saw the frown on his face, she went around the register to the other side of the counter. "What's the matter?" she asked.

"There was a man. . . . He was carrying a cat, running," he said, shaking his head as if he still couldn't believe it.

Lily raised her eyebrows. "What cat?"

"A stray. A black one." Bong gestured at the storefront window toward the sidewalk. "He lives down the street. He's always coming around with Omar, the mailman."

Lily hurried to the door and peered through the glass. "Did you see where the guy went? I know that cat. It's one of the strays that Núria feeds."

Bong shrugged. "I don't know. He went that way," he said, pointing.

"Huh." Lily continued peering through the door. "Hey, look. Is that the mailman who knows the cat?"

Omar rounded the corner and parked his cart by the door before opening it. Lily stepped aside so he could come in. "Good morning, Bong. I can't believe it's so hot already. You got some of those sparkling waters? The flavored ones?" he said with the cheeriest of smiles.

Bong rushed over to him. "Something happened to your cat. I mean, the black cat that you're always with."

"What? What do you mean?" said Omar.

Lily butted in between them. "Bong saw a guy running down the street holding the cat."

"Yes, he went that way. The cat looked hurt, maybe sick," added Bong, pointing in the direction that the big and tall guy had gone.

Omar looked worried and panicked and scared all of a sudden. In all the time Bong had known him, even before they'd become friends, he'd perceived him to be a chill kind of person. At this moment, though, he was anything but chill. "What did the man look like?" he asked Bong.

"Kind of familiar. I've seen him around the neighborhood. Tall. Really tall. Big. Broad shoulders. Curly dark hair, like a cherub."

Omar's eyes brightened. "Shit. I know who that is." He gazed across the road again, this time with his brows knitted together. "There's a vet clinic about four blocks that way. Maybe he was taking him there?"

All three of them looked at each other. Omar at Bong and Bong at Lily and Lily at Omar. "You want to go?" said Bong to Omar.

Omar nodded.

"I want to come too," Lily said. "But-But what about the store?"

Bong waved his hand in the air as if he were shooing a fly and said, "Don't worry about that, Lily. We'll lock up and be back in no time."

It was settled, then. Omar stowed his mail cart inside. Lily grabbed her purse. And Bong locked the front and side entrances of the bodega so they could track down the man who had catnapped Itim.

# SIXTY-FOUR

# Núria

Núria and Collin were at the Pet Project Veterinary Clinic. The vet tech had whisked Cat into one of the enclosed rooms so that the veterinarian on duty could tend to him. Thankfully, the clinic wasn't full of clients—the only other person in there was an old man holding a turtle. He'd politely let them go ahead since his turtle, Mel Brooks, was only there for his annual checkup.

While waiting, Collin paced the room. Núria observed him—the way he walked, the way he pulled back his shoulders when he breathed deep, the way he tensed his jaw every time the vet tech appeared, the way he ran his hand through his thick hair in frustration. It was as if she were watching a massive black panther pacing in its enclosure at the zoo. Núria hated zoos, so the image was a rather unpleasant one. She wished he would sit down. But she knew that people handled their anxieties in different ways, so she let him be.

Besides, there was still the awkward situation with the whole Guillermo thing. To be honest, she hadn't expected the Post-it note person to *actually* take her up on her suggestion. It had been a silly idea. Now there was this air of embarrassment between them. Núria was having a hard time squaring the awkward, pacing man in front of her with the person who had bared his soul to her in the notes.

Why on earth would a successful, attractive man like Collin be interested in Núria? None of her clothes ever matched, and half of them were from thrift stores and stoop sales. Her hair was either a tangled mess or pulled up into an I-don't-give-a-shit bun. Not to mention the cat fur that clung to her skin, to her shoes, to her clothes, and to pretty much every surface she owned.

She stole another glance at Collin from the corner of her eye. So the brownstone where Cat hung out must have been *his* brownstone. All along, he'd been taking care of Cat when she wasn't around. What a clueless fool she'd been! How had Rocky put up with her all these years? And why the hell was Collin Thackeray so infatuated with her?

Núria was perplexed. *And* worried.

What was wrong with Cat? How had she not noticed that he wasn't his usual self? She had let her life get messy, let herself be distracted, and neglected the creatures who were depending on her. Her stomach clenched and for a moment she felt like throwing up. Her vision blurred and the room began spinning. She closed her eyes and focused on her breathing. Then she opened her eyes and looked around the room, silently naming three things she saw and three things she could hear and moving three parts of her body—her right foot, the fingers of her left hand, and her shoulders. The 3-3-3 rule was something she'd learned from her high school guidance counselor.

It worked. The room stopped spinning. Her stomach relaxed. She stood and went over to the water dispenser, filling one of those cone-shaped paper cups several times until her thirst was quenched. When she turned around, Collin was right there staring at her. "How long does this kind of thing usually take?" he asked.

She avoided his eyes, instead looking straight at his chest, which for whatever reason seemed less awkward. "You can go home if you want. I know you must be busy with your writing. I can take it from here," she said.

"No. That's not what I meant." He stepped even closer. So close that she could see his dark chest hairs through his old, thinning white T-shirt. "I'm not leaving. Not until we find out what's wrong with him," he said.

That's when she looked up into his eyes. They were slick in the way eyes were before tears began to form. She'd never seen a man cry before, except for her dad, who had never been afraid to be vulnerable in front of her. If only he'd known how much she had cried when he'd left. How much she'd missed him. Maybe that was part of the reason why she loved cats so much. It was something that she and her dad had shared.

Seeing Collin so upset over a stray cat made her insides warm and tingly. The kindness in his eyes, and the way he'd put himself on the line for the sake of an animal that wasn't even his, confused her. Sure, she was attracted to him. But it was more than just that. It was a different kind of feeling, one she'd never experienced before with another man.

Without thinking, she reached out and placed her hand on his arm. Her skin touched his. For a split second she was tempted to pull away. Instead, she squeezed his arm. "I'm sure he'll be okay. You did the right thing bringing him to me," she said softly.

His arm twitched. His face turned pink. Yet he didn't draw his arm away. "I hope you're right," he said, a small tear snaking down his cheek. He wiped it away with the back of his hand. "I don't know how, but that damned cat somehow stole my heart," he said.

Núria smiled and then chuckled. She knew *exactly* what he meant. Cats had this sneaky way of crawling into your life and making you fall in love with them. Even if they were complete and total assholes. "I know," she said.

Suddenly, the front door slammed open. Núria, Collin, and the old man with the turtle turned to look. It was a super-sweaty Omar and an equally sweaty Bong. Behind them was Lily, her sister. For a moment, their eyes met. Núria hadn't seen her since their disastrous outing at the ice cream shop.

"Oh, thank God you're here," said Omar with a huge sigh of relief.

# SIXTY-FIVE

# Omar

Omar and Bong asked Núria every question under the sun. Except she didn't have many answers. Apparently, Collin had found Gatito in the state he was in—lethargic, dehydrated, drooling—and rushed him over to the café where Núria worked. Omar wasn't one to gossip, but boy oh boy, how he wished he could have been at the café to witness how it had all gone down. Later, he would have to pull Núria aside and get the deets.

Omar wasn't sure if he was relieved because the supposedly crazy man who had abducted Gatito was indeed Collin, as he'd suspected, or because Núria and Collin were staring at each other with goo-goo eyes. Admittedly, he was a bit of a hopeless romantic. When he'd found out that Collin had a thing for Núria, he'd secretly hoped it would work out, even though at first, he'd thought that Collin was one of those grouchy hermits who hated *everyone* and *everything*. It seemed, though, that maybe Collin wasn't so bad after all.

Besides, he also welcomed the distraction from his own relationship woes. Witnessing a budding romance made his own heart hurt a little less. It made the butterflies in his stomach flutter for the *right* reasons every time he caught Collin and Núria stealing glances at one another. It was just so damned wholesome and adorable.

However, he was also extremely worried about his little buddy.

For now, he and everyone else there, including the man with the turtle, was waiting for the vet tech to come out with some news. In the meantime, he bounced from person to person, trying to calm them all down with small talk and reassuring words. Surprisingly, Collin seemed to be the most frazzled. Maybe it was because he was the one who had found Gatito. Or maybe Omar had simply underestimated the man's emotional capacity.

When Omar finally managed to convince Collin to stop pacing and sit down, he went over to the water cooler and fetched him something to drink. Collin took the little cup and gazed at him with a warmth that Omar had never seen from him before. "Thanks. I think I needed this," he said.

Omar sat down beside him, eyeing Núria and Bong, who were huddled by the door, talking. Lily stood to the side, biting her lip with what Omar would describe as nervous energy. He hardly knew her, but he could tell that Bong was fond of her. If she was Bong's friend, well, then she would be Omar's friend too. Ever since Carl had left to stay with his brother, Omar had been feeling all sorts of lonely. To make himself feel better, he needed to be surrounded by people, even though they were people he had just gotten to know. They certainly were a motley crew. How exactly had this group ended up here? Then he thought about his little buddy and smiled. It was Gatito who had somehow connected them.

He'd grown awfully fond of Gatito over the years. Never had he met a cat so inquisitive, so astute, so willing to go with the flow. Not only that, but he was also an excellent listener. Omar could jibber-jabber about any random subject, and Gatito always seemed to be paying attention. If Omar hadn't already lived in a no-pets apartment, he probably would have adopted the cat a long time ago. He sighed at the thought of it. If Gatito had lived indoors rather than having the life of a stray, surely he wouldn't have gotten sick, right?

Collin turned to him with this pleading look of desperation. "Do you think he's going to be okay?" he asked.

All Omar could do was smile reassuringly and tell him the truth. "I don't know, man. I sure hope so." After lying to Carl, the last thing

Omar wanted to do was to lie again. Even if it would make someone feel better.

Suddenly, he remembered something that his abuela used to say quite often, especially when she knew he needed to hear it: *The truth may hurt for a little while, but a lie hurts forever.* A lump materialized in his throat at the thought of Carl. He tried to swallow it down. But it stayed put. Why oh why had he lied to Carl? Would he ever forgive him?

Finally, the vet tech came out of the examination room and cleared his throat. "Dr. Vasquez would like to speak with you," he said, looking at Núria and Collin.

Except everyone approached him, including the man with the turtle.

"Can we come too?" asked Bong, speaking on behalf of the group.

The vet tech sighed, his eyes jumping from person to person to person. After a couple of seconds, he nodded and said, "It's a small examination room. But I suppose it would be all right. *You* and the turtle stay here, though." He stared at the man until he sat back down.

"Let me know what happens. Okay?" said the man with the turtle as the group followed the vet tech.

They entered the room one by one. The space was sterile and cold. There were shelves and cupboards with medical supplies, a gray linoleum floor, and a long stainless-steel table in the center. Dr. Vasquez was by the table, dressed in her scrubs and a white doctor's coat. Gatito was lying on a rectangular white pad, conscious but not looking very well; his eyes were sunken, there was drool coming out of his mouth, and his fur was dull and matted.

"Well, this is more people than I was expecting." Dr. Vasquez made an attempt to smile, but Omar could see her concern underneath it.

They all stared at her, waiting to hear what she had to say. The air in the room was heavy in spite of the air-conditioning, as if their collective worries were sucking the oxygen out.

"It's not the best news, I'm afraid," said Dr. Vasquez, petting

Gatito on his neck as if to soothe him. "Cat has stage three kidney disease. . . . He's ten, maybe eleven years old. For a stray, that's quite old. I'm surprised he's lasted this long," she explained.

Omar glanced over at Collin. His lip was quivering; Omar could tell he was trying hard not to lose it. "Is there anything that can be done?" he asked, because everyone else seemed to be too devastated to say anything.

Dr. Vasquez looked down at Gatito and then back at Omar. "In cases like these, the most humane thing to do would be to put him to sleep. He's a stray, and putting him back on the street in this condition would be cruel."

"But what if he wasn't a stray?" Collin stepped forward next to Omar.

"Well, if he *had* an owner, I would suggest a couple of days here at the clinic so he could have IV fluids to get some of his strength back. Then he could go home and continue with subcutaneous fluids, supplements, and a special diet," said Dr. Vasquez.

Núria went over to the steel table and rested her hand on Gatito's back, petting him gently. "How long does he have?" she asked.

"I can't really say for sure, but if he had someplace to go with a person that could care for him properly, he could live another year or two."

Núria sucked her breath in. "I wish I could take him in, but my landlord has a strict three pets per household limit. If I get caught, I might get evicted. . . ."

Omar shook his head and sighed. "Unfortunately, no pets are allowed in my building."

Lily, who had been mostly quiet, observing everything that was going on, chimed in, "Sorry, my roommates would kill me."

"I could try . . . but I'm pretty busy with the store these days," said Bong.

Everyone turned to look at Collin. He must have had a lump in his throat, because Omar could see his Adam's apple bobbing as he swallowed hard. "I-I can do it. He can come home with me," he said in a raspy voice.

Omar grinned. "I can come over and help with the medical stuff. I'm used to giving Mrs. Lewis's dog his meds."

"I can help too," said Núria. "I'm a pro at giving meds to cats."

Bong bounced in place like an excited toddler. "I can bring cat food and supplies. Whatever is needed."

"Me too. I can help clean up, run errands, cat-sit. Whatever," added Lily.

Dr. Vasquez nodded and clasped her hands together. "How wonderful that Cat has so many people to care for him. We'll have to give one of you a demo on how to do subcutaneous fluids, and I'll write out the prescription for all his meds, supplements, and food. *But* I want to see him once a month for a checkup. It's important we monitor his kidney function."

Collin nodded. "Of course, anything for the cat . . . I mean, Cat."

Omar bent down so he was at eye level with his little buddy. He scratched him under his chin and said, "You're going to be all right, Gatito, my man. . . . Just a couple more days in this popsicle stand and then you'll be home. From now on you're going to be one of those fancy-schmancy indoor cats. No more slumming it on the streets for you."

Dr. Vasquez chuckled. "I don't think anyone has ever called my clinic a popsicle stand."

"No offense, Doc," said Omar with a sheepish grin.

"None taken. Why don't you all let Cat get some rest now? Enrique can do a subcutaneous fluids demo for you in the waiting area," she said, opening the door.

One by one, they filed back into the waiting area. At the sight of them, the man with the turtle got up off his seat. "Well? How is the little guy? Me and Mel want to know," he said, holding Mel Brooks.

Omar grinned. "He's going to be okay. He just needs a couple of days to recuperate, and then he's going to be livin' it large with my man Collin," said Omar, patting Collin's back.

"That is wonderful news! What a relief. Did you hear that, Mel?" he said, bringing Mel up to his face. Mel blinked and moved his head up and down.

"So, which one of you is going to be doing Cat's subcutaneous fluids?" said Enrique the vet tech, glancing at all of them.

Omar raised his hand. "You can teach me first, and I'll get everyone else caught up."

Enrique led Omar to a corner behind the reception counter, then proceeded to show Omar how to set up the bottle of fluid and attach the tubes and needle. Then he showed him where and how to insert the needle on a stuffed cat, giving him tips on how to keep the cat calm and relaxed. When he was done, he asked Omar to do it by himself. Without hesitation, he did exactly as Enrique had instructed, his movements fluid, confident, and gentle. When Omar was done, he looked up at Enrique for approval. "Was that okay?"

Enrique smiled and fist-bumped him. "That was *more* than okay. You might have actually done it better than I did," he said with a chuckle.

Omar beamed. "Really?"

"Yeah, man. Good thing Dr. Vasquez isn't here. Otherwise, she might offer you my job," he joked.

It was at that moment that Omar finally knew. He stared at the stuffed cat and the subcutaneous liquid paraphernalia, at Enrique and his vet tech uniform, at Mel Brooks the turtle, and lastly at the veterinary clinic surrounding him. It all made so much sense. Omar loved animals *and* people. He was a natural caregiver. And as much as possible, he tried his very best to be kind and compassionate.

This job, this place, was going to be his future.

# SIXTY-SIX

# Cat

Cat saw a light. Was he dead? He could still feel pain. Surely if he was dead, the pain would be gone, right? He blinked. The light was so bright. It wasn't sunlight, that much he knew. He blinked again. Other things started to come into focus.

Walls. Shelves. Nope. He wasn't dead. He was indoors, in a strange place. He blinked again. No. Not so strange. He recognized it. The harsh overhead light was the same one he'd seen when Rainbow Lady had catnapped him before. At the time, he'd been mad at her. As the days had passed, though, he'd forgiven her. Cat wasn't one to hold grudges. Especially not when he was getting fed.

Suddenly, he heard voices. Some were familiar. Some not so much. He blinked again. Faces appeared from the shadows. Awkward Neighbor Guy was there, looking rather upset. Then he spotted Cheery Mailman standing beside him. His usually cheery demeanor was gone. Rainbow Lady was there too. The crevice between her brows was deep. And her freckles seemed to hop off her face like overzealous fleas.

Cat blinked again. Another person appeared. It was Bright-Pink Person, who he now knew was Rainbow Lady's sister. In his youth, he too had had siblings. They were long gone now. He blinked again.

Was that Sad Bodega Man? It sure was. What was he doing here? He blinked again.

These people, were they all here for him? Surely not. Cat blinked again. Why else would they all be in the same little room? He managed to lift his head even though every inch of him hurt. Yes, they were definitely here for him.

"I-I can do it. He can come home with me."

Cat opened his eyes as wide as he could and stared at Awkward Neighbor Guy. Had he *really* said those words? Did he mean them? Cat was going to live with *him*, inside *his* house? Never in a million years had Cat seen this coming. He'd been more than satisfied with the cardboard house he'd been sleeping in. The idea of becoming one of those inside cats, well, it had him confused and at the same time elated. Truth be told, he'd grown tired of life on the streets. Living indoors with a human of his own might be a nice change of pace. He didn't hate the idea.

Cat was going to have a home of his own! A real home with a door and windows and chairs and beds to sleep on. A home he could be cool in during the summer and warm in during the winter. A home. Finally, a home.

There was a warmth in his body, spreading from his face to his chest to his torso to the tip of his tail. And even though he was under the weather, he could feel a vibration coming from within.

# SIXTY-SEVEN

# Collin

The minute they'd stepped outside the clinic, Collin had grown even more anxious. What had he gotten himself into? He'd never had a cat before. It was one thing to make a cardboard house for a stray, but it was another thing altogether to have one living *inside* his house. Not to mention that Cat was very sick. Part of him wanted to run back inside and tell the veterinarian that he'd changed his mind. But the way Núria looked at him made that part of him relax.

Soon, they would be alone, just the two of them. Omar was still inside the clinic chitchatting with Enrique, the vet tech, and Bong and Lily were heading back to the bodega.

"See you later, Bong and Lily. Thanks for being there for Cat, and for offering to help take care of him," said Collin with a smile and a wave.

Bong backtracked and shook Collin's hand. "No. Thank *you*, Collin, for stepping up. I am so happy that Itim—I mean, Cat—will get to live out his days in comfort. If my late wife Conchita were here, I am pretty sure she would call you a saint, and then she would crochet you something, because that's what she did for people she liked."

"Oh, it's nothing, really," said Collin, whose face had suddenly turned pink.

"C'mon, Bong. We have to open up the bodega so that Omar can get his mail cart," said Lily, gazing at the sidewalk as if she was trying to avoid eye contact.

Bong flinched. "Oh, yes. You're right. . . . Well, see you later! Please keep us updated on Cat's progress," he said with a nod.

"Wait up!" Omar burst through the clinic front door. Then he, Bong, and Lily headed down the street.

"Lily!" Núria suddenly called out.

Lily halted, turning back around, her eyebrows raised in surprise. "Y-Yes?"

"I was wondering . . ." Núria stepped closer to her. "I-I was wondering if you want to meet up at the café later? We can, you know, talk?"

Lily smiled, the corners of her eyes tilting up. "Really? Are you sure? I mean, yes. I-I'd like that. I'll come by during my lunch break."

"Great. See you then." Núria smiled back and lingered for a good minute, watching Omar, Bong, and Lily until they were gone.

Collin shuffled his feet, wondering what he should say and do. Núria, on the other hand, went back to pretending to check the messages on her phone, except every so often, she stole glances at him when she thought he wasn't looking. But Collin noticed. Every time her hazel eyes wandered in his direction, he felt a warmth on his cheeks and the back of his neck. It was humiliating. However, it also gave Collin an immense pleasure. It had been a long while since he'd felt this way. Despite all the awkward moments, he found that he was enjoying himself.

"Hey," said Núria. "I think I still owe you that Guillermo you ordered."

Collin shrugged. "No biggie. It's not like I paid for it or anything. . . . Besides, I'm not really sure if espresso and lime go well together."

"Oh yeah?" Núria grinned. "So you looked it up, huh?"

Suddenly, his cheeks were warm again. "Well, um, I mean, how could I not?"

Núria sidled up to him. "It's actually good, I promise. I'll make you one sometime." She peeked at him out of the corner of her eye, biting her lip as if she was hesitating about what to say next. "I'm curious. Do you make a habit of writing notes to women you don't know? Is this, like, your thing?"

"My thing?" Collin raised his eyebrows. "I don't really have a thing. This is the first time. . . . I just saw you through my window. And, well, you intrigued me."

Núria grinned. "Intrigued? How could I possibly be that intriguing?"

It was then that Collin's already-warm cheeks burned so hot that it felt as if they were on fire. He was light-headed. His palms were cold and clammy despite the warm weather. He blinked and looked away from her, suddenly embarrassed. "I see you almost every day from my office window. And, well . . . It's sort of hard for me to describe, but it's almost like everything I used to look at was a blur. Then suddenly, I put on a new pair of eyeglasses and there you were, so alive, so bright, so in focus. It's like I'm seeing things differently now," he mumbled. "I-I'm sorry if that sounds creepy."

"No. Not at all. I'm flattered, actually," said Núria, reaching out to touch his arm as if she sensed he needed comforting. "Most days, I kind of feel invisible, you know? It's nice to be seen for a change."

Collin made himself meet her gaze. For a moment, he sort of swayed from dizziness.

"Hey, are you all right?" said Núria, grasping his thick forearm.

He took a deep breath and steadied himself. "I'm sorry, I think I'm still in shock."

"It's okay. I know it's a lot," said Núria. She stepped even closer and let go of his arm, instead tugging on the edge of his T-shirt. "C'mon. I think you need a distraction to help you relax. . . . There's an awesome pet supply shop a couple of blocks from here. If you want, I can help you shop for some supplies."

Collin glanced down at the spot on his T-shirt that she'd tugged. She may have touched only the fabric, but he could feel his skin underneath tingling. He was flustered. "Oh, that's okay. I don't want to bother you. I can just buy everything online."

For a moment, Núria didn't reply. Instead, she reached up and twirled a strand of her loose hair. As the moment stretched longer, she let go of the strand and inched closer, so their hips were a mere inch or two apart. "Wouldn't you rather go in person so we can pick stuff out *together*?"

Collin flinched at the word "together." Oh God, he was such an idiot. Why had he scoffed at her offer? He wanted to cover his face with both hands in embarrassment, or maybe dig a hole so the pavement would eat him up. But he was a grown man. Not a little boy. *Be cool, Collin,* he said to himself. "All right. That sounds good. I'd appreciate your help. Thank you."

Núria smiled. Clearly, she was happy he'd agreed. "Well, it's a date! Let's go," she said, gesturing for him to follow.

A date? Was this actually a date, disguised as an errand?

Collin had no clue. He decided to just go with the flow. Date or not, he was going to get to spend more time with Núria. He followed her down the street, forgetting about all the nervous apprehension from moments ago.

# SIXTY-EIGHT

# Núria

Brooklyn Pet Village was divided into two sections, "Meowtown" and "Dogtown." Núria steered Collin toward the "Meowtown" section of the store. She knew every inch of the place, and the staff called her by name.

"Hey, Núria! What's new?" said one of the employees, an older man with a beard, mohawk, and tattooed arms.

Núria waved. "Duncan. It's nice to see you. My friend here has a new cat rescue he needs supplies for," she said, gesturing at Collin and his shopping cart.

Duncan nodded to Collin. "Good on you, man. Taking in rescues is hard work, but it's really gratifying," he said with a grin.

"Thanks." Collin smiled back, but Núria could tell he was still uneasy about the decision he'd made.

"C'mon, this way," she said as she ducked into the aisle with litter boxes and cat litter. "Let's get started with the necessities."

Collin stared at the various litter boxes on display. "All this for a cat to pee and poop in?" he said, widening his eyes.

Núria chuckled. "There's an entire range. From the basic litter pan to the hooded ones to rolling self-cleaning ones, and even smart litterboxes that you can sync to your phone. It just depends on how much you want to spend."

"You were right. I *do* need your help."

Núria reached for an old-school litterbox with a hood. "If you don't mind doing a little extra work, I'd recommend one of these. You can't go wrong with the basic model," she said.

"Okay . . . What about the litter?" he said, eyeing the sacks of cat litter.

She grabbed a bag. "Ignore the fancy variants and stick to good ol' clumping litter. You're also going to need a scooper to remove the clumps in the morning and at night."

"A scooper?" he said with a frown.

"Yeah. One of these." She plucked a jumbo plastic scooper from one of the shelves and tossed it into the cart.

Collin pushed the cart into the next aisle. "What's next?"

"Food and water bowls and a carrier," said Núria.

"Oh. I already have bowls. I bought some at the supermarket. And a cat bed too."

Núria placed a blue-and-gray carrier into the cart and glared at him. "So you've been feeding him this whole time, huh?"

"Not this whole time. I mean, just recently. I-I felt bad for him, living in the bushes and all. So I made him a cat house, and I got the bowls and the cat bed. He's been staying in the alley next to my house," explained Collin.

Núria crossed her arms across her chest. "That brownstone. It's yours. I should have known."

"I'm sorry. I wanted to talk to you so badly. But I-I just didn't know how."

She uncrossed her arms and relaxed. "There's nothing to be sorry about. If you hadn't been there, Cat would probably already be gone. You did a good thing," she said.

Collin exhaled. "Thanks."

"Anyway, just so you know, that cat bed might become obsolete once he's inside your place. Cats prefer *everything* that is ours. So you should fully expect him to take over your bed, your chairs, your kitchen counters . . . anything that's yours will soon be his," she said, leading him to the next aisle.

Collin didn't respond. Núria could tell by the way his brows furrowed that he was overwhelmed at the thought. But she knew not to sugarcoat the situation, especially since he was taking in a sick cat. She had to make sure he was prepared.

"You're going to need one of these." She handed him something that looked like a small duffel bag.

"What is it?" he asked.

"It's a cat immobilizing bag." She pointed at the Velcro tabs and zippers. "You put the cat inside and it keeps them still so you can give them meds more easily and safely. If you keep all the openings closed, only his head will be exposed. But if you need to trim his claws or something, you can open the leg zippers too."

Collin frowned. "Is this really necessary?"

"Yes. Trust me," said Núria.

He shrugged. "All right, then. Anything else? How about some toys?" he said, halting at the display of cat toys.

"Nah. Most cats prefer foil balls and boxes, anyways. Toys are just a big waste of money."

Collin glanced into the cart. "So that's it? I thought we'd need more stuff."

"The rest of the stuff, his prescription food, supplements, and fluids, we'll get from the vet clinic. Okay?" she said.

"Okay."

They headed to the checkout counter, where Duncan was already waiting for them. Collin reached into the shopping cart to unload their stuff. So did Núria. For a second their hands touched. Núria was tempted to pull her hand away. But she didn't. She was oddly comfortable with Collin, even though men generally made her quite uneasy.

*Twinkle-twinkle . . . Twinkle . . . Twinkle-twinkle . . .*

It was Núria's phone. She didn't have to glance at it to see who it was. It was her mother checking up on her. As much as she didn't want to answer it, especially after their heart-to-heart the night before, she knew she had to.

"Hola, Mamá," she said as soon as she answered. Except it wasn't a regular call. It was a video call. Núria pulled the phone away from her ear just as the image of her mother appeared on the screen.

"Oyé! Why didn't you pick up sooner?" she said, putting her face so close to the screen that Núria could see up her nose. "Estás bien, mija? Are you feeling better?"

Núria glanced at Collin nervously as he paid for the items with his credit card. She mouthed *Hold on* to him, her cheeks hot from embarrassment. "Hola Mamá. Yes, I'm feeling better. I'm just a bit busy right now. Can I call you later?"

Her mother squinted at the camera, her eyes darting right and then left as if she was looking for something. "Busy? Is there someone there with you? Who did you say *hold on* to? Dígame!"

"It's nobody, Mamá. I'm just shopping with a-a friend," she said, exhaling impatiently.

"A friend? Who friend? Hello? Hola? Hello? Hello?" she shouted so loud that Collin, Duncan, and the entire store could probably hear her.

Collin placed his credit card back in his wallet and chuckled. Before Núria could stop him, he leaned over so his face could be captured by the camera. "Hello. Hi. I'm Collin. It's nice to meet you," he said with a grin.

"Collin? Collin who?" her mother said, continuing with her squinting. "Oyé, espera. You're quite handsome. Are you single? Because my daughter, Núria, she's dating a mailman, but I'm *not* so sure about him—"

That's when Núria hung up on her. She was so humiliated that she was tempted to drop her phone and make a run for it.

"I take it she was talking about Omar?" said Collin, trying hard not to laugh.

Her cheeks were suddenly burning hot. "Uh, yeah . . . I might have, you know, told her he was my boyfriend to get her off my back. I'm sorry. My mother is a lot."

"Don't worry about it. Whose mother isn't a lot? It's practically their job, right?"

Núria smiled. Not only had Collin handled her ridiculous mother like a pro, but he also hadn't made her feel ashamed for making up a fake boyfriend. Her cheeks were hot again. This time, it wasn't out of humiliation. It was because the flutters in her stomach were making her warm from the inside out.

For so long, she'd told herself that the company of cats and Rocky was enough for her. Yet lately, she'd found herself wanting to open up to others. First, she'd accepted Omar's dinner invitation. Then there was Lily, her half sister whom she hadn't known existed until the day before. Now there was Collin, who'd inexplicably barged into her life with a series of notes and letters. She couldn't explain it, but it somehow felt like it was meant to be. Like it was a master plan that Cat had meticulously orchestrated. Núria knew that couldn't be true. After all, he was just one stray cat. But she wanted to believe. Because if she believed, then maybe, just maybe, they would all get their happy endings.

Collin grabbed the shopping bags and smiled. His shoulders seemed more relaxed. His cheeks weren't quite as flushed. His gaze was steady and unflinching. "I was wondering if maybe you were going to eat something later?"

"Yeah. I mean, I *do* eat," she blurted out.

He chortled and shook his head. "I'm sorry. I'm still kind of nervous. What I meant to ask is if you would like to eat dinner with me . . . tonight."

For a moment, they lingered by the exit of the shop, saying nothing while a flurry of customers passed them by.

All those back-and-forth notes and letters. All the wondering. All the unknowns. All the waiting. It had led them up to this.

It felt right.

Núria glanced up in search of his warm brown eyes. When she found them, she couldn't help but feel as if she'd been waiting her entire life to gaze into them. "Yes, I would very much like to have dinner with you, Collin."

# SIXTY-NINE

# Lily

"Ummm . . . So that's what the coffee here tastes like," said Lily after a long sip of her iced caramel latte.

Núria, who was sitting across the table from her, furrowed her brows. "What do you mean?"

"It's totally humiliating, but I used to pass by here all the time and watch you from outside. I never actually had the guts to come in. . . . Besides, the coffee doesn't exactly fit my budget," explained Lily.

"Well, if I didn't work here, I wouldn't be able to afford it, either."

Lily smiled nervously, then picked up her ham-and-cheese croissant and took a big bite.

Núria cleared her throat. "Anyway, I did a lot of thinking last night. Like, a lot. And I just wanted to talk so we could clear the air. . . . I know it may have seemed like I was mad at you. But I'm not, Lily. Not really. I was just shocked. I freaked out. I said some awful things to you. . . . I shouldn't have run off like I did. I'm sorry."

Lily put her croissant down and wiped the crumbs off her chin with a napkin. "God, you don't need to apologize, Núria. If anyone should apologize, it's me. I'm the one who followed you around like a stalker. I'm the one who lied. I'm the one who kept secrets from you. . . . Honestly, I won't blame you if you never want to see me again."

"No! Of course not!" Núria widened her eyes and leaned forward. "I don't want you to go anywhere."

"Really?"

"Really."

"You don't hate me?" asked Lily.

Núria reached out and placed her hand on Lily's. "I don't. What I realize now is that the fault doesn't lie with any one person. What happened, happened. I mean, sure, my father ran off and left me and my mom. But my mom was also to blame. She never filed a change of address with the post office when we moved. She made sure our phone number was unlisted. She did everything in her power to keep him out of our lives. . . . And I guess I can't really blame her."

Despite the hustle and bustle of the café around them, there was a palpable silence. It was almost as if Lily and Núria were in their own world.

Lily exhaled. It was the first time she'd felt like herself since moving to New York City. The imaginary boulders that had been lodged between her shoulders lifted. The burden was gone. This amazing sense of ease coursed through her body. She reached into her tote bag and pulled out a large envelope and handed it to Núria. "I found these in the basement after my dad—our dad—died. I've been keeping them for you ever since, hoping I could give them to you one day," she explained. "I ran all the way home to get it before coming here to meet you. . . . I haven't worked out that hard since my cheerleading days."

Núria held the envelope, her hands not fully grasping it, as if she was frightened by what was inside.

"Go ahead and take a look. I promise it's nothing bad," said Lily.

Slowly, Núria coaxed the envelope open. She peered inside before pulling out the items one by one. There was the children's book entitled *The Cat Who Went to Heaven*; she opened it and gasped when she saw the inscription from their father.

*Happy birthday to my dearest daughter, Núria.*
*Papa misses you very much.*

Then she pulled out a large bundle of letters.

"He wrote to you, Núria. Even though he knew they would be returned, he still wrote to you," said Lily softly.

Núria pulled the bundle of letters to her chest and hugged them, tears streaming down her cheeks. "I-I didn't think he cared. . . ."

"He did, Núria. He really did." Lily picked up the last item from the table—the issue of *Barista* magazine with Núria on the cover. "This magazine. It came out two weeks before he died. . . . I'm pretty sure he was going to come find you. In fact, the night before his accident, he suggested a father-daughter trip to New York for Christmas. He wanted us to go see some Broadway shows. He wanted us to go ice-skating at Rockefeller Center. And I'm *one hundred percent* sure he wanted us to meet. It all makes sense now."

"So, here we are," said Núria with a sniffle.

Lily squeezed her hand. "Somehow, he still got his wish."

"I'm so glad you came to find me, Lily. Thank you," said Núria.

"You're welcome."

Núria sniffled again, wiping the tidal wave of tears from her face with a napkin. "Oh God. Are my eyes puffy? Red? They are, aren't they?" she asked Lily.

"I mean, yeah. That's kind of what happens when you cry, you know?" said Lily with a frown. "I really don't think your customers will care if your eyes are a bit puffy."

Núria shook her head. "It's not that. It's just that I have, like, a date tonight. With Collin," she explained.

"What? Oh my God! *Really?*" Lily leaped off her seat as if someone had lit firecrackers under her butt. "What are you doing? Where are you going? Holy crap . . . What are you wearing?"

All of a sudden, Núria's eyes bulged out of their sockets. "Oh, no. Shit. I only have one nice dress and he's already seen me in it."

"Well, it's your lucky day, then. Because shopping just happens to be something I'm good at. C'mon, there's a really cute vintage boutique around the corner," said Lily, grabbing Núria's hand and pulling her until she was standing.

"But I'm still working," said Núria.

"Give me half an hour. I promise, that's all the time I need," pleaded Lily.

Núria glanced over at the cashier guy, who was dancing to the café music, oblivious to everything that was going on around him. "Anh, can I take thirty more minutes? Please?"

The cashier guy thrust his hips, then shooed them away with his hands. "No worries, hon. I got it *all* under control."

Viola's Closet was a trendy vintage boutique. A lot of the stuff was overpriced, but if one looked hard enough, especially in the sale racks, there were affordable treasures to be found. Lily had perused the store many a time, salivating at some of the designer dresses that were way out of her budget. She hadn't bought a single thing. But now she had an excuse to shop, even if it wasn't for herself. In fact, it was even more exciting, since Lily was a huge fan of makeover shows. Giving her sister a makeover would be a fun bonding activity—at least for Lily.

There was a problem, though. Every time Lily pulled something off the rack and showed it to Núria, she cringed.

"C'mon. Can you at least try something on? We're running out of time," Lily pleaded.

Núria pouted. "But everything is so . . . not me."

"Okay. Fine. I'm going to make another quick round and see if I find something else."

Thankfully, there was a raspberry velvet ottoman in the corner for Núria to sit on while Lily inspected each and every item on the racks. Núria closed her eyes. Lily figured that this was her way of zoning out. Clearly, this date with Collin had her stressed out to the max.

When Lily was done with one rack, she moved on to the next and the next and the next until she was left with only one rack to inspect. She sighed and crossed her fingers. There just had to be something that would work. When she was nearing the end, a garment suddenly caught her eye. A little patch of fabric that looked extremely promising. Lily tried not to get too excited as she pushed the cocktail dresses aside.

*Ahhh* . . . Lily gasped. This was it! She grabbed it and ran over to where Núria was seated. "Look!" She held up a pink cotton summer dress with a black cat print. "It's perfect, isn't it? What do you think?" said Lily.

It was then that Núria seemed to come alive. She snapped her back straight. Her hazel eyes sparkled as she studied the dress. "You did it, Lily. You really did it!" she exclaimed.

Lily hadn't been this proud of herself in a long time. It didn't matter that Núria was the one going on the hot date and not her. All these months living in New York City, and all she'd felt was envy at everyone else's seemingly amazing lives. But none of that mattered now. She was happy for Núria. And being happy for her sister was the best feeling in the world.

# SEVENTY

# Collin

As soon as Collin and Núria got out of their Lyft car, her eyes lit up. "How did you know this was one of my favorite restaurants?" she asked, staring at the *Mama Shirley's Vegan Soul Food* neon sign.

Collin shrugged. "You said you were vegan, and this place looked pretty decent. I got lucky, I guess."

What Núria didn't know, though, was that he'd spent a good three hours googling all the vegan restaurants in Brooklyn— searching images to check for ambiance, reading their menus to see if the food sounded good, checking out reviews to know which restaurants to skip. Initially, he'd envisioned something fancier, more romantic. But the more he thought about it, the more he was convinced that Núria would prefer something casual with a homey vibe.

"C'mon. I'm starving," she said, pulling him by the wrist.

The feeling of her skin on his made his insides tingly. As soon as they went inside, a hostess greeted them. "Núria, it's been a minute. It's nice to see you again," she said, glancing at Collin with interest.

"Thanks, Tamika. I sure missed your mama's cooking," said Núria.

"Follow me. I've got a nice table by the window." Tamika grabbed two menus and then led them to a quiet corner of the busy restaurant. "Busy" was really a bit of an understatement. The restaurant was alive with the sounds of talking and eating and laughter, and in the background, "Try a Little Tenderness" by Otis Redding played.

They sat and Tamika handed them their menus. "Lamar will be over shortly to take your orders," she said before going back to the entrance to greet more guests.

"Do you mind ordering for us? I'm pretty sure you know which dishes are best. It seems as if you've been here quite a few times," said Collin.

Núria smiled. "What can I say, I'm a creature of habit. I'll admit I'm not very adventurous when it comes to trying out new places. When something is good, it's good. You know what I mean?"

"I do. You should see my online grocery list. It's pretty much a carbon copy every single week. I guess I'm a creature of habit too," he said.

"Hey, Núria!" Their waiter came by and kissed her on the cheek as if they were old friends. "What's Rocky been up to? It's been a while since I've seen you both," he said.

Núria placed her menu down and glanced over at Collin, who was fidgeting in his seat. "Oh. She's fine. You know her. Work, work, work. I'm here with my frie—I mean, Collin. I'm here with Collin. Collin, this is Lamar. Lamar and Tamika are siblings, and Mama Shirley is their mom."

"Nice to meet you, Lamar. I've heard great things about your mom's cooking," said Collin, shaking his hand.

Lamar grinned. "You're in for a treat. Mama makes the best vegan food in town. Hell, she makes the best food, period. . . . So, what can I get ya'll? Is it going to be the usual?"

Núria giggled. "You know me so well."

"All right, then. One order of Mama's empanadas, one fried chik'n and gravy, one mac and cheese, one collard greens, one rice and peas, one potato salad, and two Harpoon IPAs. Is that right?"

"You got it, Lamar. Thanks."

As soon as Lamar was gone, Collin relaxed. His fidgeting stopped. And he couldn't help but stare at Núria from across the table while thinking about what a lucky bastard he was. All the months of watching her from afar, of pining after her, and there she was, seated in front of him.

"So, I take it you were never really a cat person until now?" asked Núria.

"*Am* I officially a cat person?" he said, his eyes widening in amazement. "I guess I am. My parents weren't fond of cats *or* dogs. God forbid there should be some fur on the sofa, or some dog drool on the floor. Our house was neat and orderly and full of precious antiques. It wasn't really a home for pets . . . or children, for that matter."

"I'm sorry," she replied, cringing. "If it makes you feel any better, I didn't have any pets as a kid, either."

For a moment they didn't speak. He fiddled with the cutlery on the table, trying to think of what to say next. The last thing he wanted was to blurt out something stupid or something that would make him sound like a pompous ass. But he needed to trust his gut. So he took a deep breath, leaned forward, and said the first thing that came to mind. "Cat is special, isn't he? I mean, all cats are special, but he's like *special*, special. Right?"

Núria grinned. "He sure is."

"You know, it's almost like he can understand me. Like, I'll talk to him, and there's emotion in his eyes. And he's so smart! He's quite the problem solver. . . . It's a bit embarrassing, but I must confess that the Murano paperweight was his idea." Collin blushed.

"Wait. What? How was that *his* idea?" said Núria with raised eyebrows.

Collin covered his face with his hands for a second; his cheeks were even more flushed when he uncovered them. "I know this is going to sound ridiculous, but he kept on placing his paw on top of the notecard I'd written you, as if he was trying to tell me something. To be honest, I was a bit dumbfounded. But then he picked up a fallen acorn and dropped it right on top of the envelope, looking at me with those mischievous eyes of his. And I knew. I immediately knew what he was trying to tell me. . . . Am I crazy?"

At first, Núria didn't respond. All she did was gaze at him intently with eyes that were equal parts honey and moss. They were quite possibly the most beautiful eyes he'd ever seen. Then the corners of her lips began to curl into a sly smile. She leaned toward him and whispered, "Welcome to the club, Collin."

He had no idea what club she was referring to. But the way she looked at him, the way her smile teased at something kind of naughty, made his knees go weak and his heart beat at a speed that seemed dangerously fast.

"I sure hope you folks are hungry." Lamar appeared at the most opportune moment. He arranged the various dishes in between them for sharing. "Here you go. Enjoy . . . You want me to save you an extra-large portion of banana pudding?" he asked Núria.

She grinned. "Yes, please. Thanks, Lamar."

And then he was gone, leaving them alone with their smorgasbord of delicious food. Thank God. If there was food in his mouth, he would have fewer opportunities to bungle the conversation.

# SEVENTY-ONE

# Núria

Núria had gone into the date with zero expectations. Well, maybe not zero. But her history of shitty first dates and half-assed relationships had made her quite numb to the idea of ever finding the one person she wanted to spend her life with.

Collin had surpassed her lack of expectations, though. In fact, he'd surpassed them by a lot. He'd picked the perfect restaurant and cleaned his plate, and some of hers too. He'd listened. He'd laughed and joked at the right moments. He'd gushed about Cat in a way that made her feel warm and fuzzy all over. And when they'd left the restaurant, he'd tipped the staff generously and spoken to them as if they were human beings, as opposed to faceless workers. All of those things were important to Núria.

When he'd offered to drop her off at her place, she'd agreed.

"Tonight was nice. I had a really good time," said Collin as they lingered in front of her building.

Núria smiled. "Thanks for dinner. I'm stuffed. I mean, look at my belly," she said, rubbing her stomach.

"I can't even tell. That dress fits you perfectly." Collin reached out and touched one of the black cats near her collarbone. "It looks just like Cat," he said.

She was tempted to admit that she'd only gotten the dress for their date. But she decided against it. Why ruin the moment with too much information? So instead, she eyed the smiley pineapples on his shirt and giggled. "I didn't know pineapples could smile."

"Pineapples are happy fruit. They're from the tropics, of course they're happy," said Collin with a shrug.

After that, neither of them spoke, as if the cat had gotten Núria's tongue and the pineapple had stuffed itself into Collin's mouth. He shuffled his feet. She fiddled with the loose curls around her face.

Was he going to try to kiss her?

Núria licked her lips, still tasting remnants of the banana pudding she'd devoured. Then she fluttered her eyelashes and stepped a bit closer. She *wanted* to be kissed. Wasn't it obvious? Most guys would have noticed, right? But clearly, Collin wasn't most guys.

From what Núria could tell, he liked her. A lot. So why was he hesitating? Was she that unreadable? Was she the kind of woman who scared men off? Or rather, was he the kind of man who needed a woman to take charge? Was that it?

Núria inched her way toward him. At first, she looked down at the ground. The closer she got, the higher her gaze went. Finally, she was right in front of him, the tips of their shoes touching, her eyes firmly locked with his.

"Collin," she said in a whisper.

He didn't reply. But she could tell by the intensity in his eyes that she'd transfixed him. For a second, she thought she could even hear his heart thumping in his chest. She was mistaken, though. It wasn't his heart. It was hers.

Images flashed in her mind—the neon Post-it notes they'd written to each other; the way his face had looked whenever he'd come into the café to order coffee from her; the way he'd selflessly offered to take Cat in; the way he'd groaned when he'd first tried the vegan banana pudding; the way he was standing in front of her, his eyes practically on fire.

*Fuck it.*

Núria reached up and rested her arms around his neck, and then she pulled herself up and kissed him the way she'd wanted to ever since he'd busted into the café and screamed *Guillermo! Guillermo! Guillermo!*

# SEVENTY-TWO

# Collin

*Four days later . . .*

Collin checked his watch. It was 2:10 P.M. The vet tech had already placed Cat in the carrier and given Collin a bag with medications. They were ready to go home. He needed Núria, though. Like, *really* needed her. But she was late.

"Oh good. You're still here."

He glanced at the door. Except it wasn't Núria. Instead, he was gazing into Lily's blue eyes. "Is Núria with you?" he asked.

Lily kneeled by the cat carrier so she could peek into it. "No, but she'll be here. I'm sure she wouldn't want to miss this. I'm Lily, by the way. We haven't officially met."

"Oh. Yeah. I'm Collin."

She grinned. "I know."

What was that supposed to mean?

"How is the patient?" she asked, peeking into the carrier again.

*Meow.* Cat seemed to have something to say, but his meow was raspy.

"The vet said he's got his appetite back. Thankfully, he's not dehydrated anymore," explained Collin.

Lily sat beside him. "Poor guy. You know, my dad loved cats. I always wanted a cat or a dog, but my mother hates animals."

Collin frowned, his gaze falling on her fingernails, which were still chipped. "Actually, it was the same for me too. My mom refused to allow me to get a pet because it would supposedly ruin our furniture."

She raised her eyebrows. "Really?"

"Thank God! Sorry I'm late!" Núria barged into the clinic.

Collin's eyes brightened at the sight of her. "We were waiting for you. I've got all the meds and Cat here is raring to go home," he said.

Núria gave Lily a quick hug, and then she bent down to the floor so she could be face-to-face with Cat. "Hey there, little buddy. How are you feeling? You ready to go?"

*Meow. Meow.*

This time, his meows were a bit louder, more urgent. Clearly, he was ready to blow the popsicle stand, aka the vet clinic.

"Hi, everyone. Sorry I'm late." Bong walked in, huffing and puffing. "I was getting ready to close the store, but then a rush of customers came in. I had to run all the way here," he said, wheezing for air.

Collin stood. "Is Omar joining us?"

"Not till later. He's still finishing up his deliveries. He said he would meet us at your place," said Bong.

"Well, let's go, then," said Núria. "Let's bring this guy home."

While Collin unlocked his front door, he couldn't help but marvel at how many people were standing behind him, waiting to enter his home. He'd owned the brownstone for five years, yet only delivery people, repair people, and a few family members had ever been inside. For a moment, he was disoriented. It was a brand-new feeling for him to want to welcome people into his life this way. But it felt good. *Really* good.

He pushed the door wide open and then picked up the cat carrier. "Come on in," he said with a glance over his shoulder.

They traipsed in behind him. Núria immediately marched through the foyer, past the kitchen, and into the living room, studying her surroundings. "This is a really big space. It's pretty overwhelming. Is your bedroom upstairs?" she asked Collin, who was still holding the cat carrier.

He gulped. The idea of Núria being in his bedroom made his hands all clammy. Sure, they'd already done their fair share of kissing in the last few days, but the room where he kept his bed was on a whole other level. He gripped the carrier harder. "Uh. Yeah. On the second floor next to my study."

"I think we should keep Cat in there for a few days. Once he's acclimated, you can start letting him explore the rest of the house. Is that okay with you?" she said.

Why wouldn't it be okay with him?

As if she'd read his mind, she raised her eyebrows and added, "Cats are more active at night. He might jump on your bed and walk all over you, like, *literally* walk all over you."

"Oh. That's all right. I stay up pretty late, anyways. And when I do fall asleep, I'm like a hibernating bear," he said with a chuckle.

Núria nodded. "Good. Let's go upstairs and settle him in."

Lily peeked out of the kitchen. "Bong and I will make some coffee and set out some snacks."

Ordinarily, the idea of people touching his stuff, rooting around his cupboards, and gawking at everything inside his refrigerator would have made him anxious. But he wasn't feeling that way. Not at all. "There's coffee next to the coffeemaker, you'll see the sugar there as well. And there's milk and half-and-half in the fridge. As for snacks, feel free to use whatever you find," he said.

"Oh! You have a lot of cheese!" Bong announced from inside the kitchen.

"C'mon. Cat must be getting antsy in there." Núria tugged on the hem of Collin's T-shirt, grazing the side of his torso with her fingers.

Collin could feel goose bumps, the good kind, from her touch. He only hoped that Núria hadn't noticed. "All right. Follow me."

Once they were upstairs, they walked down the hallway, past his study, and into his large bedroom with its king-sized bed, which was immaculately made with heather-gray sheets. For a moment, Núria seemed to be taking in the shiny antique wooden floors, which were covered on one side by a Persian rug in shades of blue. On the other side of the room there was a navy-blue velvet two-seater sofa, an armchair covered in brocade fabric, an ottoman, and a coffee table. Next to the bed was the door to the en suite bathroom.

"We can set up the litter box in your bathroom so it's easier to clean. And his food and water bowl can go in that corner by the window," she said, pointing at the sunny corner of his bedroom.

"Sure, that sounds good." Collin placed the cat carrier down on the rug. "So, do we just open the carrier door and wait for him to come out?"

Núria nodded. "Yup, that's the idea."

So that's exactly what they did. Collin slowly opened the metal door. They backed away and sat next to each other on the sofa, watching, like two parents waiting for their toddler to take its first steps.

# SEVENTY-THREE

# Cat

Cat was scared. Once he was indoors, away from the street, it was less scary, though. Through the metal grate in the box he could see walls and a floor and chairs and tables, some of them with fluffy cushions. There were also windows, which fascinated Cat, because he'd only ever seen them from the outside looking in, not the other way around. Would the street look the same through the glass? Would he be able to see the trees and sky? He certainly hoped so, because one of his favorite pastimes was watching birds.

After a while, the box he was in stopped moving. *Squeak!* The metal grate door opened. Cat crawled forward a couple of inches and spotted Awkward Neighbor Guy and Rainbow Lady sitting on a nearby sofa. At first, they just watched him silently. But as the minutes passed, they began to chat and laugh and smile at each other a whole lot. Maybe Rainbow Lady *did* like Awkward Neighbor Guy back.

*Huh. Well, that worked out.*

Although Cat wasn't quite ready to leave the box, he was curious to explore the giant room filled with new, strange things.

Little by little he moved his legs, inching forward until he was out of the box. He didn't have the energy to go any farther, though. He collapsed onto the rug, which was a whole lot softer than the pavement outside. It was so soft that he was compelled to dig his claws into it, kneading like he'd kneaded his mother's stomach as a kitten.

"Oh, hey, little buddy. You finally came out," said Rainbow Lady with a smile.

Awkward Neighbor Guy got off the sofa and kneeled in front of him. "You don't need to be nervous, okay? You're safe here with us," he said to Cat gently.

After a couple of minutes, Cat decided to stand. His legs were a bit wobbly. But he wanted to explore. As he walked slowly, stumbling a bit here and there, he could feel the loose skin on his belly flap from side to side. His joints ached. He had a hard time catching his breath. Every couple of steps, his muscles twitched and cramped. Eventually, he made it to the outer corner of the room, where there was a large window.

"Good job, my man! Keep on going!" Awkward Neighbor Guy cheered him on.

Rainbow Lady showed him his food and water bowl, which were already filled. Cat wasn't all that hungry, though, since he'd already eaten at the other place. Still, he sniffed the food a bit and took a couple of licks of water. When he was done, he gazed up at the two of them. They seemed satisfied, smiling at him and at each other.

"I think we should let him relax now. I'm pretty sure he's overwhelmed," said Rainbow Lady.

"Okay." Awkward Neighbor Guy placed his cat bed on top of this large wooden storage chest he had by the window. It was almost level with the windowsill. "Should we put him on the bed? So he can rest?" he asked Rainbow Lady.

She nodded. "Yeah. But we should come and check on him once in a while. He's not used to furniture and books and knickknacks. We have to make sure he doesn't hurt himself. At least until he has the lay of the land."

Awkward Neighbor Guy picked him up off the floor, carrying him like a priceless antique. "There you go, little man. Look out the window. You can see your alley from here, and your favorite hedges and that tree. If you watch, you'll see some birds. Okay?"

Cat gazed through the window. He was right. Down below, he recognized all of those familiar things. It made him feel better, somehow. Like he wasn't completely removed from the world he knew. He could still see it. If he pointed his nose up, he could even smell the air outside through the cracked-open window. After a minute, Cat tucked his front legs and hind legs underneath his body as he sank into the cushion of his bed. He was tired again. His eyelids were heavy.

"Oh, and guess what?" said Awkward Neighbor Guy, gazing at Cat with a dopey grin.

Cat gazed back at him, wondering what had him so happy all of a sudden.

"Bernie, my niece. She's coming to visit you tomorrow. When she found out what happened, and that you were coming to live with me, she insisted on coming over to give you a little welcome tea party. What do you think?"

*A welcome tea party?*

If Cat could have grinned, he would have. No wonder Awkward Neighbor Guy was so happy. As much as he hated to admit it, he was excited to see Little Human again. Would she bring him some roasted turkey? He couldn't wait to find out.

Before that, he would need some rest. His eyelids slowly dropped, even though he tried hard to resist by pulling them back up. It was a battle he was losing.

"Should we leave the door open a crack?" whispered Awkward Neighbor Guy.

Rainbow Lady shook her head. "No. He might wander and get himself into trouble. We can check in on him in half an hour." She took one more look at him, then left the room. Cat could hear her footsteps clomping down the stairs.

Except Awkward Neighbor Guy was still by the doorway, watching him. "You're not going to get into trouble, are you?" he asked.

Cat stared at him and blinked. What kind of trouble could he possibly get into in this place? Surely the streets were more dangerous, weren't they? *Nah. I'm good, dude. Don't you worry about me,* he thought to himself.

Awkward Neighbor Guy must have somehow sensed what he'd been thinking. He grinned and placed his pointer finger on his lips. "It's our little secret, okay, little buddy?"

Cat blinked again. Satisfied, Awkward Neighbor Guy tiptoed out the door, leaving it open wide enough for Cat's body to fit through. *Clomp. Clomp. Clomp.* His footsteps were heavier than Rainbow Lady's. He kind of sounded like one of those horses that Cat had seen on the street one time; their hooves had made such a racket on the concrete road. *Clomp.* He had reached the ground floor. Even though Cat was sleepy, he could hear voices and laughter.

*Ha! Ha! Ha!*

What were they talking and laughing about? What could possibly be so funny?

Of course, he would have to go investigate. He peered over the edge of the cat bed until he could see the rug on the floor below. It didn't seem that high. Surely, even in his weakened state, he would be able to jump safely?

He pushed himself off the cushion and positioned himself for jumping. *One . . . Two . . . Three . . .* Cat leaped as best he could, except when he landed, his legs buckled, causing him to tumble forward like a drunken acrobat.

*Oof.*

It wasn't the smoothest of landings, but he'd still made it. He licked one paw, then the other in an effort to compose himself. *Okay, that's better.* When he was satisfied with his grooming, he scurried over to the door. With each step, the voices got louder. He poked his head through the opening, getting a good look at his surroundings. It seemed pleasant enough. Not all that scary, really. Well, except for the stairs, which seemed quite steep.

It took Cat a handful of strides to get to the stairway landing. He stood at the very top, gazing at all the steps before him. There were so many. The jump from the cat bed to the floor had been too much for him already. He didn't dare attempt the journey to the bottom step in his condition. If he wasn't careful, he would slip and stumble and fall. The last thing he wanted was to be whisked back to that awful place when he'd just gotten here.

*Nope. Maybe another day, once I regain my strength . . .*

Instead, Cat picked a spot on the landing, where he could hide behind the banister but still have a view of the bottom floor. The rug was below him, so he would be comfortable while he listened to the commotion downstairs. It was perfect, really. Like the tree he used to like to climb in his youth—the tree that had a wide-open view of the playground down the street.

He sniffed the air. There were all sorts of smells coming from below. He sniffed again. Maybe eggs? Cheese? Bread? Definitely coffee. He could recognize that smell anywhere, since Rainbow Lady always reeked of it.

"Would you like an egg salad sandwich, Núria? It's my wife's recipe." Was that Sad Bodega Man? It sure sounded like him.

There was a moment of silence. Cat listened. He heard the clattering of plates, the clinking of glasses. Chewing. Lots of chewing. If he'd felt better, he would have ventured down the stairs and attempted to beg for food.

*Ding-dong!*

It was the doorbell.

Who could it be?

"Omar! Come on in. We have sandwiches and a cheese board and refreshments," he heard Awkward Neighbor Guy say as he opened the front door.

There were footsteps as they walked to the kitchen. Cat recognized the squeakiness of Cheery Mailman's work boots.

Then the voices amplified as everyone in the kitchen greeted him at the same time.

"Hey, everyone. Sorry, I'm kind of sweaty. It's like an oven out there." It *was* Cheery Mailman. "I stopped by the Jamaican place and got some vegan patties."

What the heck were Jamaican vegan patties? Cat had no idea, but after a couple of minutes he smelled a whiff of something delicious. He made a mental note about the Jamaican vegan patties.

"Oh God. These are so damned good!" said Rainbow Lady.

As Cat listened to the rhythm of their eating and chatting, his eyelids got heavier and heavier. Every muscle in his body relaxed, making him sink deeper into the rug. He blinked, trying to stay awake. It wouldn't work. Slowly, his eyes fluttered closed.

"Hey! I have an announcement. I've decided to enroll in the veterinary technician program at the LaGuardia Community College in Long Island," said Cheery Mailman.

There were the sounds of clapping and several *congratulations.*

Cat startled awake. *Wait. What?* What was going on? He tried his hardest to keep listening. But the force of sleep was too strong. His eyes shut again. This time, his breathing slowed as his consciousness drifted. Part of him could still hear all the voices and laughter. It was almost like music. Like a soft and gentle lullaby, lulling him to sleep.

Those were the sounds of his favorite people.

As long as he could hear them, he was safe.

The inside of the house no longer scared him. It was then, in his half-conscious state, that he realized that home wasn't necessarily a place. Home could be people too. As long as he was with them, he would be all right.

Cat had finally found a home to call his own.

# Acknowledgments

It has always been a dream of mine to write a cat book, specifically, a cat book with the point of view of a cat. But something about this idea intimidated me. Would potential literary agents and editors be interested? Was it even marketable? Would readers find the concept silly? When I finally faced my fears and wrote *Cat's People,* I was thankful to find out that my fears had been unfounded.

To my literary agent, Amy Bishop-Wycisk: I am forever grateful for your thoughtful editorial feedback, networking and negotiating skills, timely communications, boundless enthusiasm, sage advice, and your overall spunkiness. Not only are you the best possible advocate for my career, but you are also someone I can proudly call a friend and fellow cat lady.

I have huge gratitude for my acquiring editor, Anne Speyer. Thank you for giving my adult debut the very best publishing home. I knew from our very first conversation that you would be the perfect editor to help me transform *Cat's People* into an actual book. Your editorial suggestions made the story shine, and the cover you helped bring to life is truly worthy of that shine. Working with you has been an absolute joy.

To my adopted editor, Wendy Wong: Thank you for stepping in and making me feel loved and appreciated from the get-go. They say that there is always a bright side to every situation, and I can honestly say that you have brought a brightness and positivity to my publishing journey. I look forward to working on more books together.

To the entire team at Delacorte/Penguin Random House. Thank you for *everything*. Not only do you publish some of the best books out there, but you do so with an efficiency and enthusiasm that is unrivaled.

My dream book cover would have never happened without its cover artist, Leah Reena Goren. Thank you for bringing Cat and his people, or rather, his people's *hands,* to life. Not only did your art blow me away, but it surpassed all of my expectations.

To my family: I am thankful for the constant cheering as I traverse the oftentimes tumultuous publishing path I am on. To my mom, Helena, thank you for teaching me your cat-lady ways, which enabled me to write this story with the utmost genuineness, honesty, and humor it needed. To my dad, Wahoo, thank you for always being interested in my writing projects and in what's next. To my sister, Katya, thank you for always being there and telling me how proud you are of me. Nothing beats having a supportive sibling by your side. To my husband, Daemon, thank you for being a great partner in cat and dog rescue. To my única hija, Violet, thanks for always being my greatest cheerleader, even though I am totally old and uncool. Maybe one day we can finally walk that red carpet premiere together.

An author's journey would be an extremely lonely one without a group of writer friends. To my MG squad, Janae Marks, Lorien Lawrence, and Shannon Doleski: Thanks for all the moral support during the stressful querying and submissions process as I made the shift from kidlit to adult. To my long-time timezone buddy, Melly Sujitro, thank you for always being there to talk craft, books, trash, and tea. Samantha Sotto Yambao, I am so happy to finally have an agent *and* publisher sister to have lunch with in real life! To Pierra Calasanz-Labrador, thank you for agreeing to be the very first person to read *Cat's People* sample chapters, laughing at the Julio Iglesias reference, and giving it a big thumbs-up.

To everyone I've met in the animal welfare community since I started volunteering in 2008, and most especially to Nancy Cu-Unjieng and Barbara Greenwood, who were my mentors when I first began rescuing, fostering, adopting, and doing TNR work: This book wouldn't have happened without your guidance and friendship.

I have a special place in my heart for all my cat people friends and community. Thank you for sharing your many adorable and funny cat photos, memes, and stories. Seeing them always brightens my day. I hope you see a little of yourself—or maybe a lot—in the pages of *Cat's People.*

And last but not least, to my readers: Thank you for choosing to spend some time with Cat, Núria, Collin, Omar, Bong, and Lily. I hope I made you smile and laugh and cry (mostly tears of joy).

## ABOUT THE AUTHOR

TANYA GUERRERO is Filipino and Spanish by birth, but has been fortunate enough to call three countries home—the Philippines, Spain, and the United States. Currently, she lives in a shipping container home in the suburbs of Manila with her husband, daughter, and a menagerie of rescued cats and dogs. She has volunteered for animal welfare organizations since 2008, focusing on trap/neuter/return and rescue/foster/adopt. In her free time, she grows her own food, bakes, and reads.

tanyaguerrero.com
X: @guerrerotanya

## ABOUT THE TYPE

This book was set in Garamond, a typeface originally designed by the Parisian type cutter Claude Garamond (c. 1500–61). This version of Garamond was modeled on a 1592 specimen sheet from the Egenolff-Berner foundry, which was produced from types assumed to have been brought to Frankfurt by the punch cutter Jacques Sabon (c. 1520–80).

Claude Garamond's distinguished romans and italics first appeared in *Opera Ciceronis* in 1543–44. The Garamond types are clear, open, and elegant.